Readers love
JOHN INMAN

Nightfall

"This is a beautiful love story. I urge you to crack open this intensely thrilling novel and discover for yourself just what happens when the lights go out."

—The Novel Approach

"…*Nightfall* is very good and it paints a brutal picture of what humanity can become. But on the flip side, we see in Joe and Ned the best of what humanity offers…."

—Joyfully Jay

Words

"If you like a little murder with your romance, this is a book for you. It's very entertaining and very mysterious!"

—Diverse Reader

"I can happily recommend this story for its deft satire with a great balance of romance, thrills and suspense."

—Jessie G Books

Ginger Snaps

"If you like light and fluffy with an HEA, you'll love the books in this series. I highly recommend you pick up this series if you haven't already."

—Love Bytes

"For those who need a dose of sweet humour that is effortlessly timed then this is the book for you."

—Gay Book Reviews

By JOHN INMAN

Acting Up
Chasing the Swallows
A Hard Winter Rain
Head-on
The Hike
Hobbled
Jasper's Mountain
Laugh Cry Repeat
Love Wanted
Loving Hector
My Busboy
My Dragon, My Knight
Nightfall
A Party to Murder
Paulie
Payback
The Poodle Apocalypse
Scrudge & Barley, Inc.
Shy
Spirit
Strays and Lovers
Sunset Lake
Two Pet Dicks
Words

THE BELLADONNA ARMS
Serenading Stanley
Work in Progress
Coming Back
Ben and Shiloh
Ginger Snaps

Published by DSP Publications
7&7: An Anthology of Virtue and
Vice
The Boys on the Mountain
The Second Son
Willow Man

Published by DREAMSPINNER PRESS
www.dreamspinnerpress.com

JOHN INMAN

A PARTY TO MURDER

REAMSPINNER
PRESS

Published by
DREAMSPINNER PRESS

5032 Capital Circle SW, Suite 2, PMB# 279, Tallahassee, FL 32305-7886 USA
www.dreamspinnerpress.com

A Party to Murder
© 2019 John Inman.

Cover Art
© 2019 Paul Richmond.
http://www.paulrichmondstudio.com
Cover content is for illustrative purposes only and any person depicted on the cover is a model.

Trade Paperback ISBN: 978-1-64405-146-7
Digital ISBN: 978-1-64405-136-8
Library of Congress Control Number: 2018961343
Trade Paperback published March 2019
v. 1.0

Printed in the United States of America
∞
This paper meets the requirements of
ANSI/NISO Z39.48-1992 (Permanence of Paper).

CHAPTER ONE

FROM THE passenger seat, Jamie Roma slipped a hand under the shirttail of the man driving the car. He chuckled to himself when the car swerved off the road, then lurched back onto the asphalt in a spray of gravel and mud.

Derek Lee growled through what Jamie considered to be the sexiest pair of lips he had ever seen in his life. "Jesus, if that hand had gone into my pants, we'd be dead now."

"Dead but happy," Jamie whispered back.

Derek made a sound that was somewhere between a groan and a chuckle. Mostly, Jamie figured, it was a groan. Jamie didn't mind not getting a laugh at his feeble joke, because at the same time as he was groaning, Derek was also tucking his own hand under his shirt and stroking Jamie's fingers.

They were motoring across the high desert thirty miles outside San Diego. Even had there been daylight, there would have been nothing to see but rolling hills, a bunch of boulders scattered around like spilled Legos, and about a gazillion clumps of sagebrush. As it was, they couldn't even see *that* because darkness had fallen with a resounding thud about three hours back. And now not only was it night, it was a moonless and starless night, thanks to the rain clouds that had been forming overhead all day. If not for the Toyota's headlights and the gleam of the GPS system on the dashboard, they would have been floundering through a sea of bottomless black shadow—blind, directionless, lost.

It was also lonely. They hadn't seen another car for ages.

Jamie jumped, pointing through the windshield at a sudden twitch of movement up ahead on the side of the road. "Lookie! A coyote!"

No sooner had he cried out than the animal froze, every ounce of its attention trained on the approaching car. The coyote's eyes were like teeny tiny flashlights, beaming straight back at them. The beast didn't run; it didn't cower; it simply stood there with its front feet on the road and its rear end in the bushes, waiting patiently for the car to speed past so it could go on about its business.

"It's not afraid of us," Jamie said.

"Why should it be?" Derek snorted. "It's not the one that's lost. And don't say 'Lookie.' You sound like a three-year-old."

Jamie slapped Derek's arm at the exact moment he spun around in his seat to look behind them as the car zoomed past the coyote. For the briefest of moments, he spotted the creature flashing to life in the red glow of the car's taillights. Then the animal melted into the receding darkness as if it had never been there at all. Jamie swung back around and replaced his hand on Derek's bare belly.

He sighed.

"What's with the sigh?" Derek asked.

"Nothing. Just happy."

"You're not getting romantic, are you?"

It was Jamie's turn to snort. "I don't get romantic. I'm just a guy who's having fun driving along with his oldest friend in the world who happens to be an occasional trick."

"Occasional as in every single night for the last two months."

"Well, yeah."

"After all these years of friendly abstinence together, we suddenly jump into bed and pork like bunny rabbits for eight solid weeks."

"Pork like bunny rabbits. What a lovely expression. Rates right up there with fuck your balls off."

"Oh hush. I wonder how it happened."

"How *what* happened?"

"How we ended up in bed together that first night."

Jamie gave Derek time to think about it while he enjoyed the sensation of exploring Derek's tight little belly button with a fingertip. "Hormones, I guess," Derek finally said. "Horny, humpy hormones."

This time when Jamie groaned, it was a real one. "Yeah. And tequila. Lots and lots of tequila. My head *still* hurts."

"How about your ass?"

"That too. But in a good way. And that's from *last* night, not two months ago."

They laughed, and Derek stroked Jamie's hand again, making Jamie's laugh ratchet down to a dreamy little smile. He couldn't see it on his own face because he was too lazy to look in the visor mirror, but he knew it was there all the same. It was somewhat worrisome, too, that dreamy, contemplative smile he could feel twitching on his lips.

My God, what if he *was* beginning to feel romantic about Derek? What would *that* do to their lifelong friendship?

"We met in fifth grade," Jamie said, pondering out loud.

Derek cracked the window to get some air into the car. Either the night had grown warmer, or he was having a hot flash. He realized, of course, that Jamie's roving fingers so close to his groin might have something to do with that. "I know. I was there. You tried to steal my milk. Hmm," he hummed, sticking his nose through the crack, "smell that night air."

Jamie rolled his own window down, letting in a blast of air that made his hair thrash around on top his head. He stuck his face through the opening, squinting into the night. "Smells like a monsoon coming!" he yelled into the empty countryside.

"They don't have monsoons in California!" Derek bellowed. "And get back in here. You look like a Rottweiler hanging out a car door with his tongue flapping in the wind."

Jamie dragged himself back inside. He was grinning like an idiot, hair going every which way. Batting his eyelashes, he leaned against his seat belt and laid his head on Derek's shoulder. "Ooh, if I was a Rottweiler, we could do it doggy style."

Derek laughed. "And break every law of nature there is. You're impossible."

A sudden flash of lightning sizzled across the sky in front of them, making them both jump. A moment later, fat raindrops began pelting the windshield. Derek switched on the wipers. Soon their comforting song filled the interior of the car. *Whoosh, whoosh, whoosh, whoosh.* It was a pleasant sound, Jamie thought. With his head still snuggled against Derek's shoulder, Jamie returned his hand to Derek's bare belly. His fingers twiddled idly with the hair around Derek's navel. Both men grew quiet as they watched the road in front of them darken with rain.

"Any idea where we are?" Jamie asked.

With his lips in Jamie's hair, Derek gave a good-natured growl. "Oh ye of little faith. I know exactly where we are."

"Where?"

"Somewhere north of Mexico and south of the Bering Strait."

"Very funny."

Derek tapped the GPS monitor on the dashboard. "Honestly. We're right where we're supposed to be. See? There should be a turnoff coming up soon, and a few miles after that, a bridge. We'll cross the bridge and continue on down a gravel side road for fifteen miles or so, and that will lead us unveeringly toward the house we're trying to find."

"So you hope," Jamie drawled.

To which Derek didn't quibble. "Yes. So I hope."

For the space of about fifteen seconds, the rain came down so hard that even the windshield wipers couldn't keep up. The sound was deafening. The downpour pummeled the car, almost stripping Jamie's breath away. Being a Southern California boy, Jamie was more accustomed to drought. He didn't like storms. When the rain eased up a little, his blood pressure dropped. He tried to relax. Through the streaming windshield, he could see the empty highway stretching out before them, disappearing into the rainy, wind-tossed distance. Derek tapped his index finger against the steering wheel. Clearly he was about to say something important. Which he finally did.

"I know we've been over this a dozen times, but I still don't understand why we both received invitations to a house party from someone we don't know."

"From someone we *assume* we don't know," Jamie corrected. "Since the invitations weren't signed, we really don't know if we're acquainted with the person who sent them or not. Personally, I think it's some idiot friend of ours."

"But we don't know that for sure," Derek pointed out. "And still, Jamie Roma, you putz, you insisted we come anyway."

Jamie laughed. "Because it's an adventure! It's a lark. It's mysterious. It's a weekend house party in the middle of nowhere, fifty miles out of the city, cut off from the world, and being hosted by someone we may or may not know for reasons we haven't got a clue about. Besides, at the bottom of the invitations they promised heart-stopping door prizes. Quote, unquote. Who could say no to heart-stopping door prizes?"

"Anybody with brains!" Derek snarled. "I've seen horror movies that start this way. While we're tooling down this spookyass, rain-drenched highway heading straight into the maw of oblivion with thunder and lightning crashing and flashing all around us, I can imagine the opening credits of a really gory slasher movie unscrolling over our heads as we speak. *Jamie and Derek on the Highway to Hell. Three for the Road with Jamie, Derek, and Leatherface. Queers on Elm Street.*"

"That's quite an imagination you've got there. Listen. Have I ever steered you wrong before?"

"Oh please, Jamie. When have you ever *not* steered me wrong? Remember that Mexican restaurant you wanted to try last week? The one where the cockroach crawled out of my taco?"

"You should have had a burrito."

Derek ignored that. "I wonder how many guests there will be."

"Like I care. Let's just hope the booze doesn't run out." Jamie perked up. "Suppose there will be tequila?"

This time Derek's groan came from the heart. "Oh God, I hope not. One shot of tequila and you end up with your legs in the air, toes pointed straight at the ceiling."

"Why, thank you."

Derek laughed. "No, thank *you*."

Derek took their lives in his hands by leaning into the darkness and planting a kiss on Jamie's eagerly expectant mouth. At the same time, their lives were further imperiled when Jamie's fingers diddled their way south, burrowing under the buckle of Derek's belt, which he cleverly unclasped with a flick of his thumb. Houdini couldn't have done it better.

The car swerved again when Jamie wiggled out from under his shoulder harness and lowered his head to Derek's lap. Rooting around with his nose like a hog hunting truffles, he unearthed exactly what he was searching for, and for the next three miles, not a word was spoken between the two.

The silence was finally broken when Derek stiffened all over and gripped the steering wheel so tightly his knuckles went white. Far beyond his ability to do anything about it, his hips lurched upward and he emitted a delicious moan.

"That's my boy," Jamie mumbled, smiling. "Let it go. And try not to run us off a cliff when you do."

"Don't talk with your mouth full," Derek gasped, once again lifting his ass off the seat until there was a good six inches of daylight showing beneath him—if there had been any daylight *available* on this miserably stormy night. While a brand-new onslaught of rain and wind pummeled the car and rocked it back and forth, he clutched a fistful of Jamie's hair with the one free hand he dared take off the wheel.

For the next thirty seconds or so, Jamie Roma worked just as hard as the windshield wipers—trying desperately to stay ahead of the deluge.

TEN MINUTES later, Derek's clothes were once again buttoned, zipped, and properly tucked into place, thanks to a little help from Jamie, who proved to be equally adept at getting Derek *dressed* in the cramped front seat of the car as he was in getting him *undressed*. With his heart still thumping in his ears and feeling smugly self-satisfied now that Jamie had had his way with him, which was what Derek had hoped for all along, he repositioned himself comfortably behind the steering wheel and drove on through the pounding rain.

Beside him, Jamie—also licking his lips but for different reasons— leaned forward and squinted through the rainwater sluicing down the windshield. He instantly gave a *whoop*.

"There's the turnoff!" he cried, grabbing the dashboard. "Right there. Don't miss it. Turn! Turn!"

Derek jumped in response and banged his head on the roof of the car. Then he slammed on the brakes, all but strangling them both against their seat belts. The car jolted to a stop in a mudhole the size of Lake Tahoe. Outside, the rain had turned to hail. It clattered off the hood and pounded on the metal roof while Derek stared out, bug-eyed, at what lay ahead. He glanced at Jamie, and in the glow from the dash lights, saw the look of horror on Jamie's face. He was pretty sure that same horror was plastered all over his own puss. And why wouldn't it be? After all, the situation, the night, and especially *the road ahead*, looked far from promising. To say the least.

They both peered intently forward, studying the terrain.

What was labeled a county road that appeared perfectly respectable meandering its way across the map on the GPS monitor was in reality little more than two muddy ruts awash in the storm. Those ruts wove their way toward a wind-tossed wilderness of trees—some pine, some deciduous and bare. They were etched into stark relief by an occasional stab of lightning sizzling across the heavens above.

"Think this is where the Donner party got lost?" Derek mumbled under his breath.

"Don't be silly. Just keep driving," Jamie said. "What have we got to lose?"

"I shudder to think," Derek answered, but he did as directed and drove on anyway.

The road was rent with washboards and potholes, and muddy water splashed all the way up to the door handles as they bumped and lunged their way along. If not for their seat belts, they would have had their brains bashed out on the roof of the car. The chassis of the vehicle squeaked and creaked beneath them, complaining every inch of the way, and Derek wondered if his poor old Toyota would survive the journey at all.

After several minutes of this, while rain and hail pelted them from above and gale-force winds jostled them from the side, Jamie leaned forward and, with his hot breath steaming the windshield in front of him, cried out, "There's the bridge!"

Once again, Derek slammed on the brakes. This time the car slued sideways. It sloshed to a stop, still hanging on to the narrow roadway without sliding off into the bracken on either side.

Derek was just beginning to wonder if Jamie's fingernails were leaving claw marks on his faux-leather dashboard when he decided to lean forward and study what lay ahead, hoping to come up with a game plan on how to proceed. With help from the headlights and an occasional explosion of lightning, he got a pretty good idea what they were up against, and it wasn't encouraging.

Tucked in among the pine trees, the contraption that had the audacity to call itself a bridge squatted there in front of them in all its rustic splendor. In truth, it was merely a one-lane clapboard affair with no visible metal framework or overhead support beams and no railings on either side. Rickety, wooden, poorly constructed, the bridge looked like a death trap gleefully waiting for the next two gay boys to come along so it could snatch them into a premature and entirely unprepared-for afterlife.

"Is that thing *safe*?" Derek asked through squeaky, tight lips. "It doesn't *look* safe. Do *you* think it's safe?"

"Like I know," Jamie all but snarled, clearly not optimistic.

In a momentary lull in the downpour, while the precipitation once again shifted from hail to rain—which in Derek's opinion was a step in the right direction—he cocked his head to the side and breathed, "Listen!" For the space of half a dozen heartbeats they sat frozen in place, staring out the windshield. The air around them was alive with the sounds of the storm above their heads.

"If this rain keeps up," Derek said, "it could cause a flash flood in the arroyo under the bridge."

Jamie groaned. "Great. Could the water get high enough to wash the bridge away?"

"I don't know."

Jamie tried again. "Well, if we get across and the bridge *is* washed away behind us, is there a way for us to get back to where we started?"

"You mean back to the city?"

"Yeah. Back to the city."

Derek punched a few buttons on the GPS monitor, scanning the maps that popped up, tracing the lines depicting roadways with a trembling fingertip.

Finally he said, "No. If we cross this bridge, there's no way back, not on any sort of marked road at any rate."

"And if we *don't* cross the bridge, we'll miss the party. Not to mention having driven all this way for nothing."

"What are you doing?" Derek asked. "Weighing our lives against the possibility of free booze and door prizes?"

Jamie turned to him, his face suddenly lit with a familiar glimmer of mischief. It was his "it's Saturday night, let's get rowdy and raise hell, screw the consequences, I've got bail money" look. Derek knew it well.

"Well, yeah," Jamie patiently explained. "What other criteria do you need?"

"I'm vaguely appalled by that devil-may-care light in your eyes," Derek drawled. He tore his gaze from Jamie's sexy grin and back to the bridge in front of them. "Almost as appalled as I am by the prospect of driving over that ricketyass bridge. Think the other guests got across already?"

Jamie thought about that for a minute. "Actually, we don't even know if there *are* any other guests."

"You're right," Derek agreed. "We don't. What sort of idiots accept a party invitation in the middle of nowhere when they don't know who sent the invitation or how many guests will be there when they arrive?"

"Idiots like us. I say we go for it. Cross the bridge."

"What if it collapses?"

Jamie gave a dismissive wave at the structure in front of them. "Oh pshaw. It looks like it's been standing for a couple of centuries already. What are the odds of it collapsing tonight at the exact moment we're scurrying across?"

Derek chewed on the inside of his jaw. "I hate it when you say pshaw. It sounds so bucolic."

"I'm a bucolic sort of guy."

"No, you're not. You're a citified wimp! But you're right. Statistically, if the bridge has withstood the elements this long, it should be safe enough for the next two minutes."

"Exactly. And we definitely need to get where we're going, because I could really use a drink right now. If this party is hosted by teetotalers, I'm going to be extremely upset. Cross the fucking bridge."

"You're crazy."

Jamie shrugged. "So are you. Cross the bridge."

"We should have packed our *own* booze."

"You're right, but it's too late now. Oh wait, look up ahead. What's that tucked in among the brambles and the blackberry bushes? Can it be? It is! It's a liquor store!"

There was nothing ahead but trees and mud and rain. "You're being sarcastic, aren't you?"

"Who me? Cross the bridge."

Derek slipped the car into Drive. "If we die, thanks for the blowjob."

"No, thank *you*," Jamie innocently beamed, licking his lips.

And with both men holding their breath, Derek floored the car and sailed out across the bridge.

Still holding their breath a moment later, they came to a sloshing, jolting stop inside a foot-deep mudhole on the far side. They turned to peer through the rear window. In the red glow of taillights, the wooden structure gave a shudder, then seemed to settle.

"See," Jamie said. "We're fine."

As if his words had conjured disaster out of thin air, there came a horrific grinding, tumbling, rushing noise that seemed to be churning its way up from the depths of the earth itself. A surge of dark water poured down the arroyo and dashed against the side of the bridge. With a heave upward amid a tiny explosion of splintered timbers, the bridge collapsed in upon itself and disappeared without a trace. One second it was there, the next it was gone, washed away in the churning flood below.

"Well, poop," Jamie whispered in the sudden silence. His eyes, Derek noticed, were as big as dinner plates.

Less than eagerly, they turned back to study the muddy, rutted path ahead. The storm had sprinkled it with evergreen bows and pine cones ripped from the living trees. The trees themselves appeared beaten down and half stripped bare, their heads bowed in the gusting wind. Fighting to stand upright against the onslaught, they shook and thrashed on both sides of the road. Derek didn't want to think about what might be lurking among the spookyass shadows between their battered trunks. He forced his attention dead ahead at the disappearing roadway weaving a winding narrow mud-holed path through the trees toward a stormy, uncertain distance.

"This had better be a damn good party," Derek muttered.

Jamie grunted in agreement. Terse for Jamie, Derek thought, who usually blathered on endlessly about *everything*. With Jamie's fingers tightening on his thigh, Derek tapped the accelerator enough to urge the car slowly forward into that nightmarish tunnel burrowing its way between the trees ahead. The car rocked and lurched as they sloshed and splashed and squelched along, sinking hubcap-deep into every rain-glutted pothole they passed.

Derek decided on the spot that the only *enjoyable* part of this miserable night was having Jamie at his side to suffer through it with him. Creeped out by the storm and the collapsing bridge and the wind and the spooky, shadowy trees, Derek was nevertheless vaguely astounded by how *much* he enjoyed having Jamie with him. After all, Jamie was just a friend, although there was no denying they had suddenly slipped into the realm of fuckbuddydom lately. So what did that mean exactly? Did it mean Jamie had suddenly become something *more* than a friend?

Dumb question.

Derek allowed a smile to play at the corners of his mouth as he drove down the miserable, bumpy cow path. He glanced down at Jamie's hand still resting on his thigh, and his smile widened.

"Don't worry," he softly said. "We'll be fine."

Jamie didn't speak, but his fingers tightened on Derek's leg, and that was answer enough.

Turning his attention back to the road, Derek drove on through the storm. Comforted by Jamie's touch, he hummed a quiet song deep in his throat to the rhythm of the *whooshing* wiper blades.

With hail still clattering across the roof of the car and the bridge now washed out behind them, he suddenly wondered what the heck he was humming about.

He also began to wonder—all kidding aside—*if they'd really be fine at all*.

CHAPTER TWO

DEREK'S LITTLE tune died in his throat when Jamie suddenly unclamped his seat belt and leaned forward to press his nose against the windshield. Doing his Rottweiler impersonation again.

Jamie's breath fogged the glass. "You realize we're trapped, right? We can't drive out of here now, even if we want to. Plus, we've got ourselves so buried in the wilderness we don't know *where* the heck we are. I keep expecting to see Bigfoot chuck a mud clod at us as we slosh past."

Hearing an edge of panic in Jamie's voice made Derek try a little harder to wrench reason from chaos. "Hey, you're the one who told me to cross the bridge. Besides, how lost can we be? We have our cell phones. And according to the invitation, our destination is only fifteen miles down this bumpyass road. Our host will know what to do."

"Whoever our host may be."

Derek grunted reluctant agreement. "Yes. Whoever our host may be."

By wrenching the steering wheel first one way, then the other, Derek navigated around a minefield of ruts, washboards, trenches, and potholes, all the while imagining strategic nuts and bolts unscrewing themselves from the Toyota's undercarriage as they bounced along. He peered out over his clenched fists gripping the wheel and wondered anew what the hell had possessed him and Jamie to accept such peculiar invitations to begin with.

Peculiar, for one thing, because the invitations had not been mailed. They had been shoved under each of their front doors in the middle of the night—Derek's under the door of his downtown apartment, Jamie's under his apartment door in Hillcrest, just up the hill from the city proper. Perhaps it was that proof of familiarity with their individual circumstances that helped convince them to accept the invitations. Clearly a friend had delivered them, right? Who else would know where they both lived?

Not for the first time since the letters arrived five days earlier, Derek shook his head at the weirdness of it. And the weirdness didn't stop with the strange way the invitations had shown up on their doorsteps. It extended onward to the two of them *accepting* the anonymous invitations without so much as batting an eyelash. Hey, it'll be fun, they told each other. A lark. A funny wee mystery they would both laugh about some day.

Well, what with his Toyota dismantling itself beneath him, the nerve-racking collapse of the rickety bridge, and the fact that they were tooling along through the worst thunderstorm he had seen in years with no way to turn around and get the hell *out*, Derek figured the giggle factor on this bizarre enterprise had deteriorated considerably in the last few minutes.

"Don't forget this is all your fault," he griped, impatiently wiping a smear of fog from the windshield with his coat sleeve so he could see where the hell he was going. "It was the postscript on the invitation. That's really why we're here, isn't it? All that business about the host offering 'heart-stopping door prizes' to all the guests. You really are a greedy little twit, you know that?"

Jamie didn't appear to be listening. "Door prizes. Greedy," he muttered, staring out into the night. He then laid a gentle hand on Derek's arm and turned his gaze on him. Leaning close, he whispered in a sweetly questioning voice. "What if we fall in love? What happens to our friendship then?"

Derek rolled his eyes. Happily it was dark enough that Jamie couldn't see him do it. "Can we try to cope with one disaster at a time, please? Besides, we're not going to fall in love. We're merely bonking each other due to a momentary shortage of other bonkable partners. It's a matter of supply and demand. Like pork bellies and soybeans. That's all it is."

Jamie plucked his hand from Derek's arm, and Derek was pretty sure by the way he did it that he wasn't pleased. He knew he was right when Jamie said, "That's not very romantic."

"No," Derek mumbled, more to himself than to Jamie. "I guess it isn't. But then, this really isn't a romance, is it? This is simply a sexual interlude between friends."

Jamie's voice was ice. "Is that what it is? A sexual interlude?" Yep, he definitely wasn't amused.

Derek relented. "Well, maybe it's a *little* romantic."

And suddenly, as Derek manhandled the Toyota around another pothole, confused not only by what was going on outside the car, but *in*, a memory washed over him. A memory from childhood. He and Jamie standing outside Roosevelt Junior High School, saying goodbye for the day before hopping their respective school buses and heading home. It had been a very odd moment, Derek remembered now. And it was made even odder by the fact that this particular memory had come back to haunt him several times over the intervening years. It had popped up in Derek's subconscious so often, in fact, that by now he had it memorized perfectly. Every little bitty bit of it.

He and Jamie had been fourteen, each in the cast-iron grip of puberty, with all the earth-shattering astonishments that entailed. They had shot up over the summer, standing now three inches taller than they had a year ago. Their shoulders were broadening, their hips narrowing. Jamie's blond hair had lost a little of its curl, and now if there was the tiniest amount of wind, it swayed atop his head like a field of tawny wheat. Jamie had a sheen of blond peach fuzz on his chin as yet unmown, while Derek had actually started shaving twice a week due to his dark beard popping through prematurely. Derek had only recently discovered the joys of masturbation, and he found himself thumping away at his poor pecker every chance he got. It was sort of funny, and a little confusing, how often he thought of Jamie when he did.

With streams of screaming kids pouring past their quiet island of stillness, Derek had stood staring at Jamie as Jamie stood staring back at him. A strange quiet had taken hold of them both. Jamie's lips were slightly parted, as if he were equally astounded by the weirdness of the moment.

Wrapped inside their well of silence and oblivious to everything going on around them, Derek had reached out, all the while watching his hand with wide-open eyes as if it belonged to somebody else. He spread his fingers and pressed them against Jamie's chest, leaving them there as he felt the sudden intake of Jamie's breath at the unexpected touch. The heat of Jamie's warm skin radiated through the thin T-shirt he wore, and that heat was like a surge of electricity shooting through the palm of Derek's hand.

"You're growing up," Derek said in a hushed voice. "You're getting handsome."

For some bizarre reason, Jamie's blue eyes misted over in a prelude to tears. "So are you," he whispered back.

A bus horn blasted behind them, and they both jumped. Derek turned to spot his driver waving for him to get the hell on the bus, he didn't have all day.

Derek lifted his hand from Jamie's chest and stammered, "L-later, I guess."

Jamie swallowed hard and since he couldn't seem to find his voice, he simply nodded. They separated then, the moment over.

That night, as Derek lay in his upstairs bedroom touching himself beneath his NASCAR quilt, he squeezed his eyes shut and remembered Jamie's breath lifting his chest against Derek's hand, felt Jamie's heat pulsing through his T-shirt to Derek's palm. When Derek's orgasm exploded out of him, he had to bite down on his tongue to keep from crying out. Wouldn't his parents have loved that? A moment later he tasted blood while his heart hammered in his ears and his juices began to puddle and crisp across his belly and chest.

Driving now down this god-awful muddy cow path with Jamie still here, still at his side, Derek smiled to himself, reminiscing.

Without thinking, he reached over in the dark and spread his hand across the side of Jamie's face. When Jamie turned his head into his hand and laid a kiss to his palm, Derek's smile widened.

"Whatever it is we're doing with each other, I'm glad you're here," he said, his voice just loud enough to burrow a path through the storm.

"So am I," Jamie answered. Derek sat mesmerized as a spark of shimmering light flared from Jamie's eyes in the glare of the dashboard lights. A grin danced across Jamie's lips. "I have plans for later," Jamie teased. "*Intimate* plans, if you know what I mean."

Derek shook his head and laughed. This time he didn't try to hide the rolling of his eyes. "Trust me, Hot Stuff. I always know *exactly* what you mean."

JAMIE LEANED in close and checked the odometer. "That's fourteen miles," he said. "The house should be coming up."

Derek responded with a quick nod. Most of his attention appeared focused on avoiding potholes and staying on the road. "I can't really look. Can you see any lights anywhere?"

"No. Yes!" Jamie squealed, jumping up and down in his seat, rocking the car like a preschooler. "Right there! Through the trees. See? See?"

Blinding sheets of rain slapped the windshield, making it almost impossible to see anything. But off to the right, following a swipe of the wipers, Jamie's vision cleared for a brief second—long enough for him to spot an array of golden lights shimmering among an all-but-solid wall of pine trees, thrashing and swaying in the wind. The lights were spilling through a dozen or more windows, indicating the presence of a large house tucked away out here in the middle of nowhere. In the flash of a lightning bolt that almost startled him out of his socks, he caught a glimpse of ornately angled rooflines and rain-soaked, peeling clapboard walls.

Jamie couldn't believe it. "Holy cow," he cried, sounding far less excited than he had a moment ago. "It looks like the Haunted Mansion at Disneyland, only dumpier!"

"Well, that can't be good," Derek commented wryly, tapping the brakes a little too hard and causing the car to slue sideways again. It bounced to a stop inside another lake-sized mudhole. "If I recall correctly, you *hated* the Haunted Mansion at Disneyland. You whined about the ghosts being way too realistic, remember? Look closer. Are you sure it doesn't look more like the Tiki Hut? You *loved* that."

"Oh shut up," Jamie groused, waiting for the wiper to make another pass so he could examine the lights in the trees again.

Derek leaned forward too, both of them now trying to see through the driving rain and hail. "See a turnoff anywhere? A driveway?" he asked.

"I can't see *anything*. No, wait. There it is. See there, by that big boulder? It's a roadway leading toward the house." He chewed his bottom lip. "But don't turn, Derek. I've changed my mind. I don't want to go to this stupid party. I don't care about the stupid door prizes. Just keep driving forward. This road must wind up somewhere, and wherever it is, we can work our way back to civilization from there."

Derek made a clucking sound. "No can do. Where the turnoff begins, this road also ends. Look."

Jamie forced himself to look where Derek was pointing, and sure enough, there it was. A solid wall of trees just past the spot where the driveway to the mansion began. With the collapsed bridge at their backs and the impenetrable trees in front, they had no choice but to approach the creepy house stuck in among the trees. There was nowhere else to go.

"Still need that drink?" Derek asked. He sounded like he already knew the answer.

"More than ever," Jamie sighed.

He flipped down the visor and lit the light on the little vanity mirror positioned there. After giving his hair a once-over and even leaning close to check for eye boogers, he finally flipped the visor out of the way and stated flatly, "Drive on. I'm ready."

Derek grinned. "You don't *look* ready."

"Oh hush," Jamie answered, laying his hand on Derek's thigh for strength, or maybe just because he liked putting it there.

"You da boss," Derek crooned, and a moment later they sloshed through the final mudhole and made the turn.

Except for the wailing of the storm, silence descended on the interior of the car while they both craned forward, staring at the old house looming up in front of them—drawing closer and closer and closer....

IT WAS an ancient three-story mansion. Desperate to flee the storm, they quickly parked, hurled themselves from the car, and ran for the front porch, vaulting over puddles with their heads hunkered under their coats. A sudden sizzle of lightning and boom of thunder gave them wings, and they fairly *flew* for shelter, dragging each other forward, half laughing, half screaming in terror.

Leaping toward the porch steps with Derek in tow, Jamie sensed the mansion looming over them like some gigantic bird of prey. There were three stories of shadowed eaves and dormered windows—some lighted, some dark. The house appeared to be in disrepair. One of the shutters hung at an odd angle while another was missing altogether. The paint on the outer walls had peeled in places all the way down to bare wood, exposing ancient, brittle planks beneath. Far above their heads, with lightning for a backdrop, Jamie had counted no less than six chimneys poking toward the heavens, denoting numerous fireplaces scattered around inside, which told him the house was built before central heating came into vogue.

The brooding facade sweeping skyward in front of them was broken by a trellised roof jutting out between the first and second floors, sheltering a banistered porch, which was what they were shooting for to get in out of the rain.

It was a wraparound porch, with chaise lounges, covered for the winter, scattered about. Jamie and Derek scrambled breathless up the front steps and stood shivering and soaked. Derek's eyes crinkled merrily. He was clearly amused, probably at Jamie's expense.

"Your imagination is going crazy," Derek droned. "I can tell. Just bang on the knocker. I'd like to get out of this infernal rain."

A single dim bulb burned over the front door. Jamie studied the door knocker Derek had mentioned. It was brass, as big as a cantaloupe, and shaped like a gargoyle. Perfect. If Jacob Marley's face suddenly appeared in it, he'd probably have a stroke. Jamie sniffed. "The knocker's a gargoyle. I don't like gargoyles."

"Bang on it anyway. It won't bite."

Jamie didn't immediately obey. Instead he started shaking himself off like a wet dog, flapping his arms and stomping the mud from his feet. Derek followed suit.

While they tried to make themselves presentable, they gazed first left, then right, examining the building sprawled out in front of them. Golden light leaked through ancient lace curtains at either side of the door. Jamie imagined Hercule Poirot, along with some of his closest buddies from the Continent, sipping hot toddies and chomping crumpets inside. In Jamie's imagination they were being waited on by a stick-up-the-ass butler and two or three liveried flunkies who were dutifully scurrying around doling out goodies while sucking up to the nobility.

Downton Abbey meets *House of Usher* meets *Friday the 13th*. Holy shit.

"Knock," Derek groused. "What are you waiting for?"

Jamie heaved a sigh, looking none too thrilled with being ordered about, nor with the cavalier attitude coming from Derek. Visibly cringing, he grasped the brass knocker. It was cold and nasty to the touch, felt heavy in his hand, and was hanging at chin level smack in front of his face. Trying to ignore his trembling knees, he lifted the brass knocker and let it fall three times, eliciting a *bang, bang, bang* loud enough to wake the dead. Well, perhaps not the dead, he sincerely hoped before he could stop himself.

The door knocker sounded like a blacksmith's hammer pounding on a humongous fucking anvil. Echoes of its racket reverberated off in every direction, all the way out to the trees in the distance. Behind them in the rain, parked among four or five other automobiles they now noticed sitting drenched in various spots under the storm-tossed pines, Derek's Toyota clicked and wheezed and dripped its way to silence after the ordeal it had endured on the crappy road that led them here. As the door knocker's third *bang* echoed down to an eerie stillness, they stood breathless through that instant of anticipation one experiences while standing outside an unfamiliar door waiting for the approach of an answering footfall. Before the footfall came, they heard a woman scream as loud as a siren. The noise erupted from somewhere inside the house.

Jamie clutched his chest while Derek stumbled backward and would have teetered off the steps if Jamie hadn't snagged his coat sleeve and snatched him out of danger. A heartbeat later, as they stood dripping, their mouths slack with horror, the door flew open in front of them, making them jump in fear all over again.

Jamie was so startled he nearly fainted. He didn't have time to gauge Derek's reaction because in that same instant, the shadow standing in the doorway, limned with light from behind, reached out and dragged them both inside.

A moment later, the door slammed shut behind them, sealing them in. There a sea of strangers, each and every one as startled as themselves, stood gaping at the new arrivals.

"Great," someone commented wryly. "The merriment continues."

THE MAN who had opened the door turned out to be somewhat of a dish. Sun-streaked hair combed straight back off a porcelain-smooth forehead. Black-framed spectacles perched on a movie-idol nose magnified brown, inquisitive eyes. His jutting jawline was sharp enough to slice bread. He was decked out in a tweed jacket with leather patches on the elbows, which Derek thought might not be too over-the-top if he were spending a weekend at Toad Hall. Here in the Southern California boonies, of course, it simply looked pretentious. In spite of the stuffed-shirt apparel, he exuded a fairly sexy persona, Jamie thought, his gaydar beeping like crazy. He wondered idly if the man had a big pretentious dick stuffed in his herringbone slacks, along with a meerschaum pipe cooling in his jacket pocket a la *Father Knows Best*.

"Sorry about the scream," the tweedy man said, but the statement was not directed to either Derek or Jamie. It was aimed at the people standing behind him, each and every one of whom looked as uneasy as Jamie felt. In particular, he directed his words toward the blonde woman standing partway up a long staircase.

The woman shrugged by way of a halfhearted apology. "Sorry," she said. "I didn't mean to scream. I hate storms. That last bolt of lightning startled me."

"Quite all right," Jamie answered back, as gallant as a knight, although he had to admit the storm was getting on his nerves too. His hormones stopped carbonating at the sight of the sexy guy in tweed long enough to allow him to look vaguely understanding. "I almost never scream," he added for no particular reason. Hoping to lighten the mood. "And when I do, it's in a much lower register. Butch, really. Manly, if you know what I mean."

Derek bumped him with a hip. "Hairdressers aren't that manly. Don't get carried away."

Jamie grinned.

Above the group of people standing around, each with a face more anxious than the next, a pinched, older woman appeared at the top of the stairs. She was as skinny as a rail and looked in desperate need of a cheeseburger and fries.

The old woman barked out a most uncharitable laugh. "Don't worry, gay boy," she snapped at Jamie. "We knew it wasn't you."

Jamie turned to Derek, his expression somewhere between amused and appalled. "Did she call me 'gay boy'?"

Derek leaned in close and whispered, "Think of it as a compliment."

Jamie blinked. "Oh. Okay, then." Still smiling, although it was a little less natural than before, he turned back to the crowd still shuffling around in the foyer to see what would happen next. The fussy older woman in need of a decent meal and lessons in how not to be an asshat in social situations gazed down at them from the top of the stairs as if she hoped they would start an argument. *Homophobic bitch*, Jamie thought, and stuck his tongue out at her, deciding maybe butch wasn't the way to go after all.

She sniffed, hoisted her nose in the air, and turned away.

The woman who had screamed—she looked to be in her midforties—took a firmer grip on the suitcase she clutched in her hand. She descended the last three steps to the foyer and headed for the front door.

Jamie's hairstylist sensibilities kicked into high gear as he studied her more closely, and he all but clucked his tongue in sympathy at her appearance. Someone whose cosmetology license should be immediately revoked had bleached the poor woman's straw-colored hair to within an inch of its life so that it now hung dead around her face. Her bangs were so long she looked to be peering out through a bale of hay. The mere sight of those god-awful brittle bangs flopping across the woman's nose made Jamie's fingers itch for his scissors and a tub of hydrating conditioner. Industrial strength. When she passed him on her way toward the door, Jamie could see that the back of her hair looked even worse than the front. Poor thing.

"Where do you think you're going?" Derek asked her politely enough.

She answered only after yanking the front door open, letting the rain blow in. She turned back long enough to say, "Back to the city where I belong. This storm is intolerable. This house is dusty. There are cobwebs in the corners. I still don't know who our host is, and I don't like *any* of you people. So I'm going home."

"Hope you can swim," Derek said.

Every head swiveled his way. The woman at the door studied him with worried eyes. "What do you mean by that?"

Derek stepped closer to Jamie and draped an arm across his shoulders. "I mean the bridge went up in splinters the minute Gay Boy and I drove across it. So if you want to leave, you'll have to swim through a raging torrent."

Tweed Man studied each face in the room in a round-robin sort of way, spinning 360 degrees while he did so, obviously seeking consolation anywhere he could find it. "Surely there's another road, right?"

"No," said the old woman on the stairs, frowning severely. "I don't believe there is."

"I didn't notice one either," said a heavyset older man dressed in gray Dickies like a janitor might wear. He had just entered the foyer from a door in the back. Jamie saw a look pass between the man and the old woman. They were obviously a couple. And clearly the service staff. God help them all.

"Not even a hiking trail," said a young man leaning on the newel post at the bottom of the stairs, whom Jamie had not noticed before. The kid, as Jamie instantly thought of him, was even younger than he and Derek. He wore a leather jacket and boots like a motorcycle rider and looked rather grumpy, as if immensely unhappy to find himself in such a crowd of old farts, which Jamie found a little insulting. His scowl softened when hunky Tweed Man shuffled through the crowd to stand at the young man's side and slip a hand in his.

Suddenly Jamie was a little less confused about Tweed Man's sexual proclivities. Clearly he was gay as a goose. And a lucky goose at that. The kid was a real hottie, and they were clearly a pair.

"Don't bother looking. There is no other road out of here."

The last statement came from the old woman on the stairs. Only now did Jamie notice she had a mass of gray hair pushed haphazardly into a bun and trapped at the back of her skinny head under a net thick enough to catch lobsters in.

Her words seemed to dash the last hope of the woman with fried blonde hair. She slammed the front door shut, sealing out the storm, then dropped her suitcase to the floor and dug her fists into her bony hips. Gazing around from one face to the next, saving Derek for last, she all but wailed, "Are you telling me we're *trapped here?*"

DEREK SIGHED and pulled his cell phone from his jacket pocket. He dangled it in the air in front of their faces like a farmer tempting a pack of donkeys with a carrot. "Good grief, lady. No need for melodrama. I'll simply call for assistance. We need to notify the authorities that the bridge is out anyway."

Everyone froze, staring at him. Then they relaxed en masse, as if they had all been through this before. Some crossed their arms over their chests, others stared down at their feet while pursing their lips. A few even tried to hide downcast grins as they stared at the floor. The woman at the front door simply tapped her toe impatiently and allowed her eyes to skitter across the ceiling. Finally, she settled her sarcastic gaze on Derek's face.

"Try it, then," she said. "Go ahead. Phone for help. Notify the authorities. We'll all wait right here."

Derek shook his head, wondering what all the fuss was about. He tapped on his cell phone and waited for a signal. Then he waited some more. The phone flashed a single word over and over across the screen.

...searching... searching... searching....

Derek gave it a shake. Still nothing happened. He turned to Jamie, helpless, and Jamie heaved a sigh of his own. He dragged *his* cell phone from his pocket and punched a few keys.

Derek peered over his shoulder and eyed Jamie's readout. It showed the same.

...searching... searching....

After a few seconds of this, both screens went dark.

The older man who had appeared out of nowhere at the back of the foyer a moment before—he sported a severe flattop and horn-rimmed glasses—cleared his throat in an officious manner. He carried himself like a crusty old general about to send his troops to war. In other words, there wasn't much noticeable humor about him.

He directed his comments to Derek, since Jamie was still poking buttons on his nonresponsive phone. "We've been trying to call out ever since we arrived. This must be a dead zone. None of our cell phones could get a signal. Or perhaps it's the storm. Maybe the towers are down."

"Well, doesn't the house have a landline?" Derek asked.

The man chewed on his cheek as if he was still processing that information. "No," he said, giving an astonished shrug as if he still couldn't believe it. "There is no landline on the premises. Or none that Mrs. Jupp or I could find." The old woman on the stairs nodded in agreement.

The proverbial light bulb went on over Derek's head. He shifted his eyes to Jamie, who was starting to look like he'd just had the same epiphany. "But that means with the bridge out, and with no way to make a call, we really *are* trapped!"

"In the *boonies*, no less!" Jamie amended, looking even more horrified than Derek. He swiveled his head around like a snake and squinted through slitted eyes at the skinny old woman standing on the stairs who'd called him a gay boy. "And under the same roof with *her!*"

"Maybe he's not as dumb as he looks," the old woman drawled, brushing a speck of lint off her bodice. Her sarcastic glance fell on her husband, who gave Jamie a wicked leer in return.

"Great," Jamie mumbled under his breath. "*Two* homophobes."

The blonde woman at the door took a moment to stare from face to face at each of the six other people milling awkwardly about before hoisting her suitcase and clutching it tightly to her chest. Outside, a boom of thunder made her cringe. Real fear flashed in her eyes. Her gaze once again drifted up to the ceiling and out past the roof to the storm beyond. She seemed to sink in upon herself as another grumble sputtered across the heavens.

Her lips went thin and bloodless, her expression cold. "So what should we do, then? Play charades? Cook up some s'mores? Roast marshmallows and sing 'Kumbaya' around the fireplace?"

No one laughed, and she didn't look like she expected them to.

Suddenly businesslike, Derek took Jamie's hand. "Would someone like to show us to our room?"

The spinsterish old woman had descended to the bottom of the stairs. There was no welcome in her eyes, simply what appeared to be a weary acceptance of her own fate. "I'm Mrs. Jupp," she announced formally. "My husband and I will do for you while you're here. Come along and I'll show you to your room. I assume you two will be staying together," she added with a saccharine smile that appeared to be thumbtacked to her face for the sole purpose of hiding a sneer.

There was something about that smile that Derek didn't like at all. It made him feel... *dirty* somehow. And that hurt his feelings. It also made him feel less than socially acceptable. Which pissed him off.

Apparently Jamie had the same reaction. "I don't suppose your husband knows how to build a bridge," he all but snarled.

Derek offered up a wicked smile, knowing how Jamie loved getting under snooty people's skin.

"No," the woman snapped. "But if you don't believe me, you can ask him yourself. He's standing right there, you know." She tipped her chin in Mr. Jupp's direction; then she turned to glare up the staircase she had just come down. With a sigh, she began to climb.

Rather than respond, the old man simply turned and walked away.

With a barely audible "Follow me," Mrs. Jupp gripped the banister and pulled herself up the staircase at tortoise speed, one agonizing step at a time.

"So you and your husband are the help," Derek said, obediently following her bony butt up the stairs. "That means you must know who hired you and who owns this house. You know who invited us here. Who is it?"

Mrs. Jupp merely continued her glacial advance up the staircase, rather like a freight train chugging up a long, steep hill. Only when she reached the landing did she turn and gaze down at them. "My husband and I don't know any more than you do," she said. "And no one has seen the hosts. If they are here, they haven't made their presence known yet. Our orders were left in written form in the kitchen, and the keys were under the mat. As per mailed instructions."

"Well, then, who paid you?" Derek asked. "Was it by check? Good grief, woman, who signed the damn thing?"

"We were paid through the mail with cash. And please don't curse. I find it extremely offensive."

With that, she turned away once again and headed along a dreary hallway. Half-confused and half-curious to see where they were going and how things would pan out, Derek followed with Jamie's hand still clutched in his.

DEREK AND Jamie had one small suitcase between them, and that was mostly filled with Jamie's blow-dryer and hair products, along with a flat of pancake and a tube of concealer. You never know when a zit might pop up. In matters of looking one's best, Jamie believed in the Boy Scout motto: Be prepared.

Derek tossed the carryall onto the bed while Mrs. Jupp stiffly angled her bones back out into the hall before closing the door behind her. They were alone at last.

"Well, she's a barrel of laughs," Jamie grunted when she was gone. He checked his hair in an art deco mirror hanging slightly askew by the bedroom door. Derek's visage in the mirror, watching him fuss and preen, appeared amused, but Jamie didn't mind. He liked it when Derek watched him.

As soon as he was satisfied with his appearance, Jamie straightened the mirror, then spun around to survey the room.

"Hmm," he said with the tip of his index finger burrowing a hole in his chin. "It's not the Hilton, is it? Now that I think of it, I'm pretty sure I saw this place in an old Marx Brothers movie. Margaret Dumont is probably in the bathroom washing cream pie off her face."

"Funny," Derek muttered, slipping an arm around Jamie's waist and pulling him near. Jamie returned the favor, snuggling close.

Their cheeks touching, they stared at themselves in the same mirror. Derek Lee's dark hair was zipped short, his five-o'clock shadow already darkening his jawline. Brown, soulful eyes peered out from beneath high eyebrows that always seemed to be in a state of surprise. Especially when he was around Jamie. He stood at an even six feet, with broad shoulders, lean hips, and almond skin. A spray of dark hair spilled across the back of his hands, which Jamie dearly loved to sweep his fingers over.

Tearing his gaze from Derek long enough to study himself, Jamie Roma reaffirmed the fact that he was pretty much the polar opposite, standing four inches shorter than Derek. Unlike Derek's, his own hair was blond and wavy. Side by side, they were a bit like night and day. One brash and sunshiny, the other quiet and dark and if not brooding, at least with the *potential* to be. On Jamie's pale, golden face, a sprinkle of freckles danced across a delicately carved nose. Above those freckles, a pair of forest-green eyes were perpetually laughing, not only at the world around him, but at himself as well. He was thinner than Derek, and unlike his swarthy friend, his arms and legs were coated with golden hair.

Jamie considered other respects in which they were alike and different. They were both in their late twenties and native San Diegans. But while Derek worked as an X-ray technician in a local hospital, Jamie styled hair in a snooty downtown salon. Lately, their lifelong friendship had somehow morphed into an ongoing sexual event, which astonished Jamie. The ferocity of their affair sometimes left him breathless.

They had been close before. Now they were closer. *Way* closer.

And having the time of their lives.

Until tonight. Jamie pulled back far enough not to go cross-eyed studying Derek's expression.

"What the hell are we doing here?" Jamie asked.

"You wanted a door prize," Derek answered. "They are supposed to be heart-stopping, remember?"

He gave his eyebrows a waggle. "I soitainly do."

Derek leaned around him and poked a finger into the mattress on the bed. The springs squeaked.

"Looks like we'll be keeping a few people awake tonight."

Jamie fisted the front of Derek's shirt. He pulled him into a kiss with such force that their belt buckles clacked together.

The kiss could have led to almost anything, and Jamie knew it, but for once in his life he had other priorities. He slipped out of Derek's arms and pulled off his coat. Standing at a hinged, full-length mirror, this one along the opposite wall and looking like an honest-to-God antique, he adjusted his clothes.

Meanwhile Derek dug through their overnight bag until he exclaimed "Aha!" and extracted a toothbrush.

When Derek peeked around a doorway to scope out their private bath, Jamie's chin was burrowing into his shoulder. Derek's sigh of relief matched Jamie's when they saw the bathroom was fairly clean. A stack of matching towels sat on a closed commode, and of the three light bulbs over the sink, only one was burned out. Could have been worse.

Jamie flushed the toilet just for the hell of it. Thankfully it worked. Then he stuck his head around an opaque sliding glass door and checked out the tub and shower. He turned back to Derek and with a wicked glint in his eye started plucking at the buttons on Derek's shirt. Thirty seconds later they were naked and soaping each other down under a spray of deliciously hot water.

Once they were clean and thoroughly turned on, they made love on the squeaky Amish-quilted bed, lazily, as if they had all the time in the world. Later, as they were pulling on their clothes and making themselves presentable once again, a rumble of thunder rolled across the roof of the old house. It sounded like an avalanche of bowling balls tumbling down an escalator. Jamie sucked in his breath and cringed until the thunder ended. Then he cast a guilty glance at Derek and laughed at himself.

Ten seconds later they pranced down the staircase on legs still wobbly from sex. They were laughing quietly and holding hands. The other guests were in what could best be described as a formal parlor just off the main foyer. Each and every one of them looked as skittish as colts. Clearly, the storm was getting on everybody's nerves.

Thank God from whom all blessings flow, Jamie thought, their fellow guests had not gathered for high tea, since there wasn't a teacup in sight. There was, however, a serve-yourself bar set up against the far wall, and not a hand could be seen that wasn't cradling a big fat cocktail.

Not bothering to look guilty about it, Jamie scuttled quickly toward an amber shimmer of smoky liquid that beckoned to him from among its multicolored brethren like a gleaming sunrise. Words, Jamie thought, that were appropriately poetic for a bottle of eighteen-year-old Glenfiddich scotch.

Especially when it was free.

CHAPTER THREE

THE PARLOR where everyone had gathered was large and a little run-down. There were a couple of stains on the brocaded wallpaper. The carpet was worn in spots, the furniture well used. Yet the room was warm and cozy thanks to a massive fire burning in the grate.

While Jamie sloshed alcohol into two glasses in sufficient quantity to marinate a couple of cows, Derek began working the room, trying to get to know his fellow guests. Not because he wanted to, but because he felt he should. Plus, he was dying to learn why he and Jamie had been invited here to this run-down old house in the middle of nowhere. What was it that all these strangers had in common that they should be singled out for such an honor? That last thought engendered a silent, sarcastic chuckle, since so far the whole experience had been a little less than festive.

He ignored Jamie shooting him a sexy wink from across the room and homed in on the elderly gentleman, Mr. Jupp, who was built like a 200-gallon drum of crude oil. The old man's colorless hair was squared off in such a severe flattop that the crown of his head was shorn down to nothing. In that shiny patch of bald skin in the middle of his head, the reflection from the parlor's chandelier twinkled and danced like Christmas lights. Mr. Jupp's white eyebrows blended so perfectly against his pale forehead they all but disappeared entirely. Icy blue eyes, neither friendly nor unfriendly, were magnified by thick bifocals perched low on a bulbous, red nose. Derek figured if he could only borrow those spectacles for a couple of minutes, he might be able to take a gander into next week.

After a perfunctory introduction, during which he reconfirmed the fact that Mr. Jupp was the housekeeper's husband and therefore one of the serving staff, the first words out of Derek's mouth set the tone for the rest of the evening. "Any idea who our host might be?"

It seemed Derek's voice had carried farther than he intended. The room fell silent but for the tinkle of ice as Jamie continued to construct cocktails at the bar, all the while humming a merry little tune, oblivious to everyone else. All eyes fell on Mr. Jupp. Even Mr. Jupp's wife, who stood off to the side arranging tiny sandwiches on a sideboard, narrowed her eyes and glared at her husband, as if leery of what he was about to say.

Mr. Jupp, for his part, didn't appear to mind being the center of attention, although his gaze did settle guiltily on his wife for a moment before he finally answered.

"As I believe my wife already told you, sir, we were contacted by mail after running an ad in the employment section of the *San Diego Union-Tribune* offering our services as household staff to anyone who needed help. Retirement doesn't set well with my wife and me. We prefer to keep busy."

Derek gave Jamie an appreciative nod as he accepted the drink he offered, which was a tall scotch and water, just as Jamie had poured for himself. Neither drink looked like they had been diluted much—which Derek suspected was a bad sign for the night ahead—but he took it anyway.

Quickly turning back to Mr. Jupp, he tried to ignore all the eyes upon them. Except for the rumble of thunder outside and the continuous pounding of rain washing across the windowpanes behind the drapes, the room was so quiet one might have heard a pin drop.

"In that first letter by mail, was there a return address?" Derek asked.

Mr. Jupp did not appear surprised by the question. "Not per se. There was, however, a PO Box where we were instructed to send our response."

"Didn't you think that was odd?"

"Not particularly," Mr. Jupp answered, his expression droll, like someone imparting secrets he really shouldn't. "My wife and I have worked for several eccentrics in our years of service."

"But there must have been a way for you and your new employer to contact each other in person."

The old man sighed. "Why? As instructed, we responded to the PO Box. That was personal enough to get things rolling. In the next correspondence from our new employer, directions to the house were sent. Also our pay. In cash. As far as we were concerned, the deal was made. Is there anything else you'd like to know?"

Those last words were not delivered kindly. Mr. Jupp had clearly begun to resent being cross-examined. Derek could see it in the way his back had stiffened. Also in the way he shot a trapped glance at his wife as she stood on the other side of the parlor, listening to every word, the platter of sandwiches forgotten in her hand.

Finally Mr. Jupp refocused his attention on Derek's face. Derek noticed he made a point of ignoring Jamie altogether. Maybe because Jamie was staring back at him as if he didn't believe a word he had said, which secretly cracked Derek up. Jamie was always seeking mysteries where they didn't exist. Of course, this time there really was a mystery, so Jamie was in hog heaven trying to piece it all together.

Mr. Jupp heaved another sigh. This one came all the way up from the soles of his feet. "Like I said before, all arrangements were made via the PO Box. Our employer's wishes were made clear. We had been paid a goodly amount to come here and open the house. The food and linens and wood for the fires were already here, as we were told they would be." He glanced down at the drink in Derek's hand. "Even the liquor had been stocked. All we were told to do was wait for all of you to arrive and to do what we could to make you comfortable."

"Did the employer say when he would be joining us?"

"He did not. But one would assume…."

"Did he say if he was coming at all?"

Another sigh, but a small one. "No, sir, he did not."

Derek frowned. He wasn't learning much. Even Jamie had lost interest. He was now staring over at the window and watching the wash of rain streaming sideways across the pane, carried by the gusting winds. Occasionally a flash of lightning would illuminate the storm-tossed trees in the distance. It was almost as if someone were running stock footage on the other side of the glass of every horror movie ever made.

Derek turned back to Mr. Jupp and tried once again. "When do *you* think our host will arrive?"

It was Mr. Jupp's turn to frown. His frown was considerably grumpier than Derek's had been.

"If the bridge is now out as you and your friend implied, I'm afraid I don't expect him to arrive at all. How can he? Unless he is hiding somewhere in the house, which is a preposterous notion, then I believe it is like everyone has already said. We are trapped. Perhaps once the storm has ended, we can try to decide what to do. Or perhaps our host will send help when he learns of the bridge's collapse."

"Yes, I suppose that's reasonable," Derek said. He reached out and touched Mr. Jupp's arm. Just a friendly, appreciative tap. "Thanks for answering my questions, sir. I won't keep you any longer."

Mr. Jupp ducked his head and immediately stalked off. He headed straight for the french doors leading into the hallway and exited the room. A moment later, his wife followed him.

Derek turned and studied Jamie. For lack of a better plan, he clinked their glasses together and took a long pull of scotch.

"You'll be happy to know that all is not lost," Jamie announced, smacking his lips. "The bar is well stocked. Whatever horrors we'll need to face, we won't be facing them sober."

Derek snorted back a laugh. "Well, that *is* a relief!"

He watched in wonder as Jamie poured the rest of his drink down his throat. So it was going to be one of *those* nights, then.

Smiling gaily, Jamie rattled the ice in his empty glass. "Ready for seconds, honeybunch?"

"DR. OLIVER Banyon. Pleased to meet you."

"Doctor of what?" Jamie asked.

"History."

"So you're a teacher."

A slight frown accompanied the good doctor's response. "A professor. Yes."

"Cool."

Jamie, well into his second drink, was feeling congenial. Expensive scotch did so put him in a pleasant mood. He nestled close to Derek's side while the tweed hottie with the leather patches on his elbows formally introduced himself. Jamie was struck again by how handsome the man was. While he didn't have a British accent, he somehow *looked* British. Like he should be at Oxford, touting his doctorate every chance he got, lecturing on the Tudors with a brolly under his arm or passing out sonnets in a centuries-old classroom overlooking the Thames while high tea waited to be served down the hall and his Aston Martin idled at the curb.

Jamie's imagination tended to run wild when he was half-snockered.

"This is my friend Tommy Stevens," Banyon added, stepping obsequiously aside to let his young, leather-clad paramour have his three seconds in the spotlight. While Banyon was perhaps ten years older than his "friend," Jamie thought he had the logistics of their relationship neatly hammered out already.

Friend my ass, he decided on the spot. Tommy was probably one of the doctor's students. A simple matter of cradle robbing. And he had to admit the kid was damn sexy in those tight jeans with the prominent bulge in the crotch, not to mention his snugly fitted Marlon Brando leather jacket. Hell, he even had the collar flipped up at the back of his neck like a proper juvenile delinquent from the fifties. After quick and careful consideration, Jamie decided it was probably a smart move for Mr. Rob-the-Cradle Banyon to let the kid have center stage for a while. He would undoubtedly be well rewarded for it later in the sack.

What bothered Jamie about young Tommy Stevens was the sheen of his oily hair, which had been meticulously combed back on either side with a damp curl left dangling over his forehead like a disjointed body part. It begged the question: *Has he found a hidden trove of Brylcreem in a time capsule somewhere, or do they actually still sell that shit? And does his mother still wear a beehive?* Derek did his socially polite bit, first shaking hands with Banyon, then with Tommy. And was it Jamie's imagination, or did the young Brando wannabe drag an alluring fingertip over Derek's palm as if he thought nobody would notice?

Jamie, never a slave to shyness when it came to protecting what was his, leaned in close to the kid's face and whispered, "Hands off, Rent Boy. This one is mine."

Tommy Stevens laughed, not even bothering to look embarrassed. Jamie was pleased to see two bright splotches of anger appear on each of Banyon's clean-shaven cheeks, however. Perhaps this wasn't the first time his young trick had put the moves on someone smack in front of his daddy's face. And suddenly Jamie honestly *did* wonder if Master Stevens really *was* a rent boy being paid for his services, which Jamie suspected would be quite intimate and most certainly enjoyable as hell.

If one was into young, hot guys and that sort of thing.

With his ten-second snit of jealousy, self-righteous anger, and downright nosiness out of the way, Jamie shot a glance at Derek, who was smiling broadly. He was clearly amused by Jamie's fit of pique. Not particularly shy about protecting his possessions either, Derek leaned in close and dragged his lips over Jamie's ear, whispering, "Don't worry, he's not my type."

"Liar," Jamie huffed back, turning away from the two men in front of them and whispering softly so they couldn't hear. "Little Tommy is *everybody's* type." His gaze slid away from Derek and back to Tommy Stevens, whom he nailed with a pointed glare that might have been shot from a nail gun for all the warmth it offered. He molded a totally artificial smile over his front teeth like he was stretching a glob of Play-Doh across his face. "So nice to meet you both. Now if you'll excuse me, I'm off to the bar. These free drinks don't make themselves, you know." Aiming his words directly at Tommy, he sweetly cooed, "I trust you'll keep your tongue out of my boyfriend's ass while I'm gone."

With that he did an about-face and flitted merrily off, leaving Derek to clean up the conversational mess he'd left behind, which was considerable.

"DEREK LEE," Derek offered, extending a hand in greeting.

Reluctantly, the woman with fried blonde hair extended her fingers, but pulled her hand back before actually making contact with Derek's hand. "Cleeta-Gayle Jones," she said, shooting a puff of air upward from the corner of her mouth to blow her bangs out of her eyes. She had removed her coat and now wore a sleeveless cotton shift with simple, straight lines. Nothing stylish about it. Her bare arms and what little Derek could see of her legs below the knees, were thin and freckled. He suspected that under her horribly bleached hair, her tresses had once been red. Red would have been a vast improvement over what she had now. He wondered why she'd changed it.

"That's a name I've never heard before," Derek commented, pulling himself out of his thoughts. He tried to be friendly since the woman still appeared terrified by the storm. He felt sorry for her and hoped he could help alleviate the shimmer of panic that still lingered in her eyes. "It's lovely, really," he said, casually stepping to the side to put himself between her and the window she kept eyeing with such dreadful fascination. "Your name, I mean."

"It's Appalachian, I suppose," she answered with a slight frown, swinging her gaze back to him. "People there have nothing else to offer their children, so they anchor them with impossible names for the rest of their lives." If the comment was meant to be amusing, it didn't show. As soon as the words were out of her mouth, a crash of thunder pounded the sky overhead, making her slap her hand to her chest and cry out with a startled yelp. "Oh, this storm!" Her face was once more riddled with panic and no small amount of impotent fury.

Feeling protective, Derek laid a gentle hand on her arm and said, "Wait here. I think you need a drink."

"Thank you," she said, her expression softening in her first display of warmth. "That would be nice."

"Any preferences?"

"Something strong."

She and Jamie should get along, Derek thought. Aloud he said, "Gotcha" and hustled off to the bar.

He returned a minute later with a gin and tonic, wedge of lime and all. A lady's drink, or so he hoped. He had bumped into Jamie at the bar, so he dragged him along as well. He introduced the two amid fears that Jamie would lecture the woman on hair care and the importance of follicle maintenance and a decent cut, but Jamie was well into his second or third drink already and obviously feeling expansive. He merely clicked his heels together and brushed his lips over the woman's hand in greeting, making her blush. Clearly, Cleeta-Gayle Jones was smitten with Jamie from that moment on, which Derek understood completely. He was rather smitten with Jamie himself.

The storm outside had not let up one little bit. If anything, it was bashing the house more brutally than it had before. Derek stared at the parlor windows and counted the seconds between lightning strikes and the ensuing booms of thunder. The time lapse was brief, since the storm was directly over their heads. The walls of the old house rattled around them. Inside the parlor where they were all milling around, the noises of the storm were augmented by the crackling of the large fire burning in the flagstone fireplace. Derek decided that without the fire and without the booze, there would have been a major shortage of good cheer to be had. He was pretty sure Jamie agreed.

Cleeta-Gayle emptied her glass with two long swallows, and even with two ounces of gin under her belt, her eyes never lost their fear of the storm. Derek couldn't help wondering if there was some sort of emotional trauma in her past that contributed to her terror. A beloved uncle beaned in the head with a bolt of lightning, maybe? A favorite brother blown away to a neighboring county and impaled on a fencepost while sitting in an Appalachian outhouse relieving himself in the middle of a storm such as this?

Derek shook his head and stared down at the drink Jamie had mixed him. Jesus, his imagination was getting the better of him. Maybe *he'd* better pour the next round of drinks.

"Why are you here?" Jamie asked the woman. When she looked startled by the question, he tried to clarify. "I mean, why were you one of the ones invited? Do you know any of these people?"

Cleeta-Gayle cast her eyes about the room. Although clearly still unnerved by the storm, she also seemed to understand what Jamie was really asking. In fact, she appeared as determined as he was to find a reason for their presence there.

"I've never seen any of these people before in my life. Have you?"

"No."

They both took a moment to survey the room before their eyes found each other again. "Then why did you accept the invitation?" Jamie asked. "A single woman and all."

She let her gaze drift back to Derek. "Are you boys together?" she asked shyly.

It was Jamie who answered, and Derek liked the words he chose. "We're working on it," he said, edging closer to Derek and taking his hand.

Cleeta-Gayle gave them a quiet smile. "I—I hope it works out for you."

"Thank you," Derek and Jamie said in unison. Jamie expanded on the sentiment. "Not everybody in this house would agree with you."

When she settled her gaze on Jamie, Derek was surprised to see such sadness in her eyes. She made a concerted effort to hold her emotions in check even as the words spilled from her lips. "There's a lot of hate in the world. People should try to be kinder."

Derek and Jamie exchanged a glance, then just as quickly turned their attention back to her. As carefully as he could, Derek asked, "Why did you come here? Why did you accept the invitation if you didn't know who had sent it?"

With an impatient flick of her hand, she scoffed at his wondering. "I could probably ask the same question of you." She glanced about the room, at the faces of all the strangers around them. "I suppose I was bored," she said. "That's why I'm here. That's why I accepted that silly invitation. I simply wanted to get away."

"And you know absolutely no one here," Jamie ventured yet again.

She gave him a shrug. "No. I don't. But I've talked to everyone. Not one guest knows who sent the invitations or why the seven of us were on the list." Her gaze flickered back to Derek. "Why did you two come?"

Derek hooked a thumb at Jamie. "The brilliant one here thought it would be a lark."

"Plus I wanted the two of us to go somewhere on our own," Jamie added. "Away from our friends and families. Off somewhere different, where we could get to know each other better."

Derek sidled closer to Jamie and bumped him gently with a shoulder. "What a lovely thought."

With a shuddering intake of breath, Cleeta-Gayle focused her attention on each of them in turn, visibly pushing her own troubles away to do it. For the first time since meeting her, Derek began to suspect the woman was stronger than she initially appeared to be.

"So you've only been together a short while," she said, gracefully turning the conversation back to them.

Jamie chortled. "We've been together since we were ten years old. It's only in the biblical sense that we're new to each other."

Her gaze drifted from their faces and centered once again on the storm outside the parlor window. "I wasn't always alone," she muttered quietly. "I had a child once. A boy."

"Oh. How old was he when he….?" Jamie faltered midquestion as if unsure how to proceed.

She didn't appear to mind the question. "I lost him when he was a baby. His life had barely begun." Tears shimmered in her eyes. Her chin trembled. "If only…."

"If only… what?" Derek softly asked.

But whatever the thought was that touched her at that moment, it was too much for her to share. Or quite possibly even bear herself. She shoved her empty glass into Derek's hands and offered a hurried apology. "I'm sorry," she stammered. "I'll go to my room now." Following a final glance at the storm outside, she gave a quiet gasp, quickly turned away, and hurried toward the stairs.

Derek and Jamie stood side by side, watching her go.

"Poor woman," Jamie whispered. He clutched his empty glass and shuddered.

"Yes," Derek agreed. "It must be hard to lose a child like that."

"Actually," Jamie said, "I was talking about her hair."

Derek took his arm. "No, you weren't. You were thinking the same thing I was. You don't always have to be a hardass, you know."

Jamie looked surprised. "I thought I did."

Derek shook his head. "On my account? No. I like you even when you're gooey and soft and sweet."

Jamie's smile slipped away. His dimple evaporated from view. "Really?"

"Really," Derek said.

Jamie opened his mouth to speak but quickly closed it again, leaving his thoughts unspoken.

For a moment, Derek wondered what Jamie had been about to say. And if it had anything to do with the two of them. As a couple. Or whatever it was the two of them were working toward becoming.

He slipped his hand over Jamie's. "You're cold," he said. "Let's move closer to the fire."

Jamie's breath stilled. His eyes widened as he studied Derek's face. It was almost as if he had suddenly figured something out he had only been wondering about before. "You take care of me," he said around a gentle smile.

Derek blushed. His heart did a pattering soft-shoe inside his chest, taking him by surprise. "Well, somebody has to do it," he stammered.

SOMETHING HAD been bothering Jamie for a while now as he stood with Derek near the fire. It wasn't the fact that none of the people knew each other, or that they all seemed so impotently mystified by the fact that they'd suddenly found themselves in this spooky old house with a bunch of strangers. In truth, Jamie didn't quite know *what* it was that bothered him so, but whatever it was, it kept pecking away inside his brainpan like a pestering woodpecker, trying to get out.

He shook his head and tried to push it all away, more intent on drawing comfort from Derek, who was standing silently at his side. Jamie had noticed moments like this creeping up on him lately. Moments when the quiet times he spent with Derek were almost as emotionally satisfying as the livelier, sexier, more intimate times.

They stood with their backs to the fire. At their feet the burning logs popped and crackled in the grate. The heat of the flames caressed the back of his legs. It felt good.

Before he knew he was going to speak, he heard the single familiar word slip from his lips. "Derek?"

Derek turned to him with a lazy smile on his face. He had that dreamy look he always got after drinking a couple of Jamie's stiff cocktails. Derek never had been much of a drinker. "Hmm?"

"I like being with you."

Derek's smile widened. "I like being with you too."

Before coming downstairs, Derek had donned a cardigan sweater, since the house was chilly in spots. Jamie reached out now and slipped his hand inside one of the sweater's broad pockets, not because he was cold, but because it brought him closer to Derek.

"You're beautiful, you know," Jamie said. Derek's dark-eyed gaze settled on him. Jamie's breath gave a hitch; he almost squirmed under the look. He stood absorbing the heat from those luscious brown eyes and the sweep of the long black lashes encircling them. A smile still played at Derek's mouth, but there was a touch more warmth in it now. Sexy warmth. Like the warmth radiating from the fire at their feet. It caused Jamie's cock to shift as veins began to fill. He thought back on the close moments they had shared during the last few weeks of their burgeoning affair. The wonderful discovery of it all. The newness. The need he felt to simply touch Derek at odd times during the course of each day.

"You're the one who's beautiful," Derek said. "In fact, those are exactly the words I say inside my head every time we make love."

Jamie edged closer. "Make love…," he murmured as his cock shifted again. "I like the sound of that."

His words were almost drowned out by a sudden surge of violence in the storm outside. A clattering of hail peppered the windows, halting conversation and causing the four remaining in the room to turn toward the sound. A mournful, wolflike howling crept in through the walls of the old house as the exploring winds tore under the eaves as if seeking a way in. The flames in the fireplace sputtered and stirred when a foraging finger of that wind swept down the chimney, gleefully scattering ashes and sparks. Everyone jumped when a limb, torn by the gale from a nearby tree, struck one of the automobiles outside, setting off the car alarm. They all ran to the nearest window to see which car had been struck, but the slanting rain and hail made it impossible to see past the house's front porch. Then Derek and Oliver pressed the buttons on their key chains, and the screeching car alarm fell silent. It was Derek's car or Oliver's, then, and not one of the others, but they were left none the wiser about which of their alarms had been responsible for the racket.

Through it all, Jamie's probing blue eyes had not left Derek's face for an instant.

And now, being forced to break that connection was proving to be one of the hardest things Jamie had ever done. But he'd had a thought. A realization, really. About the predicament they were in. And about the house that both protected them from this rampaging storm—and held them captive at the same time.

"Pictures," Jamie said. "Of people."

Derek blinked. "What?"

"There aren't any," Jamie explained. "Look around. If someone lives here, shouldn't there be pictures? Family photos? Framed snapshots sprinkled here and there?"

Derek blinked again and finally tore his eyes from Jamie's face. He did as Jamie asked. He looked around. At the tabletops. There were knickknacks galore. Fussy little ceramic doodads and statues. Dusty books lined up on shelves. Cloth doilies pinned to chair arms and artificial flowers, as dusty as the books, poking up from pots and vases—each bouquet looking as if it hadn't been moved or cleaned in months. Cheap store-bought landscapes decorated the walls, but none of the pictures showed actual people.

Jamie pointed to the wall opposite the fireplace. "Look there," he said.

Derek trailed his gaze to where Jamie pointed and saw immediately what Jamie was trying to tell him. What he didn't understand was why he hadn't noticed it before.

"Certain pictures have been taken down," he said.

"Yes," Jamie answered. "And quite recently, I'd say."

With his hand still tucked cozily in the pocket of Derek's cardigan, Jamie stood motionless, staring at three squares of fresh color on the parlor wall where pictures had been removed, pictures that had hung there long enough to protect the wallpaper from fading.

"Who do you suppose those pictures were of?" Jamie wondered out loud.

It was Derek who tossed another log onto the fire of mystery. "And who do you suppose removed them before the lot of us arrived?"

"And why?" Jamie added.

They stood quietly pondering that question as the flames sputtered at their feet and the storm raged over their heads.

Chapter Four

"Follow me," Jamie whispered.

With a plateful of sandwiches and fresh drinks, they ducked out of the parlor and parked themselves halfway up the staircase leading to the second floor. They wiggled their butts around to get comfortable, then set their drinks aside and lit into the little sandwiches Mrs. Jupp had prepared. It was nothing fancy. Tuna salad. Ham and cheese. Jellied triangles of toast. But they were hungry. They scarfed it all down without saying a word.

While they ate, Jamie pondered their situation. Half a dozen strangers—not counting Derek, of course—wondering, perhaps, how the hell they had allowed themselves to be lured to this drafty old house, then managed to be trapped here with a bunch of people they had never seen before in their lives and wouldn't much care to see again.

Jamie covered a delicate burp with his fist and scooched closer to Derek on the stair. With a delicious groan, he stretched his legs out in front of him. His muscles still felt cramped from the long car ride. He spoke softly, not because he didn't want to be overheard but because he was feeling lazy and relaxed and he didn't have the energy for grand oration.

"Next time I accept an invitation from someone I don't know, for reasons I can't explain, to a place with only one escape route and *it's* blocked by a fallen bridge, just shoot me, will you?"

Derek leaned in to press his lips to Jamie's neck. When Jamie gasped a little laugh, then ducked his head to meet those lips with his own, he was gratified to feel Derek's smile in the kiss.

"If I shoot you," Derek mumbled, "it won't be until I'm done with you."

"When will that be?"

"I'm not sure. Hmm. You taste like raspberries."

"It's the jam. I think it was homemade."

"Do you suppose there are still door prizes?"

Jamie's groan was a little less delicious this time. "Oh, do shut up."

Jamie watched Derek ease himself away. Their lips separated and Jamie missed Derek's kiss already. They settled comfortably against each other on the stair, shoulders touching, hands clasped. Derek found his drink and took a sip. Jamie did the same.

"Why do you suppose the pictures were taken off the walls?" Jamie asked, twisting his head around to stare at another square of clean wall space that had been recently exposed at the side of the staircase.

"And if our host lives here, why wasn't he already in the house, waiting to welcome us?"

"I don't think he does live here," Jamie said.

Derek gave him a sidelong grin. "I don't think so either." He cocked his head. "Say, is that *Twilight Zone* music I hear?"

Jamie kicked him in the foot. "Stop it. I'm a nervous wreck already. Don't make it worse."

A not unpleasant calm settled over them. Jamie cleared his throat and edged a little closer, even though he was practically in Derek's lap already. "Derek?"

"Hmm?"

"If we get out of this alive and actually find ourselves back in the city in one piece, can we keep seeing each other? I mean, the way we're seeing each other now?"

Derek's warm eyes reflected the light from the sconces on the wall that followed the staircase upward. In their amber glow, the brown in Derek's eyes had deepened. Their color was like chocolate now. Luscious, melted chocolate. Jamie thought he wouldn't mind spending the rest of his life staring into those eyes. Or was that being a bit too romantic for the circumstances? And while he was on the subject, what exactly *were* the circumstances? What the hell were they doing, he and Derek? How the hell did they think this was all going to end?

There had been humor in Derek's expression before, but it suddenly evaporated. One second it was there, the next second it was gone. Suddenly, Jamie was sorry he asked that last question.

"If we do keep seeing each other," Derek said, all laughter gone from his eyes, "I'll probably fall in love with you. Is that what you want?"

Jamie could only stare back at the open expression of trust that radiated from Derek's eyes. They had quickly gone off script here. This wasn't the usual repartee they engaged in. This wasn't one of their little conversational gambits they so often played with each other.

Swapping insults. Teasing. Trying to get a rise. Trying to get a laugh. Jamie understood immediately that Derek had changed the rules. What he asked now, he asked from the heart. And the intensity of his words, along with his melted chocolate gaze, caused goose bumps to explode on Jamie's arms.

Jamie sat there, entranced, as the tip of Derek's tongue came out to brush his lips, which still sparkled with the moisture from their kiss. Those were his own juices moistening Derek's mouth, and with that gentle swipe of his tongue, he realized, Derek had retasted him.

Jamie knew if he said what he wanted to say, it would change things even more than things had changed already. He and Derek would never be the same again. Not with each other. Not with their friendship.

Jamie also knew he didn't care about that. Not really. He only cared about how he felt.

"I think it's what I've always wanted," he said in a whispered hush, unsure how it would sound until he actually heard the words coming from his own lips. When he did hear them, he knew they were true.

"Since we were kids?" Derek asked, his eyes wide and searching now. Studying Jamie's face. Humorless. Sincere.

And somehow it was that sincerity in Derek's eyes that made Jamie really understand. Derek was right. They had been leading up to this moment from day one of their lifelong friendship. For years, even when they were children, that friendship had camouflaged what was actually happening between the two of them. Now the camouflage had been swept away. And it had happened the very first time they stumbled into bed together.

Jamie imagined a little cartoon light bulb blinking on over his head. My God, how could he have been so blind for so long? Without hesitation, he echoed Derek's words right back at him. "Yes," he said with his heart hammering in his ears. "I've wanted to be with you since we were kids."

Derek smiled then. Just a tiny one. At the same time, the fire in his chocolate-brown eyes flared to glorious flame. Sparks of gold bubbled in their depths. They blazed to life, burning like the flames on the grate in the other room. Only brighter, hotter. Derek's hand came out and covered Jamie's cheek. Jamie all but melted beneath the touch.

"It took us long enough to figure it out." Derek smiled.

Jamie tried to swallow the lump of emotion swelling in his throat. He succeeded, but the emotion found another escape route. A tear spilled from his eye. He felt the heat of it as it slid down his cheek to the corner of his mouth, where he licked it away.

"Are you saying what I think you're saying?" he asked with a tremor in his voice.

At that, Derek gave a tiny shake of his head. "If I have to translate, maybe I didn't say it very well. Or maybe you're just not ready to hear it."

"You're wrong," Jamie said, his fingers tightening on Derek's hand. "I'm ready." He twisted his head into Derek's other hand, the hand caressing his cheek. He pressed a kiss into Derek's warm palm. Derek's thumb stroked his cheek when he did.

Oddly enough, at that moment Derek turned away, directing his gaze back to the square of pristine paneling on the wall where one of the pictures had been removed. As if on a cue from the prop master tucked away in the wings, a crash of thunder shook the house around them, startling them both. A blinding flash of lightning seared the window panes that bordered the front door, strobing through the foyer, throwing everything into stark relief.

"I think we should search the house," Derek said out of the blue.

Jamie frowned. "What? *Now*? I think I'd rather finish this conversation. You were saying something about… us. Remember? I think it was kind of important."

But Derek pulled him to his feet. He didn't even try to be gentle. "Something's wrong," Derek said. "Don't you feel it? Listen."

Jamie glanced around and tipped his head to the side, concentrating on all the noises inside the house. The hushed murmur of voices in the parlor. The tinkle of cutlery. The roar of the storm battering the forest outside the foyer windows. A branch, thrashing in the wind, scraping against the porch roof somewhere. The rattle of window blinds in some far-off room, perhaps where the wind from the storm had crept through an unsealed window. The pop of an ember exploding in the fireplace in the other room. The thump of an outside shutter, loosened from its moorings and banging against the side of the house.

Jamie heard it all but didn't care.

"Sorry," he said. "I only hear my hormones begging me to take you to bed."

He reached out to pull Derek up the stairs, and at that precise moment, a woman's scream tore through the house.

The scream was sharp, piercing. It sliced through the night like the point of a knife penetrating the tender flesh of an eardrum. Cruel, invasive. Jamie shrank from the sound, it was so awful, so *operatic*. A chill crept up his spine. Terror erupted inside his head like a frightened heartbeat. Without thinking, he moved closer to Derek, where he felt protected. Where he felt safe.

As the echoes of the scream diminished, a strange quiet engulfed the house. It was as if the walls had suddenly ceased to breathe, waiting to see what would happen next. Jamie imagined the entire structure crashing down upon itself, crumbling to the earth under that eerie barrage of deafening silence.

Jamie reached out again for Derek, and Derek snaked an arm around his waist to hold him close. They stood frozen for a moment, listening. Waiting. Trembling in expectation.

Then the scream came again.

RUNNING FOOTSTEPS thundered across the hardwood floor in the parlor. Oliver Banyon burst through the parlor door with Tommy Stevens hot on his tail. They skidded to a stop when they spotted Jamie and Derek on the stairs. Both men were still clutching their drinks. Banyon's hand was dripping where most of his cocktail had sloshed out as he ran. He looked stunned, while Tommy wore a strange grin on his face that didn't seem to fit the circumstances at all. It was a fun-house grin. Like Tommy thought maybe it was all a game. A trick.

The kid's in shock, Derek thought.

A moment later, Cleeta-Gayle Jones appeared at the top of the stairs. Her eyes were as big as silver dollars, her face pale. One trembling hand clutched the bodice of her dress, the other embraced her throat.

Derek quickly altered his opinion. Tommy Stevens wasn't in shock. *She* was.

"Who was that?" she wailed. "Who screamed?"

The answer was obvious.

"It had to be Mrs. Jupp," Derek said. "She's the only other woman here."

"Where is she?" Jamie asked, not caring what anyone thought about him standing there in Derek's arms. If they had a problem with it, fuck 'em. "Where's her husband? Where's Mr. Jupp?" Banyon stepped forward. He was clutching Tommy's hand. Tommy wasn't grinning anymore. He seemed to have finally caught on to the fact that something was wrong. Whiz kid.

Clearly rattled, Banyon spoke louder than necessary. A professor trying to reach the students in the back. "He told me they were going to check the basement for a generator in case the storm took out the electricity. That must be where the scream came from."

"I guess we should find them," Jamie said, his eyes centering on Derek as if Derek's opinion was the only one he cared about. Derek had to admit he liked that. He ignored the sudden urge to kiss Jamie's trembling lip in front of everybody in the hall.

Instead, he tugged him down the stairs. They were only a few steps into their search to find the quickest route to the basement when a door slammed deep inside the house. Footsteps approached. They seemed to be rising up toward them, coming from beneath the staircase.

A triangular door under the arch of the stairs, one that Derek had not noticed before, squeaked open. Mrs. Jupp stepped through it into the hall. She looked even more terrified than Cleeta-Gayle. Her hair had escaped the bun at the back of her head and hung in long gray tendrils across her shoulder, swinging under the weight of a couple of fat bobby pins that were hanging on for dear life. Her pale cheeks were wet with tears, and the tears had not yet stopped falling. Her eyes were brimming with them. She spotted everyone watching her and pulled herself up short.

Mrs. Jupp opened her mouth to speak, but only a sob came out. A noise behind her made her jump, then turn. Her husband stepped into the hall from beneath the stairs. One side of his trousers was covered in blood.

Cleeta-Gayle finally released the scream she had been holding in for so long. Even Derek had to admit it was a pretty good time to let it go. Immediately she tried to swallow a second scream, succeeding to some extent. "What's happened?" she cried. "Why is he bleeding?"

Mr. Jupp looked down at himself, then back up into the gaping faces. Derek couldn't tear his gaze away from the old man's eyes. Magnified, as always, behind his thick glasses, they radiated shock and fear. His jowls were slack with terror. His mouth sliced a thin scar above his chin. Somehow he looked twenty years older.

"It's not my blood," he said on an intake of breath, as if the very act of speaking had pulled the air from his lungs. "There was—so much. I—I slipped in it and fell."

"If it isn't yours, whose blood is it?" Derek asked, taking a step forward.

Mr. Jupp opened his mouth to explain, but a movement to his left caused his eyes to skitter sideways. For a large man, he moved quickly and gracefully, catching his wife before she hit the floor.

He knelt with a groan on aged knees and, carefully cradling Mrs. Jupp in his arms, lowered her frail body gently to the floor. He laid a skillet-sized hand over his wife's meager bosom as if feeling for a heartbeat. Apparently satisfied she had only fainted, he lifted his gaze to the people watching. In the end, his old, weak eyes settled again on Derek, just as Derek somehow knew they would.

"Whoever they are, or were," Mr. Jupp said, straining to calm his voice, "they're both dead now. I think they were murdered."

THE TWO bodies lay side by side in a dirty back corner of the old house's basement, in a small enclosure about ten feet square that used to be a coal bin. There was a hinged door, closed to the elements now and no bigger than a window, inserted in the wall above the bodies where the coal was once shoveled in from outside.

The corpses were older. Probably in their seventies. A man and a woman. Their lives had clearly been snuffed out by cruel blows to the head. First one, and then the other. Their bodies had been neatly laid out on the filthy, blackened floor, the old woman's skirt modestly folded over her legs, the man's shirt and tie neatly smoothed out across his still chest. Neither corpse could have weighed much in life, for in death, they appeared almost skeletal. Jamie suspected it would have taken very little effort to end their lives.

On both corpses, the eyes were closed, as if in spite of all the blood and violence, they had merely dozed off in the coal bin, of all unearthly places. Jamie wondered if the murderer might not have closed their eyes for them. But why in the world would he—or she—do *that*?

A small hand shovel lay on the floor beside the woman's head. Its blade was covered in blood.

The murder weapon.

Jamie stood stunned by what he was seeing. After a startled intake of breath, he quickly placed a hand over his nose and mouth, for he suddenly smelled the bodies. They must have been dead a while.

"Oh my God," Banyon exclaimed, as if he had suddenly found his voice. He stood with Tommy, next to Jamie and Derek, as they all stared down at the two corpses on the floor. Cleeta-Gayle hung far back, over by the ancient furnace in the corner, refusing to come any closer.

The basement was a mess, as basements usually are. Cobwebs trailed from the rafters overhead. A lifetime of discarded items were piled here and there. The only light came from a bare bulb hanging from the end of a cord in the middle of the ceiling. The light bulb swayed, causing shadows to roll back and forth, bringing everything in the basement to imaginary life but for the two bodies in the corner. No amount of imagination could have resuscitated them.

As Jamie watched, a spider crawled out of the dead woman's hair and skittered across her face, disappearing into her hairline on the other side.

Jamie almost barfed.

A pool of blood had spilled from the coal bin and meandered out onto the basement floor. At a spot six feet or so from the bodies, the blood was smeared in a wide swath. Directly beneath the bare light bulb, footsteps could be seen in the shimmering liquid. That was where Mr. Jupp had fallen. Jamie didn't need Hercule Poirot to tell him that.

The fetid basement air had been moistened by the storm, which was probably why the blood on the floor had not completely congealed. It took Jamie a few seconds to realize that what he originally thought was the smell of decomposed bodies, was really not that at all. Perhaps the two victims had not been dead long enough for that. What he smelled was the effluvium of loosened bowels where the victims' waste had spilled from their bodies at the moment of death.

Jamie really wished he hadn't figured that out.

The pressure of Derek's hand at his back eased the shudder welling up inside him.

"These two must be the owners of the house," Derek said.

"You mean our host and hostess?" Jamie asked, still trying not to gag at the stench and the memory of that goddamn spider.

"I don't think so," Derek answered. "I don't know them. I've never seen them before. And unless you're keeping it a secret, I don't think you know them either, or you'd have mentioned it by now."

"No, I don't know them," Jamie muttered through the hand still clapped over his mouth and nose. If Derek had been trying to make a joke, Jamie hadn't found it amusing. Derek turned to the others. Banyon and Cleeta-Gayle were carefully watching him, as if they didn't need another glimpse of the two dead people, thank you very much. Only Tommy Stevens still stared at the bodies, his eyes bright with wonder, his expression oddly blank, as if he couldn't quite interpret what it was he was seeing.

"Do any of you recognize these people?" Derek asked.

He was answered by a couple of muttered no's and then silence. Just as Jamie expected.

"I have to get out of here," Jamie said, and Derek quickly agreed.

He steered Jamie back toward the basement steps. "Come on, babe," he said. "I think we need another drink." Cleeta-Gayle was no longer in the basement. She had already left. Back upstairs. Back to the light. Back where no head-bashed old people had been left to bleed to death on a filthy basement floor.

DEREK SUCKED in a breath of clean air as he led Jamie back into the foyer through the strange little Harry Potter door under the stairs. He studied Jamie's eyes and realized he had never seen such sadness in them before, but it wasn't surprising. What they had witnessed in the basement was truly the saddest thing either one of them had ever seen.

Jamie brushed his hair out of his eyes with a trembling hand. His gaze found Derek's face. "I don't think we should have left them alone down there. Shouldn't we at least cover them up?"

Derek sighed. "I don't think we should disturb the evidence."

Jamie nodded. "I guess you're right."

"Are you okay?" Derek gently prodded.

Jamie nodded again. As if shaking off the fetid cold of the basement, he headed straight for the fire in the parlor. He stood in front of the flames, washing his hands in the heat, while Derek took it upon himself to pour them each a drink. God knew they needed it.

Banyon, Tommy, and Cleeta-Gayle had positioned themselves around a settee in the corner of the room, where Mr. Jupp was tending to his wife, who had woken up. He held a hand towel filled with ice cubes to her forehead, as if he thought that would make her feel better. Derek thought she looked more annoyed than appeased by his attentions, but she didn't say anything. She simply let her husband do what he felt he needed to do. Derek supposed that was the result of spending a lifetime together. Letting the other do what they thought needed to be done, whether it pissed you off or not.

Drinks poured, Derek nudged close to Jamie in front of the fire and handed one to him.

Jamie took it but didn't bring it to his lips. Instead, he simply stared into the flames. A moment later, he said, "We have to get out of here. We have to notify the police."

In the background, Derek noticed for the first time, the soft sounds of Cleeta-Gayle sobbing into her hands. Banyon was awkwardly patting her shoulder, trying to get her to stop, while Tommy stood over by the sideboard, chewing on a sliver of tuna sandwich. His eyes weren't on Banyon or Miss Jones; they were on Jamie and Derek across the room. Mr. and Mrs. Jupp looked at no one but each other.

Unintentionally, Derek overheard Mrs. Jupp fussing about the state of her husband's trousers. "I need to soak those, or we'll never get the blood out."

"Maybe we should wait until the police come?" Mr. Jupp replied, his voice low, as if he didn't want the others to hear. He used almost the same words Derek had used only moments before. "One isn't supposed to mess with evidence at a crime scene, you know."

Mrs. Jupp bristled at that. "You watch too much TV. Just when do you think the police will come? After the bridge rebuilds itself? After the phones miraculously start working again on their own? When Batman swoops down in his Batcopter and carries us all away to Gotham City?"

For all her griping about her husband watching too much TV, she herself was clearly a movie fan. Derek bit back a giggle.

Mr. Jupp, on the other hand, sounded like every henpecked husband Derek had ever known. "Sorry," he said, "I wasn't thinking."

"Nothing new there," Mrs. Jupp snapped back. "And before you say it, no, I *don't* think that poor dead couple downstairs are the ones who hired us."

"Oh," Mr. Jupp managed to say, making it clear that was *exactly* what he'd been thinking. Too cowed to argue about it, he redirected his attention to fussing around with the ice bag on his wife's head.

Pitying them both, although in truth pitying Mr. Jupp a little more than his wife, Derek turned his attention back to Jamie. The drink seemed to be helping. Half of it was gone, and Jamie's eyes didn't appear quite so shell-shocked. He had some color in his cheeks again.

Standing close, Derek sipped at his own drink and stared down into the fire. The heat felt good on his legs. Thinking on it, Derek decided Mrs. Jupp was right. The dead couple in the basement probably weren't their hosts at all. Which begged the question—why were they killed? And by whom?

And more importantly, what did it have to do with him and Jamie and the other people invited here? How was it all connected?

A shudder coursed through him. He raised his drink to his lips and took a deep swallow to calm himself down. While the wheels in Derek's head began to grind into action, working to figure it all out, it was Jamie who managed it first.

"You don't suppose those two old people were killed just so the house could be used to lure us all together into one place, do you? This *is* their house, don't you think? They *were* the ones who lived here, right? The dead couple?"

Derek stared into the fire. "I would imagine so, yes." He turned to Mr. Jupp, still sitting with his wife across the room. "When did the two of you arrive?"

"Yesterday afternoon," Mr. Jupp answered. "We drove down from Oceanside."

"And the storm hit this morning," Derek mused.

"Yes."

"And without the storm, you would probably have never checked out the basement at all. Right?"

Mr. Jupp considered that. "Well, yes. There would have been no point. Like I told you earlier, I went down there to see if there was a gas generator around in case the power went out."

"And did you find one?" Derek asked.

"No."

Jamie shuffled his feet beside him. "Great. Now if the lights go out we'll be stuck in the dark with a killer."

Derek studied his face. "You think the killer is still here?"

Jamie let his eyelids droop to half-mast. Sarcasm was one of Jamie's talents. "Good grief, Derek. I think the killer is in this very room. Don't you?"

That snagged everyone's attention. Every soul in the room within earshot swiveled their head around to stare at Jamie. More than one of them gave the impression they thought Jamie was being a drama queen. On the other hand, more than one of them also seemed to think Jamie was probably right.

"No need to gawp," Jamie said, straightening his posture and squaring his shoulders as if prepping for an argument, focusing his attention on the doubting faces first. "Where else do you think the killer is? If he's roaming around the house on the sly, I think we would have heard him by now. I haven't walked across a floorboard yet that didn't squeak."

"You're not as dumb as you look," Derek said, eyeing him proudly.

Jamie gave a nod, accepting the praise as if he knew he deserved it. "Thanks."

"Now wait a minute!" Banyon barked, but then his outrage seemed to peter out as quickly as it had come. A look of confusion crossed his face, like maybe he couldn't think of an argument against Jamie's theory after all.

Derek eyeballed everyone in the room, his gaze sliding from one face to another. He wondered if one of them really *was* the murderer. His gaze fell for the umpteenth time on the squares of unfaded wallpaper where several pictures had been removed from the house. He had already seen the same clues in the hallway and on the staircase. He didn't doubt for a minute that if he searched the house he would discover others.

There had to be a reason for it. It had to be a clue.

For lack of a better plan, he decided to ask. He pointed to the closest spot on the wall where the wallpaper had been protected until recently. "Why were certain pictures removed from the walls? Anybody know?" Every face turned to the place where he was pointing. He could tell no one had really noticed the anomaly before and were slightly taken aback by the implications of it. *Well, that didn't take long.* If anyone was being insincere in their surprise, it didn't show. But then, he supposed he hadn't expected it to be *that* easy to weed out the killer.

Jamie stared at the unfaded squares on the walls as well. It didn't take him long to figure it out. "The killer must be *in* those pictures. He must be hiding his own identity." Jamie's eyes narrowed, and he scrolled warily from one face to the next. "Or *her* identity," he added.

Derek took Jamie's theory a step further. "And if the killer is in those pictures, it means he was close to the old couple in the basement. A family member, more than likely. Why else would he—or she— have to remove so many pictures from the house in a bid to protect his identity?"

Cleeta-Gayle took belated umbrage at Jamie's, and now Derek's, suggestion. "That's ridiculous! If you think a woman killed that poor old couple, then you must think either myself or Mrs. Jupp are the prime suspects, since we're the only two women here. How can you even imagine such a thing?"

Jamie took umbrage in return, bristling like a bantam rooster. "Well, somebody had to do it! And anybody can swing a shovel!"

From over by the sideboard, Tommy Stevens poked a cookie in his mouth and laughed. "So the lions are eating each other now. I suppose it had to happen sooner or later." He appeared vastly amused. Derek suspected a quick poll would have shown Tommy was the only one who found humor in the situation.

Mrs. Jupp at long last yanked the towel-wrapped ice cubes from her husband's hand, rose to her feet, and tossed it into the fire. She stared at the fresh square of wallpaper directly over the mantle. With her back still to the room, she said, "We have to get out of here. I read once where you can call 911 on a cell phone that isn't even hooked up. Someone try their phone again. My husband and I can't seem to find ours."

"Mine's upstairs," Derek said.

"Mine too," Jamie said. "I'll go get them both." He immediately left the room. Banyon slapped his jacket pocket, looked vaguely startled, and announced, "I was sure I had it with me. Maybe mine's in our room as well. Tommy, you want to go check?"

Tommy gave a reluctant grunt, then walked toward the stairs. Behind him, Banyon explained, "Tommy doesn't have a phone. By the way, even if the phone isn't hooked up, you'll still need a signal to reach 911, and a signal is the one thing we don't have. Still, we might as well try."

All eyes turned to Cleeta-Gayle. She met their looks with an almost guilty expression. Acting like she was doing them all a massive favor, she dipped into her sweater pocket and removed a cell phone. Even from across the room, Derek could see that the face of the phone was shattered.

"It's broken," she said. "I left it on my dresser after arriving. When I went back for it later after I decided to leave, I found it on the floor. The fall cracked the screen, and now it won't turn on. I'll have to buy a new one when I get home."

At that moment Jamie and Tommy Stevens both rushed through the parlor door. They stood side by side with startled expressions on their faces. "Our phones have both been stolen. They're gone."

Derek took a single step toward Jamie. "Even mine?" he asked.

Jamie stared back through troubled eyes. "Yes, baby. Even yours."

A flash of lightning strobed the room. Thunder cracked like a bullwhip over their heads and everybody jumped.

Cleeta-Gayle stared through her chemically fried bangs at the shattered cell phone in her hand. She didn't look happy.

CHAPTER FIVE

JAMIE WOKE up in one of those moments of total disorientation and panic, not knowing where he was or what he was doing there. The accidental brush of his hand across the familiar velvet skin of Derek's forearm brought everything back.

It was the middle of the night. Dawn was nowhere near. The house stood silent. It hovered over him like a crusty old vulture waiting for Jamie to take his last breath so it could swoop down and start pecking him to pieces.

Cheery thought.

Jamie stretched and quietly yawned. He and Derek had gone to bed early, exhausted from everything that had happened since they'd arrived. They had undressed and showered together, then tucked themselves into bed. Derek had fallen instantly asleep in Jamie's arms, and Jamie had followed soon after.

It was the first time since their affair began that they had lain down together and not made love.

Now that he was awake, and with a host of unfamiliar shadows looming up around him, not to mention his macabre imagination going a mile a minute, Jamie's mind began to roam. Derek's presence beside him brought to mind a night long ago. He and Derek were in their freshman year of high school. Derek was sleeping over. Jamie had found a straight porno magazine in his brother's room, hidden deep in a closet. Brothers being what they are, he pilfered it without a twinge of guilt. He and Derek were naked and flat on their backs side by side in Jamie's bed, beating off while Derek slowly turned the pages for them both with his free hand.

But for the brush of a furry leg down below and the occasional bump of an elbow, the two did not touch each other. Still, Jamie remembered every erotic moment of that night. He remembered them lazily stroking their young cocks and giggling, and he remembered when the giggling stopped and the touch of their hands on their own bodies had turned more heated, more unstoppable. He remembered their breaths quickening, their hearts pounding. He also remembered it was the sight of Derek arching his back as his juices exploded from his body that made Jamie erupt as well. Derek in orgasm, he remembered thinking later, and still thought to this very day, was the most beautiful thing he had ever seen in his life.

The memory of it now made Jamie's cock lengthen under the covers. He eased closer to Derek and laid his lips to that velvet-soft arm. Not to disturb, but to carefully touch and breathe in a little of Derek's heavenly heat, while at the same time letting him sleep.

But Derek was already awake. At the first touch of Jamie's lips on his skin, he rolled over and gathered Jamie in those strong, sexy arms. With a hand at the back of Jamie's head, Derek pulled Jamie against his chest. The hair there tickled Jamie's nose and made his cock grow even harder.

"You're as squeezable as a roll of toilet paper," Derek crooned, his voice grumbly from sleep.

Jamie stared up into his face in the darkness. "Is that supposed to be romantic?"

"Yeah."

"Well, it needs a little work."

Derek snuggled closer, pulling Jamie's face back to his chest. He didn't sound apologetic at all when he said, "Sorry."

Jamie relished everything about being in Derek's sleep-warm embrace. Derek's leg hair bristling against his own. Their toes twining around each other down at the foot of the bed. The way Derek's broad hand rested on the rise of Jamie's ass, his index finger burrowing comfortably and unobtrusively into the warm valley of flesh he discovered there.

"Listen," Derek breathed.

Jamie's lips brushed Derek's nipple as he whispered back. "Listen to what?"

"The rain."

"I don't hear it."

"Exactly."

Jamie lifted his head and truly listened. Derek was right. The storm had stopped. It was the first time nature had been silent since they entered this old house, and the quiet seemed somehow unnatural. Wrong. This house was built for thunder and lightning and lashing rain—sound effects, gliding ghosts, the wail of banshees somewhere off in the shadows. Peace and quiet didn't suit the place at all.

"What are we doing here with all these old people," Jamie asked, lowering his mouth back to the welcoming forest of hair on Derek's chest. He burrowed deep so he could breathe in Derek's delicious scent. In Derek's arms was his favorite place to be, for only there could he hear the gentle rumble of Derek's waking heart drumming softly against his cheek.

Derek's lips brushed through his hair. "Oliver 'the Hunk' Banyon and his leather sidekick, little Tommy Stevens, aren't so old. In fact, Tommy's younger than we are."

Jamie didn't have an answer for that, so he let it slide. He had other questions rampaging through his head at the moment anyway. Questions of a little more importance.

"There is no host, is there? No one is coming, even if they could get here."

"No," Derek said. "I don't believe there is. I think whoever was meant to be here has already arrived."

"So whoever killed the old couple in the basement is here too. It's one of our fellow guests."

"I think so. Yes."

"And the invitations were just a ruse to get us all here together so he can kill us too."

Derek's lungs went silent as his breath stopped. He lay motionless, still clutching Jamie close. Jamie could imagine Derek trying to decide whether to make a joke or not. In the end, Derek said, "We don't know that for sure."

For Jamie, it was like picking at a scab. He couldn't let it go. "But we don't *not* know it either."

"No, I suppose we don't."

Jamie wormed deeper into Derek's arms. "So any way you look at it, we're in a spot of trouble here."

While Jamie's words clearly did not comfort either one of them, the nearness of their bodies did. Derek breathed a heavy sigh as he dragged a lingering kiss over Jamie's forehead. The nestling finger down below came, as if by accident, to rest on Jamie's heated opening, sending a tremor of lust coursing through him.

Derek's long cock lay pressed against Jamie's thigh, even while Jamie's own erection pulsed atop the thatch of crisp dark hair covering Derek's belly. Derek's voice was huskier now, and probably not from sleep. He offered Jamie his best Jack Webb impersonation, even while his mouth worked its way downward to slurp at Jamie's throat, which always appeared to be one of *his* favorite places to be.

"Those would appear to be the facts, ma'am, yes. A spot of trouble indeed."

A growl erupted deep in Jamie's throat, below Derek's kisses, as another shudder of desire rattled through him from the top of his head to the soles of his feet. It took him a minute to find his voice. "There are corpses in the basement and a murderer running loose. How weird is it for me to want you inside me right now?"

"Well, it probably isn't normal."

"Is that a problem?"

"Not for me," Derek growled sexily as he eased Jamie onto his stomach and burrowed down beneath the covers. When his warm searching mouth found Jamie's On button and triggered it with a flick of his tongue, the conversation abruptly ended.

Other pursuits began.

DAWN HAD barely chased the shadows from the house when Jamie and Derek stepped through their bedroom door. Treading softly, they headed toward the staircase leading down to the first floor. Derek's head was thumping from too much scotch and too much excitement, but he didn't let that slow him down. Besides, the time he had spent in Jamie's arms in the middle of the night had calmed him. Making love to Jamie always did. Remembering, he reached out and clutched Jamie's hand as they descended the stairs.

They passed the dining room, which was situated across the hall from the parlor where they had met everyone the night before. A large dining table had been set for breakfast.

Derek raised his hand in silent greeting to Mrs. Jupp, who was fussing with a coffee urn and a tray of cups and saucers. Mrs. Jupp glanced his way but made no response. Without speaking she went back to what she was doing, her back as stiff as always. She was obviously not in a social mood. Derek wondered if the dead people in the basement had something to do with that, or if Mrs. Jupp was always a pain in the ass in the morning.

Hearing a clatter, Derek peeked deeper around the doorway and spotted Mr. Jupp arranging logs in the fireplace. Mr. Jupp looked inquisitive for a moment, as if he thought Derek and Jamie were about to ask for something. When they didn't, he simply said, "Good morning, sirs. Breakfast will be ready soon."

"Thank you," Derek said and immediately pulled Jamie toward the front door.

They stepped outside and stood on the broad wraparound porch, staring out on a dripping gray morning. The air was cool, the grounds beyond the porch's sodden planks a vast field of mud. Tree branches were scattered all over from last night's wind, and the mottled sky was still packed tight with rain clouds. Derek's original conclusion that the storm must be over took a major hit. Eyeing those black-and-gray thunderheads roiling overhead, he suspected they were experiencing more of a lull in the storm than an end to it. A far-off bark of thunder reaffirmed his suspicions.

"It's not over, is it?" Jamie asked, craning his neck back to scan the sky and looking none too happy about what he was seeing.

"Afraid not, kemo sabe."

"Well, poop."

Side by side, they stared out at the dripping trees. Over by the tree line where the cars were parked, the gleam of rain-washed chrome sparkled amid the gloom. Derek could hear the *plunk, plunk, plunk* of raindrops slipping from the branches and hitting the roofs of the cars. Somewhere among the trees, an owl hooted softly. Or was it a dove? He was never sure.

He glanced at Jamie, and Jamie glanced back.

Derek smiled. The lower half of Jamie's face had been rubbed red from Derek's five-o'clock shadow when they made love. Jamie's lips were still puffy and tender from other endeavors, but he gamely offered a smile in return.

"I know," Jamie grinned, rubbing his shiny pink chin. "Rug burn." His eyes softened as he reached out and stroked Derek's cheek, which was now smoothly shaven.

"Thank you for last night," Derek softly growled.

He corralled Jamie against the wall of the house as the wind began to pick up again, whipping their hair around and sending a chill up Derek's spine. Although it was late spring, the storm had left a nip in the morning air. With the tempest trying to drag itself back to life, the cool air had turned even chillier. A fine rain began to fall, but the porch roof shielded them from it. They stood in each other's arms, watching the distant trees grow dim behind the mist. The proximity of their bodies blocked the wind a bit, and Derek smiled again when Jamie tucked his hands inside Derek's jacket pockets instead of his own to keep them warm.

"Tell me again why we're here," Jamie said.

Derek pushed Jamie's hair from his eyes, but the wind blew it back a moment later. "It's like we said last night. You wanted your damn door prizes, and you wanted—we both wanted—to spend some time alone without the distraction of friends and family. If I fall in love with you, Jamie, I want to know that I did it on my own without any outside influence. In other words, with nobody's help but yours."

Jamie dropped his head to Derek's shoulder. With his hands still inside Derek's pockets, he clutched Derek's hips, locking them together. "You have no idea what it does to me when you talk about falling in love."

With his mouth at Jamie's ear, Derek faintly crooned. "Tell me, then. Tell me what it does to you."

But Jamie didn't answer. Instead, Derek felt Jamie stiffen in his arms. He pulled back to gaze at Jamie's face to see what was wrong. He found Jamie staring out at the cars again. His expression was more than troubled. He looked—confused.

Derek whirled around to see what had so captured Jamie's attention. "What?" Derek asked. "What are you seeing?"

"The cars," Jamie said. "They look like they've sunk into the mud. They're sitting too low."

Derek blinked and peered more intently into the mist. Jamie was right. The chassis of every car, all four of them, appeared to be almost resting on the ground.

Derek eased himself from Jamie's arms, and the two of them stepped out into the rain, where fat drops were now plunking in puddles already standing from the night before. Behind them, the raindrops clattered across the house roof and plinked against the window panes. But they ignored it all. They ignored a sudden streak of lightning slicing across the sky as well. And the sharp crack of thunder that instantly followed.

Derek began to run, pulling Jamie along beside him. He slid to a stop three feet from his car. Panting, Jamie stumbled to a halt right next to him. They both stared down at the wheels of the Toyota. Then their eyes wandered to the other cars, gazing disbelievingly at each of them in turn.

It was true, Derek realized. The chassis of every automobile *was* setting too low to the ground, and the reason for it was obvious.

Someone had slashed the tires.

SOAKING UP rainwater and grappling with why someone would go to the trouble of slashing all the fucking tires, Jamie spotted something silver lying in the mud beside Derek's front bumper. He leaned over and picked it up.

Wire cutters.

Derek said, "Oh, shit," and leaped inside his car to pull a lever by the door. Jamie watched, confused, as Derek swung back out of the car and manhandled the Toyota's hood open. He stood there with one arm up, holding the hood out of the way, while the rain pummeled the top of his head and his hair became slowly saturated.

"What is it?" Jamie asked, moving closer. But he knew. He already knew.

He and Derek stood side by side, staring into the engine well. There, what had once been a plethora of neat little doodads and gadgets (which was all Jamie knew about the workings of an internal combustion engine) had been reduced to a tangle of snipped wires and sundered connections.

A sudden fury welled up in Jamie. The fury didn't come because they were now really and truly stranded, or because the icy rain was dribbling down his neck, or even because there were two bodies back at the house and someone might very well have it in their plans to kill a few more, including themselves. No, the fury came simply because someone had dared do this to Derek's car.

He snuck a peek sideways to see Derek's reaction. He was surprised to see Derek's cheek sucked in like he was chewing on it, trying to work things out inside his head. He didn't appear mad, which scared Jamie even more than he was already.

"Are the other cars ruined too?" Jamie asked.

Derek slowly nodded, still gazing into the ruins of his Toyota's engine. "They pretty well have to be, don't they," he said. It wasn't a question. It was a statement of fact. "It wouldn't make any sense to dismantle one car and leave the others. And even if the engines *aren't* ruined, the tires are all flat. We wouldn't get very far on the rims. Even if there were a bridge behind us still standing."

They stared at the ruined engine for a long minute, listening to the rain, getting wetter by the second. Finally, Jamie couldn't stand it anymore.

He stepped forward, once again tucking his hand into Derek's pocket, for the connection more than anything else. It would take more than one dry pocket to warm the chill in his heart.

"Tell me what you're thinking, Derek. Tell me what we're going to do."

Derek slid his gaze around to settle it on Jamie's face. There was something in Derek's expression Jamie had never seen there before. It was a cold and calculating thing. Where before there had always been warmth and humor, and sometimes immeasurable lust, in those chocolate-brown eyes of his, there was now an icy, rising awareness. And Jamie knew exactly what it meant.

"We're really in trouble here, aren't we?" Jamie asked. "Someone is really out to kill us. *All* of us."

Derek slowly nodded. "I couldn't believe it at first, but, yeah. I think that's exactly what's happening. We're being systematically hemmed in. All routes of escape are now cut off."

Jamie turned and stared back through the rain at the old house half-hidden in the mist. Smoke rose from two of the chimneys. Golden light shone through the dining room windows, and now and then a shadow passed in front of them. People were milling about, gathering together, partaking of a half-wanted breakfast, perhaps, wondering what they were going to do. How they would get away.

Derek's next words did not surprise him at all. "It's not only us, Jamie. I think everyone inside that house is in danger."

"Except for the killer," Jamie said.

"Yes, except for the killer."

Derek took Jamie's hand and pulled him toward the house, if for no other reason, maybe, than to get in out of the rain. Thunder and lightning was booming and flashing across the sky again, the storm working itself up to round two. The rain was so heavy now Jamie could hardly see the house in front of them until they raced up the porch steps.

There they found a fellow guest. Waiting.

CLEETA-GAYLE'S EYES were puffy and her complexion more pallid than usual. Derek thought she looked like she hadn't slept very well, or possibly not at all. Her frazzled hair was a bird's nest on top her head, as if a brush hadn't touched it since she'd crawled out of bed. She was dressed in the same simple dress she wore the day before, but now she had a long raincoat pulled over it, unbuttoned in the front. It was flapping in the wind. Derek expected to see a suitcase in her hand again, but perhaps she knew better this time around. Maybe she knew as well as they did just how trapped they really were.

When she spoke, the earliness of the hour and her obvious weariness somehow managed to accentuate her Appalachian drawl. Or maybe it was simply the terror Derek spotted lurking in her eyes.

Derek figured they were all well past the point of wishing each other a good morning. Cattle in the queue at the stockyards waiting to be turned into ground beef probably didn't say good morning to each other either.

"Are you all right?" he asked, while he and Jamie shook themselves off after ducking under the porch roof to escape the rain.

"What's wrong?" she asked through pinched lips. There was a distinct tremble in her chin, like a subterranean earthquake jarring her skin from within.

Derek didn't see any reason to mince words. "Someone disabled the cars. Unless there's a mechanic hanging around I haven't met yet, not to mention a bridge builder, no one is going anywhere anytime soon."

Cleeta-Gayle didn't seem surprised. "Someone tried to get in my room last night."

Jamie stiffened at Derek's side. "What do you mean?"

She wrapped her arms across her chest as a tremor rattled through her whole body. The shiver was either from fear or cold. Derek didn't know which. She tucked in her quivering chin and glared out at them.

For the first time, Derek thought he saw a glimmer of spunk shooting out of those wounded, weary eyes. Behind the fear, the faintest glimpse of anger lurked.

"I heard footsteps in the hall. Then someone jiggled the doorknob to my room. They did it gently, like they were trying not to be heard. I had the lights out, so they probably thought I was asleep."

"And you weren't?" Jamie asked.

Her glare intensified. "I was praying."

"Did it help?" Jamie asked, unimpressed.

She glowered at him but didn't answer.

"Was your door locked?" Derek asked.

She gave a reluctant shrug, as if it didn't matter one way or the other. "Yes. There's an old skeleton key in the lock. I twisted it when I got inside. But these old houses *always* have a single key that opens every door. My key surely isn't the only one."

"No," Jamie said. "Our door had an old skeleton key too. And they're probably all interchangeable."

As if the same urge suddenly fell on each of them simultaneously, they all turned their eyes to the rain. It was really coming down now. They could hardly see through it to the cars and the trees beyond. Thunder was a continuous rumble overhead. When lightning seared the sky, they each stepped farther back from the edge of the porch, as if afraid they'd be barbecued in their tracks.

Cleeta-Gayle at last turned her back on the storm. After a quick glance through the window to the dining room, where the other occupants of the house were huddled, eating breakfast, gossiping, complaining, she focused her attention once again on Jamie's and Derek's faces.

"Someone here isn't who they say they are," she said. "How are we going to find out who it is?"

"Are you absolutely sure you don't know any of the other guests, or Mr. or Mrs. Jupp for that matter? Have you really never met any of them before?"

"No," she said. "I told you that before. Why, have you?"

Jamie and Derek answered in unison. "No."

A silence settled over them, a silence only interrupted by the rising storm. The rain seemed to draw them like a magnet. After each of them had spent a little time lost in their own private thoughts, watching the sky unload before their eyes, Derek finally turned to Miss Jones and asked point-blank, "Why did you tell us about someone trying your door? Why did you trust us? Why didn't you go to one of the others?"

Her answer came without a beat of hesitation. "You have honest faces." She centered her attention on Derek then, gently weeding Jamie out of the equation. His contempt for prayer had clearly rankled her. "And you look like someone who would know how to take care of himself."

Jamie turned to him and grinned. "My butch baby."

Derek laughed. Cleeta-Gayle did not.

She did not look amused by the sweet talk between Jamie and Derek. She did, however, businesslike and without preamble, ask the question that was paramount in all their minds.

"So tell me. What exactly are we going to do?"

CHAPTER SIX

IN THE dining room, they found everyone sitting disconsolately around the long polished table. Many of them sipped coffee, but most of the plates were clean, so not much food was being consumed. Jamie speculated that appetites were at a minimum. No surprise there. The only exception was Tommy Stevens. His plate was piled high with bacon and eggs. He was working at it with his full attention, seemingly ignoring everyone else in the room.

Oliver Banyon, seated beside him, looked up when Derek and Jamie and Cleeta-Gayle Jones entered the room.

"Now what?" he asked. There was a bruise on his cheek.

Jamie stared at the bruise. "What happened to you?"

Tommy Stevens looked up from his plate. "We had a fight. He lost." Banyon remained silent, but he didn't look happy. He looked, if anything, embarrassed.

Mrs. Jupp spoke up from the end of the table where she was seated by her husband. Apparently with murder being added to the program, the line between staff and guests had been forever obliterated. They were all in the same boat now, so social distinctions were moot.

"Lover's tiffs are the least of our worries." She scowled as if the words were distasteful on her tongue, and turned her steely glare on Jamie as if he were the cause of all her misery. "We saw the two of you out by the cars. What has happened now?"

Jamie didn't like the way she stared at him, so he was less than gentle with his answer. "The cars have been messed with. Tires slashed, engines destroyed." He reached out and snagged a strip of bacon from a platter. "Would anyone like to confess to the crime? Or perhaps tell us why you beat that poor old couple to death in the basement?"

Banyon hurled himself to his feet. "You're out of line! What makes you think one of us killed those unfortunate people?"

Before Jamie could snap back, Tommy Stevens laid down his fork, propped his elbows on the table, and clasped his hands under his chin. He gazed up at Banyon trembling in fury beside him. "Geez, Ollie. For a college professor, you're not very smart. The pool of suspects is rather thin, don't you think? Since there is no one else on the premises, who do you *think* did the killing if not one of us?"

Banyon glowered back. "Those killings happened before any of us arrived here. How do you know it has anything to do with us at all?"

Tommy all but clucked his tongue at the level of rose-colored naïveté spilling from his lover's mouth. "What else could it be? Do you really think we were all invited here and then some random murderer just happened by? Someone must have come here twice. Once to kill the old couple, and the second time to innocently arrive with the rest of us. It's the only thing that makes sense."

Jamie felt Derek's hand brush the small of his back. "I think your friend is right," Derek declared to Banyon. Then his eyes traveled to the other faces in the room. "Unless someone has a better theory."

At that moment, a crash of thunder as sharp as a hammer blow jolted the house. Everybody jumped. A water glass tumbled to the floor and shattered. It was Banyon's. Mr. Jupp wearily dragged himself to his feet and set about sweeping up the broken glass with a tiny broom and shovel he plucked from among the fireplace tools.

Jamie stared at the tiny shovel in Mr. Jupp's hand. "That looks like the murder weapon we found in the basement."

All eyes turned to Mr. Jupp. "Jamie's right," Derek said. "If we look around, we'll find one of the fireplaces short of its shovel. Not that it really gets us anywhere."

While everyone else continued to stare at the shovel, Cleeta-Gayle stifled a sob and moved to stand beside the fire. Derek and Jamie parked themselves at the table and began filling their plates. Mrs. Jupp, perhaps more out of habit than anything else, rose and filled their coffee cups from the urn.

They offered polite thanks, and she gave a reluctant nod to show she had heard. Jamie noticed her hands were shaking as she delivered the cups.

Mr. Jupp poured the shards from Banyon's water glass into a trash bin by the sideboard. He quickly replaced the fireplace shovel in the rack of tools by the grate as if he couldn't wait to get it out of his hands. Turning to Derek with bright, hopeful eyes, he asked, "Did you two find the phones you misplaced?"

Derek shook his head. "They weren't misplaced. They were stolen. And no. I'm sure they're gone for good."

"Someone seems to have thought this through pretty well," Jamie added.

"So you think the killer means to murder us too." It was Mrs. Jupp. Again, a clump of hair had slipped from the net at the back of her head. She seemed to notice it as soon as she spoke and set about with a bobby pin, tucking it back into place. With her hands shaking, it was no easy task.

Cleeta-Gayle spun from the fire and faced them all, her face taut, her eyes flashing. "Well, of *course* he means to murder us too! Why do you think we've been lured here?"

Tommy Stevens smiled around a mouthful of eggs. "Seems to me it didn't take a lot of luring. One simple invitation and we fell all over ourselves RSVPing the shit out of it."

"Watch your language," Mrs. Jupp snapped.

Banyon laid a gentle hand on Tommy's arm. "Please," he said. "Let's try to be civil. Being at one another's throats isn't going to help. We need to work together."

"And do what, exactly?" Tommy asked. In the same instant, he brushed his thumb across Banyon's cheek, the one with the bruise. "I'm sorry," he said. "I shouldn't have hit you."

Banyon smiled. "Don't worry about it. It's not the first time a boyfriend has popped me in the puss. I'm pretty sure I'll live." His gaze traveled to the little shovel still swinging on its rack by the fire. "Maybe."

Mr. Jupp stood at the dining room window, staring out at the rain. His back was as straight as a fence post. With his massive hands clenched into balls of muscle and bone, he looked like he wanted to hit something. Jamie wondered if it was the tender moment between Tommy and Banyon that irked his homophobic sensibilities, or whether it was the fact that he was on the menu for slaughter like the rest of them that was pissing him off.

"Can we walk out?" Mr. Jupp asked, his tone thoughtful, as if he were thinking out loud. But once the words were actually uttered, he turned to face the room. "What do you think? Is there a chance?"

Jamie shook his head. "Not on the road, at least. The bridge is destroyed, remember. With the rain still coming down, the stream will be a torrent like it was last night. I suppose we could trek through the woods, but it might take hours to reach the nearest house or highway. Even if we knew which way to go."

Tommy blew the biggest hole in the question of whether or not they could simply walk away from it all. "Even if we do leave," he said, his hand now resting in Banyon's, "the murderer will just pick us off in the trees."

"What do you mean?" Mrs. Jupp asked, a distaste for the young man, or more precisely his sexual proclivities, clearly written in her eyes. "Why would you say that?"

Tommy leveled a mocking gaze back at her, as if he couldn't believe what he was hearing. "Because if we leave, the killer leaves. Why wouldn't he? With his prey boogying off into the woods, there wouldn't be much motivation for him to stay behind."

Mrs. Jupp studied Tommy's face. Her dislike for him seemed to have fallen by the wayside all of a sudden. Fear was in her gaze now. Jamie could see it from across the room. Tommy could probably see it too, Jamie thought, but if it affected him he didn't let it show.

Mrs. Jupp's thin fingers danced at her throat like a dying bird. "You said... prey."

"Yes," Tommy answered, unmoved by her obvious terror. "Prey."

But Mrs. Jupp could not be completely cowed. Her face grew stern. She persisted. "So you really think the killer is one of us? Someone in this very room?"

Tommy's handsome young face turned mean in an instant. He squeezed Banyon's hand until Banyon winced. "How many times do we have to go through this? Unless it's a ghost, of *course* the killer is one of us! We're the only people here." His eyes lasered in on Mr. and Mrs. Jupp, one right after the other. "And while we're on the subject, some of us might be a little old to go traipsing through the stormy forest for miles on end, don't you think? We really have no choice but to stay here inside this house until help arrives. To suggest leaving is *nuts*!"

Mrs. Jupp flinched in the face of his fury. Defensively, but with hurt in her eyes, she said, "I know my husband and I aren't young. I just thought...." But she didn't finish. She let her comment slip to silence. Gathering her plate and cutlery, she rose and left the room without a backward glance, heading presumably for the kitchen where she would begin washing up.

Tommy Stevens watched her go with no sympathy on his face.

"My wife is frightened," Mr. Jupp spat bitterly, leaning across the table and aiming his words directly at Tommy's face. "There's no need to be cruel." With that he rose and followed his wife from the room.

Tommy looked surprised, although the two rising spots of color in his cheeks might have suggested a wee touch of shame was working its way through his system whether he wanted to admit it or not. He turned to the others in the room. "What'd I say?" He seemed abruptly surprised by the cool reception he got from his fellow guests. "Why are you looking at me like I'm an asshole?"

Jamie smiled to himself when no one denied they were doing exactly that.

"WHY DID they fight, do you suppose?" Derek asked. "Banyon and Tommy. I thought they were all lovey-dovey together."

"Together means different things to different people," Jamie said. "Together for us means fucking like rabbits. Maybe together for them means punching each other in the face. Frankly I like our way better."

Derek grinned. "So do I."

"Think Professor Banyon culls through the student roster to find his latest trick?"

Derek's grin hadn't faded yet. "Looks like it."

Jamie returned the grin with one of his own. "I suppose Tommy's shooting for an A."

"After popping the professor in the jaw, I doubt he'll get it."

They were in their room again. Jamie, for the tenth time, was digging through their stuff trying to find their cell phones.

"They aren't here," Derek kindly insisted, pushing away all thoughts of Banyon and Tommy. "The phones were stolen. They had to be. There's no sense looking for them. They're gone." But Jamie continued to search.

The storm had reached a crescendo again. Lightning sizzling, thunder booming, wind and rain lashing the house and trees. Timbers deep in the walls creaked and moaned. Since they were on the second floor, they could hear shingles rattling above their heads and floorboards moaning below. The house was a fucking symphony.

Derek thought of the bodies in the basement. Leaking abominable fluids. Decomposing. He wondered how long it would take for meat to begin sloughing from lifeless bones.

He gave himself a shake to chase that last macabre thought away. When it steadfastly refused to go, he sat on the edge of the bed and stared morosely out at the rain lashing the bedroom window.

His silence must have attracted Jamie's attention. He quickly crossed the room and knelt at Derek's feet.

Jamie's words nudged at Derek like a probing kiss on the cheek. "Don't worry. We'll get through this."

Derek smiled down at him as Jamie laid his head in his lap. He ran his fingers through Jamie's hair, which was still damp from the rain. "We've come a long way, you and I," Derek said. "I don't want to lose you now."

Jamie gazed up, his eyes dreamy. He seemed to be enjoying Derek's fingers in his hair. "What do you mean, lose me *now*?"

"Now that we've found each other," Derek explained. "Now that I'm starting to realize what you mean to me."

"What *do* I mean to you?" Jamie asked, brushing his lips over the tender skin on Derek's wrist, as if savoring the taste.

Derek blinked. The answer was so obvious he was surprised he had to explain it. "Everything," he said. "Don't you know that? You mean everything." Jamie's eyes misted up. A tear gathered, shimmering on the long sweep of his blond lashes, then fell with an almost audible plop, sliding down the side of his nose. Derek bent and kissed it away before it was lost forever.

"Please don't break my heart," Jamie whispered.

"Never," Derek whispered back. He laid a second kiss to Jamie's cheek, as if the residue of his tear might still linger and he wanted to taste it again. With his lips still on Jamie's skin, he muttered careful words. "I want you to come with me."

"Come with you where?"

"Down to the basement."

Jamie jerked back, his eyes no longer dreamy and soft. They were wide and worried now. "The basement? Why?"

Derek felt color rise to the back of his neck. He wasn't sure why what he was about to say embarrassed him so, but it did. Still, there was no way around it. This was something he had to do. "I want to cover the bodies. I can't just leave them lying there on that filthy floor. They were old. They must have loved each other for decades. They... deserve better."

Jamie's gaze bore into Derek's eyes. The faintest of smiles touched his lips. Derek, unable to stop himself, leaned in to kiss them, one after the other. When he was finished, Jamie claimed his hand.

"Let's go, then. Let's do what we can for them."

Derek's heart gave an odd lurch inside his chest. His pulse quickened at his temple.

"Thank you," he said, pulling a kitchen knife from his trouser pocket.

Jamie's eyes got big and round. Wary all of a sudden. "What's *that* for?" he asked.

"Protection. I swiped it from the dining room."

"Oh."

"Unless you have an Uzi we can use."

Jamie patted his pockets and frowned. "Sorry. All out of Uzis."

"Then the knife will have to do."

"I don't suppose you swiped one for me too?"

Derek pulled a second knife from his pocket. "As a matter of fact, I did. Try not to stab yourself. Or me. Or anybody who isn't trying to kill us."

Jamie's eyes narrowed to beady slits. "What am I, twelve?"

Derek studied him fondly. "I remember you at twelve. You were sexy then too."

The snarl slid from Jamie's face like a scoop of ice cream sliding off a plate. He slid his fingers under Derek's shirttail, ruffling through the hair on Derek's belly. A purr entered his voice.

"What else do you remember from when we were twelve?"

THE STENCH of human waste was stronger now. It was mixed with the acrid scent of old blood, ancient coal dust, and woodsmoke. The bodies of the old couple had not been moved since Mr. Jupp discovered them the evening before. The only difference was a string of ants that now crossed the coal-bin floor from the trap door high in the wall and disappeared beneath the hem of the old woman's skirt.

Jamie almost passed out looking at them. He desperately tried not to imagine what they were doing under there.

He and Derek had blankets tucked under their arms, gleaned from the linen closet off the second-floor hallway.

Jamie stared at the ants again. Busy little bastards, scurrying back and forth. Doing God knows what. "We need a can of Raid."

"Hush."

Jamie hushed. Derek carefully spread a blanket over the old man, neatly tucking in the edges. When he finished, Derek plucked the other blanket from Jamie's grasp and spread it over the woman. Jamie imagined the ants lighting little tiny candles and wondering what the hell had happened.

It was a relief not to see the corpses' faces anymore, but the two blankets did nothing to quell the reek of corruption that seemed to have burrowed into the basement walls.

"Can we go now?" Jamie pleaded, patting his pocket to make sure the knife was still there.

Derek was staring at the bloodied shovel lying at his feet. It *was* exactly like the one in the dining room upstairs, Jamie decided. Derek nudged it with his toe but didn't try to touch it. Fingerprints, Jamie supposed.

Jamie's gaze wandered back to the bodies. "Do you still think they were killed so the house could be used as a staging area for murdering the rest of us?"

Derek eyed him with what looked like renewed respect. "I hadn't thought it through quite that clearly," he said, "but yes, Jamie, now that you mention it, that's exactly what I think."

Jamie tried not to preen under Derek's admiration for his acumen. As long as he was on an intellectual roll, Jamie figured he might as well shoot for another brilliant deduction. "It means whoever the killer is, he already knew about this house, so it stands to reason he already knew the owners." At that, his gaze fell again on the bodies at his feet.

Derek nodded. "Yes. That's what I think too."

"It also explains why the pictures were removed from the walls."

"Yes. Something in the pictures would have given the killer away. But we've already been over this."

"I know," Jamie said. "But there must be more to it."

Jamie chewed on the inside of his cheek as if it were a fat ball of bubble gum. He tried to order his thoughts, while at the same time struggling to ignore the stench of death and human waste. An idea struck him out of the blue. He snapped his fingers.

"So many pictures have been removed from the house, it must mean the killer was a relative of the old couple. Surely a mere friend wouldn't be so prominently displayed."

"No," Derek agreed. "Surely not."

Jamie blinked. Still thinking. "We need those pictures, don't we?"

Slowly, Derek turned and aimed a smile right at him. "Bingo, Sherlock. That's exactly what we need."

As one, they turned away from the coal bin and its unholy contents and glanced about the basement. If Derek was expecting to immediately spot a bigass pile of discarded family portraits, Jamie was afraid he would be sorely disappointed.

"There!" Derek cried, and Jamie jumped two feet straight up into the air.

Derek strode forward and scanned a shelf filled with odds and ends: light bulbs, tools, a huge roll of twine, paint cans, and other assorted junk.

Alongside the shelf in the middle of the floor stood something covered with a large black tarp. Jamie stepped forward and lifted the corner of the tarp to expose a motorcycle that looked shiny and new. A helmet dangled from the handlebar. He and Derek stood side by side staring at the thing for a moment, and then Jamie rearranged the tarp the way he'd found it. They had other things to worry about.

Jamie forgot about the motorcycle quickly enough. He was just glad he hadn't found another body. While Derek fiddled with the junk on the shelf, Jamie edged up close behind him and tucked his hand in Derek's back pocket for anchorage.

"That's good," Derek whispered. "Stay close."

"Don't worry," Jamie whispered back. "I fully intend to. Where's your knife?"

"In the other pocket," Derek said.

"Oh good. I won't cut my fingers off."

JAMIE TRAILED along behind Derek as he searched the basement further, still looking for clues, of which there were damn few. Aside from the bodies and the shovel, there were none, in fact. Not one damn clue anywhere. Jamie still had his hand tucked securely in Derek's back pocket, and frankly, Derek was happy to feel it there.

Strangely, Derek's mind was only partially focused on the search and the murders. The bulk of his brain matter was contemplating his future with Jamie. That was assuming they would *have* a future after the killer got through with them.

His thoughts a maelstrom, he bent and once again began rummaging through a pile of crap stacked haphazardly in a basement corner. Derek hated spiders, and he cringed at every unexpected twitch of fabric or material, but he doggedly plowed on, hoping to find the missing pictures.

He was about to suggest they move their search up the basement stairs and into the house itself, but instead he found himself turning and taking hold of Jamie's shirtsleeves. Jamie looked startled but waited patiently for whatever Derek was about to say. The trust Derek saw burning in Jamie's eyes at that moment reconfirmed the fact that he was right to say it.

He also knew he would never be happy if he didn't.

Derek cleared his throat. He shuffled from one foot to the next, seeking the words to begin.

When Jamie reached out and rested his hand on Derek's chest, Derek edged closer, cupping Jamie's face in his hands.

"If we die in this fucking house, I want to know that I did one thing right before it happened. Jamie Roma, I've been crazy about you since the fifth grade. I have no idea why it took us fifteen years to finally crawl into bed together, but now that you're *in* my bed, I'll do whatever I can to keep you there. God, Jamie, please tell me you're crazy about me too, and that you're not just in it for the pheromones."

He finished in a tongue-tied flurry of disjointed vowels and consonants, his face so hot he must be red as an apple. Within moments, tears were dribbling down his face, and he had the hiccups. He stood meekly—half-embarrassed, half-terrified—waiting for Jamie to respond. He also needed to pee, but he was trying his best to ignore that.

Jamie stepped forward and tucked his head under Derek's chin. With his warm breath on Derek's throat, he pressed a gentle kiss to Derek's Adam's apple. It bobbed up and down in Derek's throat while he tried not to sob out loud. At that moment, he was more scared of the hope in his heart than he was of the killer in the house. The one controlled his happiness; the other only his death.

In any contest, happiness would win hands down.

"Thank you," Jamie muttered against his skin. Jamie nibbled on the little V of bone at the base of Derek's throat. He slid a hand under Derek's shirt and caressed his side, tucking his fingers in the slots between Derek's ribs. When Jamie's lips traveled up his neck and found his ear, Derek shivered and tilted his head to the side to let Jamie have his way.

Jamie's breath blew across his temple, and Derek's shiver became a tiny laugh. Or was it a baby sob? Jesus, was the guy ever going to answer?

"I have to admit," Jamie breathed, "the pheromones are great." He dragged his lips over Derek's cheek until they reached his mouth, and there Jamie came to rest. His kiss was sweet and gentle and wetter than usual. It took Derek a moment to realize it was moistened by both their tears.

"I am crazy about you," Jamie finally whispered. His voice sounded weak and fractured, like it had been taken out and beaten like a rug, but he managed to make himself understood.

Derek grinned beneath the kiss.

"And you'll stay with me when we get home?"

"What do you mean, stay with you?"

"I mean live with me."

Jamie's jaw fell open, and he blinked six times. "You mean honest-to-God *live* with you? Like cohabitation? Like you take out the trash and I'll scrub the toilet live with you?"

"Something like that, yeah."

Jamie still hadn't finished blinking. "Well, yeah, I guess I could do that." Desperation swelled up inside Derek. He wasn't getting the enthusiasm he'd expected.

"But do you *want* to live with me?"

"Yes, Derek, I want to live with you."

"In my apartment? I hate yours."

"Are we talking forever here?"

Derek hesitated for less than a heartbeat. "Maybe."

Jamie huffed but didn't balk, to Derek's relief. "Fine. But we'll get a new apartment. A bigger apartment. We'll split the rent. And I want a dog."

Derek tried to pout, but Jamie's sharp little teeth snagged his bottom lip and wouldn't let him do it. He squirmed and flapped around like a worm on a hook. "Ouch! That hurts. Fine, we'll get a dog."

"A big one. And a cat."

"Oh Jesus…."

Jamie laughed and pulled back far enough to study Derek's eyes. "Just so you know, the dog's a must, but I'm flexible on the cat."

Derek reached up and squeegeed a tear from his own cheek. When he was finished doing that, he took pity and squeegeed one from Jamie's.

"I'll make you happy," he said gently.

"You'd better," Jamie threatened.

"Our mothers will be thrilled. They'll pick out our curtains."

"They probably think we're lovers already."

Derek felt his smile welling up. "We sort of already are."

In tandem they each inhaled a deep, shuddering breath. Derek's tongue came out to lick the residual taste of Jamie's kiss from his lips. It was his favorite flavor—after butterscotch. He circled Jamie's back with his arms and pulled him close. With his mouth on Jamie's neck, he mumbled something that sounded like an aardvark slurping up ants.

"I missed that," Jamie said.

Before Derek could respond, a loud crash shook the house. The stunned silence that followed lasted no more than a second. Suddenly there were running footsteps everywhere. They pounded on the floor above. Doors slammed. Floorboards creaked and popped. A fine rain of gray dust sifted down on their heads through the cobwebs on the basement ceiling.

A woman's voice cried, "No!"

"Oh shit!" Derek spat. Stripping Jamie from his arms, Derek hurled them both toward the basement stairs. Before they reached the first step, a wailing scream erupted. It pierced the basement walls, slicing the air like a knife. Goose bumps rose on the back of Derek's neck.

"This can't be good," he said.

"Dammit!" Jamie groused. "I was just getting a boner too."

At that precise moment, a crack of thunder split the sky outside, and both men gasped. Derek pulled himself together. With his heart in his mouth, he flew up the rickety basement steps, dragging Jamie behind him. They threw themselves through the little Harry Potter door under the foyer stairs. And almost tripped over the body on the floor.

CHAPTER SEVEN

WITH ARMS and legs flung wide and the swell of his massive torso rising off the foyer floor like a foothill, Mr. Jupp looked far larger than he did ordinarily. Far larger, and far quieter.

For he was clearly dead.

He lay chest down, his head turned to the side at an impossible angle. The only sign of movement on the body was a rivulet of blood, still traveling, still seeping from Mr. Jupp's ear and oozing down the side of his cheek. Already a small puddle of shimmering crimson had gathered on the hardwood floor beside his open, sightless eye. Even that pool was still traveling, still spreading, as tiny streams branched off from it to follow the cracks between the floorboards, elongating slowly in perfectly straight lines like the careful strokes of a pen filled with deep red ink.

Jamie, with Derek clutching his sleeve, stared down at the body in shock.

There was a rawness to Mr. Jupp's death that Jamie had not encountered before. It was, after all, the first time he had seen death as fresh as this and still working its magic. His prior experience with the end of existence consisted of vaguely familiar people who never looked quite the way they did in life. Most often they were spiffily dressed, packed into expensive coffins, and engulfed in silk. Sometimes they even wore eyeglasses, which Jamie *never* understood.

He knew violent death existed, of course. Hell, look at the two bodies in the basement. Yet even they had been long-enough dead by the time Jamie came on the scene to cause a bit of a disconnect between the act of violence that smote them lifeless and the way they presented themselves now. Cold to the touch, stiff, no trace of humanity remaining. They didn't even smell like people anymore. They smelled like… *waste.*

Poor Mr. Jupp was different. He was still warm. He still reeked of Old Spice. And he was still spilling blood.

Derek dropped to his knees at Jamie's feet and laid his cheek to Mr. Jupp's back, listening for a heartbeat. Everyone else stared on. Mrs. Jupp had pressed a handkerchief to her mouth, her eyes wild and frightened. She was gasping for air as if her breath had been literally snatched from her body. Her tear-filled gaze never once left her husband's face.

At long last, Derek sat back on his haunches. He gazed up at Jamie and shook his head.

"There's no heartbeat," he said softly, keeping his eyes trained on Jamie's face. Avoiding Mrs. Jupp's gaze at all cost, clearly not wanting to be the one to legitimize her grief, he added, "Look at the way his head is positioned. I think maybe his neck is broken."

Oliver Banyon stood in the dining room doorway. He still cradled a cup of coffee in his hand. Tommy Stevens peered around him from behind, one hand resting on Banyon's shoulder.

Cleeta-Gayle stood with her back to the front door. She was wearing a raincoat, as if she had just ventured outside to watch the storm, which was still raging over their heads. At that moment, a searing flash of lightning strobed the foyer walls and lit the body on the floor, making poor Mr. Jupp almost appear to move. It startled everyone so that Mrs. Jupp cried out and Cleeta-Gayle began to cry. She covered her face with her hands as if she couldn't bear to look anymore. At the storm, at the body, at her fellow houseguests, at any of it.

"The killing has started, hasn't it?" she mumbled into her hands.

Clearly referring to the bodies in the basement, Derek answered, "The killing started before we ever got here."

"It might have been an accident," Jamie said, staring blandly at Mr. Jupp lying silent at his feet. "He could have stumbled coming down the stairs."

Derek stood and took his hand. Together, they carefully stepped over the body and turned to gaze up the staircase.

Derek sighed, still averting his eyes from Mrs. Jupp, who was watching him like a hawk. Listening closely to every word he uttered. "Look where the body is positioned, Jamie. It's not at the foot of the stairs. It's off to the side of the staircase." Derek sucked in a deep breath, as if what he was about to say made him uneasy, but there was really no getting around it. "Mr. Jupp didn't trip coming down the stairs. He tumbled over the railing at the top of the landing. He came crashing down at the *side* of the staircase, not at the foot of it."

"So it couldn't have been an accident," Jamie said quietly.

Derek answered reluctantly, but his words captured the attention of everyone present. "No," he said. "It couldn't have been an accident."

Jamie, and everyone else in the foyer except the unfortunate Mr. Jupp, stared upward. No doubt they were all imagining the fall, picturing what it must have been like. The last rush of wind on a gasping face. The horrifying sight of the floor hurling upward. Startled eyes. A voiceless scream. And the moment of impact, when all sensation ended. Leaving nothing behind but... what they were seeing now.

It was Cleeta-Gayle who asked the question. Her drawl slowed the words to a crawl, and her face still sparkled with tears. "But how could he do that?" she asked. "Unless...."

Tommy Stevens filled in the blanks. "Unless he was pushed." Tommy seemed to have finally realized the peril they were all in, for even as he spoke, his eyes never left Mr. Jupp's body. His cockiness had fallen by the wayside. Maybe it fell to its death at the same time Mr. Jupp did. Suddenly Tommy Stevens looked as young as his years. Banyon's eyes darted from face to face. "Where was everyone when it happened? I was in the dining room." He glanced down at the coffee cup in his hand, then back to all the faces watching him. "There was no one with me, so I'm afraid my alibi isn't worth much. Where was everyone else?"

"Jamie and I were in the basement covering the bodies of the old couple. You know that's where we were. You saw us coming through the door under the stairs. After Mrs. Jupp screamed."

"I was exploring the house," Tommy said. "I came back through the dining room when I heard the commotion in the hall. Oliver was at the door looking out."

Cleeta-Gayle wiped the tears from her face with the sleeve of her coat. She still stood before the front door, her shoulders peppered with raindrops, her god-awful chemically fried hair a damp and lifeless mess.

"I was outside on the porch watching the storm," she managed to utter, before another sob rattled through her. She once again buried her face in her hands.

All eyes turned to Mrs. Jupp, who stood motionless, gazing down on the body of her husband. She appeared to have no desire to reach out and comfort him, or to say goodbye, perhaps, with a touch, a caress, or even a gentle word. The tears still fell from her eyes, but there was an emptiness in them too. A vacancy of emotion that gave Jamie the creeps.

Instead of mourning, he thought, she looked… *analytical*. As if she were trying to figure out the cold logistics of how her husband managed to do a swan dive off the second floor landing.

She seemed to suddenly realize everyone was waiting for her to speak. She did so, but not graciously. "I was in the kitchen, if you must know. Cleaning up after the lot of you, washing the breakfast dishes." Her eyes narrowed. A flush of anger tinged her cheeks. "Do you really think I'm strong enough to push my husband over that railing on the stairs?"

It was Jamie, then, who reached out and patted her arm. "Of course not," he said kindly. "I'm sorry. I think we're all in shock."

He turned back to the group and, finding no comfort there, focused his attention on the body. "Well, we can't leave him here."

"No," Derek agreed. "We can't."

"Jesus," Tommy groaned. "The guy isn't even cold yet. Plus he must weigh 300 pounds. What are we supposed to do with him?"

Jamie shot him a nasty glance. "He's not that heavy. We can move him if we work together. But move him where?"

"Not the basement, please," Mrs. Jupp pleaded. At long last she cast sympathetic eyes on her husband's lifeless body. "I couldn't bear to think of him down there with… those others."

This time Derek tried to comfort the woman. "We'll find a different place," he said. "I promise." He turned to Jamie and pointed down the hall, deeper into the house past the door under the stairs. "There's what looks like a sewing room down that way. There's a daybed in there too. We can put him on that."

"What about clues?" Banyon asked. "What about disturbing the evidence for the police later?"

"There's nothing to be done about that," Jamie said. "Don't forget the road is out and our cars have been trashed. We could be here for days. We can't be continually tripping over the guy." He suddenly realized what he'd said and shot an apologetic moue in Mrs. Jupp's direction. "Sorry. I didn't mean that to sound so cold."

Mrs. Jupp resurrected the steely countenance she had used often enough before where Jamie was concerned. Without saying a word, she turned away. From her husband, from the group, from everyone. Giving her husband's body a wide berth, she stepped around it and slowly began to climb the stairs, step by agonizing step, as if the weight of the world now rested squarely on her shoulders.

"I'll be in my room," she said without looking back. "Please leave me in peace. I'll spend time with my husband's... body... after you place him in the sewing room."

Tommy Stevens whispered just loud enough for everyone, including Mrs. Jupp, to hear. "Does that mean she's not cooking for us anymore?"

Cleeta-Gayle threw a disgusted look his way. Also skirting the body carefully, she hurried to the foot of the stairs and then pulled herself up the steps to join Mrs. Jupp. She tried to give the older woman a hand, but Mrs. Jupp shook her off. Flushing, she left the old woman to her own devices and hurried on up the stairs without looking back, presumably heading for her own room.

Neither woman took any more notice of the men below. Seconds later, Jamie heard two separate doors open and close upstairs. But for the roar of the storm and the intermittent crash of thunder, a renewed silence settled over the house.

Jamie and Derek turned to the corpse on the floor. As if seeing no gracious way out of what was expected of them, Banyon and young Tommy stepped forward like the two most reluctant volunteers in the world.

Footsteps above drew Jamie's attention to the top of the stairs once more. He found Cleeta-Gayle standing there, looking down. Her eyes were as big as fried eggs, and she waved a newspaper clipping in her hand.

"I suppose," she said, "you should all come look at this. I found it on my bed."

"What is it?" Jamie called up. "We're a little busy here."

Cleeta-Gayle's brows furrowed. Then she seemed to have second thoughts. The concern on her face morphed into a nasty little smirk that tweaked at her cheeks. She dangled the newspaper clipping over the side of the banister between thumb and forefinger—at the exact spot where Mr. Jupp must have sailed off into oblivion not ten minutes earlier.

"In that case I'll save you a trip up the stairs," she said.

Releasing the clipping, Cleeta-Gayle and everyone else in the foyer watched the slip of newsprint waft soundlessly downward, sliding on air currents from one side to the other, slipping through the air until it came to rest, as light as a feather, on Mr. Jupp's lifeless shoulder.

It was Derek who reached down and delicately plucked it off.

"HOLY SHIT!" Tommy Stevens cried, scaring the bejesus out of Jamie, who almost leaped out of his shoes.

He and Tommy and Oliver Banyon were staring over Derek's shoulder as the four of them read the newspaper clipping in Derek's hand. Once it was read, they looked down en masse at the body on the floor.

"Well, golly!" Jamie declared. "I didn't see *that* coming."

Tommy snorted back a laugh. "If he wasn't already dead, I'd swear the butler did it. Killed the old couple downstairs, I mean." He turned to Banyon, a gleam of mockery in his eyes. "What do you make of *this*, Mr. PhD Banyon? Presumably you're the brains of the outfit. Who's the killer now?" Banyon opened his mouth, then closed it without making a sound, clearly at a loss for words.

Still looking pleased with himself, Tommy turned to Jamie and Derek. "Ollie was telling me earlier he thought Mr. Jupp was the murderer. Had it all worked out, you see. Fancies himself a proper sleuth, I guess."

"Well, Jupp is clearly *not* the killer," Derek said, still staring down at the clipping in his hand.

"No," Tommy grinned. "Unless he murdered himself, I'd say he's pretty much off the hook."

"But what does it mean?" Cleeta-Gayle called down from the landing above.

No one answered. Once again, all four sets of eyes were drawn to the clipping in Derek's hands.

It was a news item dated four years earlier. Published in the *San Diego Union-Tribune* on April 12 of that year. It bore a photograph of Mr. Alphonse Jupp, the very same man who now lay dead as a mackerel on the floor at their feet. He was standing downcast at a long table in a San Diego courtroom, surrounded by a small ragtag team of attorneys who were clearly public defenders since there wasn't a suit among them that cost more than two hundred dollars. In truth, the defense team looked just as depressed as their client.

Behind them, seated in the first row of spectators, sat a prim, small woman clutching a wrinkled handkerchief in her lap. Her face was stoic, her head held high. It was Mrs. Jupp. The only word to describe the look on her face was... unrepentant. *Easy to stay on your high horse*, Jamie thought, *when you're not the one facing the jury.*

The snapshot captured the exact moment when a female judge, unnamed in the article, threw the proverbial book at Mr. Jupp. His crime—the practicing of gay conversion therapy on a sixteen-year-old boy who, in the midst of a savage weeks-long treatment at the hands of Mr. Jupp, committed suicide by swallowing Drano. The article alluded to one other suicide as well, but that victim was not named, nor were charges filed on his behalf.

Proven culpable for the one boy's actions in ending his own life, Mr. Jupp had been charged with involuntary manslaughter. He received a sentence of two years behind bars.

His wife was not charged.

"What the hell!" Derek stammered, reading the clipping again.

It was Jamie who took it upon himself to state the obvious. In fact, he was rather amazed that no one thought of it but him. "I hope you all realize that today is the twelfth of April. It's the fourth anniversary of his conviction. Looks like somebody wanted to commemorate the occasion by teaching the bastard how to fly."

Three gawking faces traveled from Jamie to the landing above, then back to the body on the floor.

The body Jamie had suddenly lost all sympathy for.

MRS. JUPP snatched the clipping from Derek's hand. She glanced at it only briefly before crumbling it in her fist and demanding, "Where did you get this?"

Cleeta-Gayle was the only one who hadn't entered Mrs. Jupp's room with the others. She answered Mrs. Jupp from out in the hall, raising her voice enough to be heard. "Someone left it on my bed."

Mrs. Jupp stared at her, hatred seething in her eyes.

Derek took that moment to glance around. The Jupps did not have a single bedroom like he and Jamie had, and like the others probably had as well. They had a suite containing a sitting room, a bedroom, and a large private bath. The furniture was old, as it was throughout the house, but it was clean and bright… or would have been had there been sunlight pounding the windows instead of rain. A cheery fire burned on the grate in the sitting room. The woodsmoke smelled faintly of pine on the air.

Clearly, since they had arrived at the house before the other guests, the Jupps had commandeered the best accommodations for themselves.

Derek turned his attention back to the woman. Mrs. Jupp strode across the room and tossed the balled-up newspaper clipping into the fire. Turning back, she faced them all with that same expression of defiance she had shown in the photograph. Clasping her hands in front of her, she stared from face to face, waiting for whatever would happen next.

"I think you'd better tell us about that news article," Derek said. "It might be a clue as to why your husband was murdered. A clue you purposely destroyed, I might also mention."

"That's ridiculous!" she spat. "My husband served his sentence honorably. He paid his debt, if there was actually a debt to be paid. It wasn't his fault those two boys killed themselves. My husband was only trying to give them a happy life."

Jamie stepped forward, snagging Derek's hand. Derek could feel Jamie's fury. He stood silent and proud while Jamie spoke. Jamie's voice was as tautly emotional as Derek had ever heard it.

"Give them a happy life?" Jamie all but hissed, carefully keeping his voice down although it was evident he didn't want to. "Those boys committed suicide because your husband—and I imagine you had a hand in it too—because you both tried to destroy their true selves. To make them deny who they really were."

Mrs. Jupp's mouth was a thin, mean line dissecting her face. "Sinners! Yes, I know. And that's exactly what we wanted them to deny. It was not my husband's fault that their weaknesses…."

Jamie bristled. "Their *weaknesses*? Are you going to stand there and tell me you're blaming *those boys* for their own deaths? You don't think your husband had anything to do with making them feel they had nowhere to turn, no one to offer help? Where were their parents? Why did they let their sons be put through that? Or did they consider their boys to be sinners too?"

Mrs. Jupp raised her chin and straightened her shoulders. She stared at Jamie with pure hate. "They did indeed. The parents of the sixteen-year-old asked for our help. The other young man came to us on his own. We did what we could, my husband and I. But the boys were too far gone. They could not be turned."

Tommy stepped into the conversation. If anything, Derek thought, he appeared more furious than Jamie. "So you still blame the victims and not yourselves. How is it you weren't sent to prison along with your husband? Did he protect you from the law? Did he lie and say you had nothing to do with it? Do you still feel no guilt about what happened? Do you still honestly think it was the boys' fault and not your own?"

Mrs. Jupp appeared to have no problem whatsoever in shifting her hatred from Jamie to Tommy. She did it without missing a beat. "I won't stand here and be barked at by the likes of you. My husband and I were doing the right thing." She cast her gaze into the fire, where the newspaper clipping chronicling her husband's crime had now been reduced to a little black sliver of ash.

When she looked up, Derek realized that tears had found her again. They shimmered on her cheeks. She seemed to suddenly wilt before their eyes. As if she was too tired to argue anymore. "Whatever happened back then," she said wearily, "had nothing to do with what is happening now. I'm sure of it."

"Then you're as blind as you are heartless," Tommy snarled.

Mrs. Jupp stared at him for a long moment, and turning away to face the fire once more, she mumbled, "Maybe I am. But it doesn't alter the fact that it was already too late to punish my husband for what you think he did. He managed to punish himself, you see. He punished himself by dying in prison. He lost his religion. He lost everything. He was dead long before he ever got out."

"But he did manage to hang on to his hatred for gays, didn't he?" Jamie said. "He didn't lose that."

Her lips twisted minutely at the corners. Derek couldn't be sure, but he thought it looked like the beginning of a smile. And a particularly nasty one at that. "No," she said, her words clipped and precise. "He didn't lose that."

Jamie and Tommy were so mad, they were shaking. Derek had to pull them both through the door to make them leave the room.

When they were all in the hall, Derek softly closed Mrs. Jupp's door behind them, as much to allow her some privacy as to eradicate her from Jamie and Tommy's line of sight.

"She thinks her husband killed himself," Banyon said.

All eyes turned to him. Tommy actually laughed. "My God, you may be right."

Derek stepped forward and pulled Jamie into a hug, while Banyon did the same with Tommy.

"Do you think it's possible?" Derek asked, but no one answered. He suspected it was because no one really needed to. The idea was preposterous.

In the distance, they heard the gentle click of a door. Cleeta-Gayle had returned to her room.

CHAPTER EIGHT

THE WOMEN in the house—Cleeta-Gayle Jones and Mrs. Jupp—did not show themselves for the rest of the day. The storm meandered back and forth in its intensity. One minute it was a simple downpour, the next minute it was a vicious bombardment of house and forest with everything in nature's arsenal. Hail, lightning, thunder, gale-force winds. The storm was so violent at times that shingles were stripped from the roof.

When the ceiling in Derek and Jamie's room began to drip, they found the source of the leak in the third-floor attic directly above, accessed by a second flight of stairs not connected to the one where Mr. Jupp had fallen. In this attic room, they discovered toys. A tricycle. An electric train on a round track. A collection of children's books with titles like *Shiloh* and *Black Beauty* and *Bambi.* A cedar chest stood in the corner, filled with balls and plastic dinosaurs and comic books and all the other flotsam of a forgotten childhood.

The strategic placement of a child's beach pail solved the problem of the dripping ceiling for now, but Jamie wondered how long the house would remain standing under nature's relentless assault.

With Mr. Jupp's corpse rolled up in a quilt and laid out like a mummy on the daybed in the sewing room, it was Derek who took it upon himself to wash the blood from the foyer floor. He knew the police would not be pleased with the evidence being repeatedly destroyed, what with cleaning up after Mr. Jupp and covering the bodies in the basement, but he figured there was no way around it. God alone knew how long they would be trapped inside this house. They didn't need to be looking at pools of blood and murdered bodies all the time. Nerves were shattered enough already.

While Jamie played detective, searching the second-floor landing for clues, Derek descended to the basement once more. He was determined to make amends for destroying so much evidence. So upon arrival at the coal bin where the older couple lay moldering, he placed the murder weapon, the small shovel, in a plastic trash bag he had brought with him to preserve the prints and blood.

His first inclination was to put the shovel, now securely wrapped in plastic, back where he found it. Then he had a better idea. If the murderer was indeed inside the house, as everyone suspected, what would prevent him from attempting to dispose of this weapon himself, thus inhibiting the police from finding the very prints Derek was trying to protect?

Clutching the bag guardedly in his arms, he looked around. In the dim light cast by the single light bulb hanging from a cord in the middle of the room, he spotted a shadowy corner. Above the top shelf of the dusty shelving unit behind the spot where the tarp-covered motorcycle stood, Derek noticed what amounted to a tiny inset, mere inches of space between the rafters and the top of the unit. Fringes of cobweb swayed from the ceiling like a veil, and hardly any light reached the space at all. Standing on a rickety stool, he tucked the shovel as far back into the shadows as he could, making sure to leave a tail of black garbage bag hanging out in plain sight to lure the police—but hopefully not the murderer—to the location where the murder weapon was hidden.

Stepping down off the stool, he eyed the results. From a few feet back, you couldn't see the smidgeon of black plastic at all. It blended too well with the shadows. The police, however, when they carried out their investigation, would have the place lit up like an operating room, so they would be sure to spot it.

Satisfied, Derek replaced the stool in the corner where he'd found it and, in spite of his best efforts not to, turned to stare down at the unfortunate couple in the coal bin one more time.

They looked so small and pathetic tucked under their blankets. Derek wondered how long they had lived together in this house. How long they had been married, if they actually were. He wondered too if they truly loved each other as much as he wanted to believe they did. Had they no children? No relatives? If not, then why were there toys stored in the attic? Why had no one tried to reach the old couple to find out if they were surviving the storm?

Pulling his T-shirt up over his nose to filter the smell of death, he knelt at their feet and reached out to touch the toe of the old man's shoe.

"I'm sorry," he whispered softly.

The scrape of a footstep behind him startled him so, he almost toppled onto his side. He awkwardly hurled himself to his feet and spun around, arms flung out in a defensive posture.

To Derek's surprise, he found Tommy Stevens standing in front of him. His arms were crossed casually over his chest, and he had the embryo of a grin on his face, as if he found Derek's reaction to his arrival amusing.

"Oops," he said. "Didn't mean to scare you to death."

Derek lowered his arms. He was not appeased by Tommy's sarcastic apology, and he was pretty sure his face showed it.

"What do *you* want?"

Tommy shrugged. His eyes fell to the couple on the floor, then returned to Derek. "What were you doing?" As if his words suddenly seeped into his own ears and he realized how they might be misconstrued, his face softened. A forced innocence smoothed his features. "I mean, what are you doing down here all alone? It seems a little dangerous for any of us to be wandering around on their own."

"In that case," Derek replied, tactfully skirting the question and not falling for Tommy's innocent routine one little bit, "what are *you* doing down here all by yourself?"

Again Tommy's eyes slid to the bodies on the floor. If he noticed the murder weapon was missing, he made no mention of it. "I'm not alone," he said. "I'm with you." He tilted his head toward the two corpses. "And them. I saw you come down here, Derek. I followed you."

A chill crawled down Derek's spine. "Why?"

Tommy Stevens took a long, shuddering breath. He once again focused his gaze on Derek's face. "I'm worried," he said.

Sensing no threat now, Derek relaxed his stance. He tried to convey a friendlier tone. They were all in the same boat, after all. If someone wanted to talk, he should be willing to listen, to help.

"About what, Tommy?"

Hearing the kinder tone in Derek's voice, Tommy visibly relaxed as well. "I'm worried about Ollie," he said. "I think he lied earlier."

This caught Derek's attention. "Lied about what?"

"He said he had been in the dining room having coffee when the old man flew off the landing. But he wasn't. He only reentered the dining room a few seconds before I did."

"And where were you?" Derek asked. "I've forgotten. Tell me again."

"I was exploring the back hallway. Back where nobody goes. I think there are old servants' quarters back there."

"Is that on the first floor, or the second?"

"The first," Tommy said. "If you're wondering if I was on the second floor when old man Jupp was pushed, I wasn't. But I don't know where Oliver was."

Derek studied Tommy's worried expression. Finally he said, "I thought you guys were an item. Why are you ratting him out like this?"

Tommy stared back. Squarely. Unintimidated. "I'm not ratting him out. I'm just saying I don't think he was where he said he was when the old man fell." Tommy gave a minute shrug, spinning his torso to the side as if he were trying to answer something for himself. "See, it's just that I haven't been with Ollie that long. We're tricks. We're not lovers like you and Jamie."

"What makes you think Jamie and I are lovers?"

Tommy looked startled. "I don't know. The way you act together, I guess. Like you, you know, *love* each other."

Derek refused to be led into that conversation. His feelings for Jamie were his own. He had no intention of sharing them with Tommy Stevens. "And you don't love Oliver?"

Tommy rolled his eyes. "Except for fucking each other's brains out, we hardly know each other. I don't owe him my allegiance. Especially if he's up to something we don't know about."

"You should stay close to him," Derek said. "Keep an eye on him, then."

"What if he's the killer?"

Derek considered that. "Well, chances are he won't kill you when the two of you are in bed alone. That would be pretty hard for him to alibi himself out of."

Tommy grinned. "True."

Derek studied Tommy more closely. "If you two barely know each other, how is it you both received invitations? Or did you?"

"We did," Tommy said. "But don't ask me to explain it. I can't. Neither can Ollie. In fact, that's one of the reasons we came. We wanted to know how we both ended up on the same invitation list when we really didn't know each other that well to begin with. We have no past together. We don't move in the same circles. We have no mutual friends."

"Are you in one of Oliver's classes at the college where he teaches? Is that how you met?"

"Yes." A smirk crossed his face. "The things we'll do for an A, huh?" The smirk dissolved and his expression grew wily. "Please tell me you don't think I'm the killer," he said.

Derek was surprised by the question. "Of course not."

Derek tensed when Tommy reached into his back pocket and pulled out a knife. The knife reflected a blade-shaped sliver of light onto the basement wall. "I'm armed, you know. Mama didn't raise no fool."

At that, Derek pulled the knife from his own back pocket. "My mama didn't raise no fool either."

Tommy stared at each of their blades and laughed. "Yours is bigger than mine."

He stepped closer. Tucking the knife back into his pocket, he reached out almost casually below Derek's waist. He splayed his fingers lightly over Derek's crotch, caressing gently.

"Let me go down on you," he whispered.

"Take your hands off me," Derek said, his voice icy. "It's bad enough you make a pass at me in front of Jamie. This is even worse. There are dead people here. Show some respect."

Tommy reluctantly pulled his hand back, but he didn't seem embarrassed. In fact, he looked amused. He didn't bother to glance at the corpses on the floor. "Fine. I'll meet you somewhere later."

Derek glared at the young man in front of him. "As you damn well know, I'm with Jamie."

"And you don't cheat, I suppose." He slid his hand over the erection outlined in the front of his own jeans.

"That's right," Derek said, resentment swelling inside him. "I don't cheat. Stop touching yourself."

Tommy ignored that. "Are you saying Jamie wouldn't cheat on you?"

"Yes," Derek said, with only a beat of hesitation. "That's exactly what I'm saying. And while we're on the subject, don't you think we have more pressing matters to worry about than getting our rocks off? Like not getting ourselves murdered, for instance?"

"A blowjob won't change anything," Tommy cooed, easing forward again, a lustful simper twisting his mouth.

Derek stepped firmly back, well out of reach. "It would change me," he said. "And I don't think I'd like myself very much afterward."

"Pity," Tommy sniffed. Shifting the bulge in his crotch to make it less noticeable—or maybe because he thought it would turn Derek on, which it didn't—he turned and headed for the stairs. He gave the hanging light bulb a gentle slap as he passed beneath it, sending it swinging.

Seconds later, Derek stood alone. As the light bulb ceased to sway, the roiling shadows slowly stilled around him. He willed his anger to seep away.

Calmer now, he turned to the corpses at his feet and said, "What a jerk."

JAMIE WONDERED if Derek was having any better luck than himself at finding clues. He had spent the better part of twenty minutes crawling around the second-floor landing, where he found little of interest.

The runner on the floor was bunched up, but that didn't really tell him anything. He had also found a deep scratch in the waist-high oak railing at the edge of the landing at what must have been the very spot where Mr. Jupp tumbled over. The scratch looked fresh, and it had likely come from Mr. Jupp's belt buckle, since thinking back, that was the only item of metal Jamie could remember the old man wearing.

He supposed the rucked-up runner and the deep scratch on the banister indicated there might have been a struggle, but it certainly didn't point a finger at any specific perpetrator. All it truly hinted at was that whoever chucked Mr. Jupp off the landing must have either overpowered him or caught him by surprise. And Mr. Jupp was no lightweight, so it must have been someone strong.

Scratch Mrs. Jupp. And you could probably scratch Cleeta-Gayle too, although she did look wiry and might be stronger than one would imagine. But she was such a nervous wreck all the time he was loath to suspect her. Hell, she practically passed out from fright every time a streak of lightning sizzled past. Unless she was a master of deception, he couldn't see her having anything to do with the deaths inside this house.

As for the old couple in the basement, any of the people here (aside from Derek and himself) could have been their killer. It didn't matter that the Jupps were the first to arrive. The couple had been dead before that, possibly for several days, so any of the guests, including the Jupps, might have tooled up here to the boonies, offed the old couple, then split and rearrived later, looking innocent as lambs.

Jamie noticed the niggle of an approaching headache stirring in the back of his brainpan. He rested his elbows on the banister at either side of the deep fresh gouge in the wood and stared down at the foyer below. From this distance, he could still see the bloodstains in the hardwood floor, even after Derek had so diligently tried to wash them away. He had an overpowering desire to spit and watch it fall, as one does when looking down from a great height. But the last thing he wanted was the police to find his DNA mixed up with the residue of Mr. Jupp's blood, so he resisted the urge.

The storm was taking a breather outside, and the unfamiliar stillness carried Jamie to other thoughts. To last night, for instance, lying in Derek's arms in the middle of the night in a strange bed in this weird old house. Leaning heavily on the banister, Jamie dropped his head, closed his eyes, and remembered every word they spoke, every movement they made. Every sensation he'd felt.

A lazy smile touched his mouth when he thought of Derek asking him to move in with him after they got back to the city. *If* they got back to the city. The way things were going, it wasn't exactly a sure thing.

He wondered if he and Derek should simply take off through the woods. Right now. This very minute. A long hike in any given direction other than the one where the rampaging stream blocked the road should take them back to civilization. But he also knew the woods were deep and thick. With no sun in the sky, and with the storm bombarding them at every step, how would they know they weren't going in circles? Yet what else could they do? Lock themselves in their room until help arrived? That wouldn't work. If the killer was as dead set on doing them in as Jamie suspected he was, he could just murder everybody else first, then burn the house down around them to get them too.

A movement caught Jamie's eye. It was Oliver Banyon, walking surreptitiously across the foyer below, heading toward the back of the house. Thinking he was unseen, Jamie jumped like a rabbit when Banyon suddenly stared straight up at him and motioned for him to follow.

Jamie glanced around to see if anyone else was present, but they were clearly alone. The women were in their rooms. Derek was in the basement. Banyon was in the foyer. And who knew where the hell the little horndog Tommy Stevens was. He'd better not be in the basement cruising Derek, Jamie knew that much.

Pulling himself upright, Jamie waved a silent hello to Banyon.

Softly, Banyon called up to him. "Meet me in the sewing room."

Jamie nodded in agreement, wondering as he did so if it would be the dumbest thing he ever did in his life. Or maybe even the *last* thing he ever did in his life.

He traversed the carpeted stairs lightly and quickly, his fingers skimming the banister as he descended. When he reached the bottom step, he grabbed the newel post and pivoted himself into a turn to follow the foyer along the side of the staircase, past the little Harry Potter door and the point on the floor where Mr. Jupp's blood still showed in the cracks.

The sewing room was three doors down. The door was ajar when he arrived. Banyon stood inside, eyeing Jamie expectantly, his hand on the knob, clearly eager to get Jamie alone.

"Come in," he said, and Jamie obeyed. Guardedly.

There was no one else in the room. No one alive at any rate. Jamie casually touched his back pocket and felt the outline of the knife to reassure himself it was there in case he needed protection.

Satisfied, he turned to Banyon, who now stood in front of the closed door, having successfully penned them both inside the room. Jamie tried not to think about the mummy-like body wrapped in a blanket on the daybed behind him.

"What is it?" he asked, studying Banyon's handsome face, and more particularly studying his sexy brown eyes, looking for a hint of impending malice.

Of which he saw none.

More gently, he asked again, "What do you want?"

"Where is your friend?" Banyon asked.

Jamie shrugged as if the matter were unimportant to him. "He's around somewhere. Why?"

"Because I'm not sure any of us should be alone."

"Why did you lure me here? If you know something," Jamie said, "spit it out."

Banyon heaved a sigh, as if battling within himself whether to speak or not. Finally, he did. "Tommy lied earlier when he said he was downstairs at the time Mr. Jupp fell from the landing." Here Banyon tilted his chin at the body on the bed. His eyes lingered there for a second.

"How do you know?" Jamie asked.

Banyon tore his gaze from the corpse and refocused on Jamie's face. "There is another staircase behind the dining room. It leads down from rooms up above, then on up to the attic as well. I heard Tommy's feet on the stairs. He said he was on the first floor when he heard the fall, but he wasn't. I'm wondering why he would lie about something like that."

"He's your boyfriend. You're the one who knows him best. Why do *you* think he'd lie?"

"That's just it," Banyon said. "Tommy is one of my students, but I don't really know him. He put the moves on me a couple of weeks ago." Here Banyon had the good grace to blush. "And I succumbed to his charms. He can be a fairly persuasive young man."

"But you both received invitations to this little wingding at Hell House?"

Banyon snorted an unamused laugh, acknowledging the joke. "Yes. Neither of us could figure that out. We barely knew each other. How could we both know the person who sent the invitations? And how could they know us? Our addresses and everything. It was practically a fluke we were together at all, and now suddenly we were getting joint invitations to a party."

Jamie thought about that. "I see your point. Derek and I thought the same thing."

Like the professor he was, Oliver Banyon popped a finger in the air and wagged it back and forth. "*Unless*," he stated with a hint of Sam Spade in his voice, "he planned it all."

"You're saying you think Tommy's the one who sent the invitations. You think Tommy's the one who's doing all this. Luring us here. Killing people."

At that Banyon appeared to lose his sense of mental direction. He suddenly looked unsure of himself. Uncertain. Flailing. "No," he stammered at last. "I can't really believe that. Tommy's just a rambunctious kid. Great in the sack, but that's about the limit of his usefulness. I don't think he's really cruel. Nor do I think he's crazy. I just think...." His voice trailed away. "Oh hell, I don't know what I think."

"But he did lie about where he was when Mr. Jupp died?"

"Yes," Banyon said, certainty back in his eyes. "That much I'm sure of."

"Then we'll have to ask him why he did," Jamie said. "We'll have to ask him why he lied."

He glanced down at Banyon's arm. There was a scratch there, just above the wrist. A scratch that appeared as fresh as the one on the banister upstairs.

Jamie took a step back and pointed to it. "Where did you get that?"

Banyon glance down at his arm. He ran a quick thumb over the wound as if thinking he might wipe it away. With his other hand he touched the bruise on his cheek.

"Tommy did it last night when we fought. We told you about that."

"What did you fight about?"

Banyon's eyes narrowed. His chin came up. "That's really none of your business. Let's just say it had to do with… sex. Tommy can be fairly forceful when he wants to be."

Jamie stared into Banyon's eyes but saw no lie in them. He was telling the truth. His embarrassment was enough to convince Jamie of that.

He was suddenly aware that not only the storm but the approach of evening had begun to infiltrate the house with shadows. Where had the day gone? He twisted the switch on a Tiffany-style floor lamp that stood at the edge of the unlit fireplace. A myriad of colored lights brightened the room, bringing it some much-needed cheer.

As if the subject of Tommy's possible deceit had brought it to mind, both men turned mute attention toward the body on the daybed. Jamie saw for the first time that blood had seeped through the blanket they had wrapped around Mr. Jupp's battered head. He thought back to the long fall between the landing and the floor below and gave a shudder.

"Someone under this roof is a murderer," Banyon said with sadness in his voice. "None of us is safe."

"No," Jamie said, tearing his eyes from the corpse to stare at a sprinkling of cold ashes in the fireplace grate. "We aren't. But what the hell can we do about it?"

DEREK FOUND Jamie in the dining room, rummaging through the leftovers from breakfast, trying to make a meal since the cook still seemed to be secluded in her rooms. Not that anyone could blame her, being suddenly widowed and all.

They stood companionably next to each other at the sideboard, creating sandwiches from half-stale scones and cold sausage links. The platter of leftover scrambled eggs looked like it had been sitting on a sand dune in the Sahara Desert for a week or two, so they ignored that.

They were talking about Tommy and Banyon.

"Why are they turning on each other? Do you think they are both in on the murders?"

Derek stared at Jamie. It was a thought that had not occurred to him before. "Why? Do you?"

Jamie thought about it for three seconds. Maybe less. "No. I don't believe that at all."

"Neither do I," Derek said, for some reason immensely relieved. "But I wouldn't put it past *one* of them to be the killer."

"What about the scratch on Banyon's arm? Do you think it's true what he said about Tommy inflicting the wound during an argument over sex? Or do you think he got it scuffling with Jupp on the stairs?"

"Nothing about having sex with young Master Stevens would surprise me," Derek said, not bothering to mention what had taken place in the basement because he knew Jamie would be upset that Tommy had come on to him.

Jamie nodded. "Yeah, he's a real piece of work, that one."

Derek snorted back a laugh. *You have no idea.*

With their sandwiches eaten, Derek motioned Jamie to follow. "Let's go talk to the little bastard."

A sneaky grin lit Jamie's face. "Yes. Let's."

They found Tommy Stevens on the front porch. He was wrapped in his leather jacket with the collar turned up to protect him from the wind. Or to look cool. Who knew what the hell his motivations were? Oliver Banyon was nowhere around. The storm beyond the eaves of the porch roof was gearing up for another hissy fit. Already the wind was whipping past the house like a typhoon, making the pine trees flail in the distance, splattering raindrops on Tommy's leather jacket even though he was four feet from the edge of the porch, and making Jamie and Derek huddle close together and squint against the spray.

The first thing Jamie noticed were the cuts on Tommy's knuckles.

"When you guys fight, you really fight," Jamie said, tossing it casually out there.

Tommy saw where he was staring and stuffed his hands in his jacket pockets. "Yeah. We do. So what do you want? I was trying to get two minutes alone."

If he was wondering whether Derek had told Jamie about the pass he made in the basement, he didn't allow himself to look worried about it. *He's a cool one*, Derek thought. *But is he a killer?*

"When Jupp fell," Derek began, "you said you were back by the old servants' quarters on the first floor."

Tommy eyed each of them in turn, finally settling his gaze on Derek. They had all turned their backs to the rain. Derek's and Jamie's hair thrashed about in the wind, while Tommy's Brylcreemed locks didn't move an inch. They had to raise their voices to be heard above the storm. "That's right. What about it?"

Derek edged closer to Jamie, but his eyes never left Tommy's face. "What if someone says they saw you coming down the stairs at the back of the house at that time?"

"What stairs?" Tommy asked.

"There's another flight that comes down from the second floor. Past our rooms, the hallway we use on the second floor turns right and leads around to the other smaller staircase which leads back down to the first floor and also up to the attic. It's nothing as grand as the main staircase in the foyer. This one was probably used by servants."

"I didn't know about it," Tommy said. "These old houses are sometimes a labyrinth of hidden passages and rooms and walkways and stairs. With a murderer running around, I haven't been exactly comfortable exploring on my own." He ran a thumb over the scratches on his knuckles. "Who told you they saw me upstairs?"

"Doesn't matter," Derek said. "They must have been mistaken."

"They were."

Jamie cleared his throat. He ducked as deep into his collar as he could to avoid the spray of rain peppering their heads. "What were you doing out here?"

Tommy turned and, shielding his eyes against the elements with his hand, nodded toward the automobiles in the distance. "I was wondering if I could get one of the cars running, but I suppose it's pointless with the tires cut and the bridge out." His face brightened. "Did either of you find your phones?"

Jamie and Derek both shook their heads. "No," Derek said, and Tommy instantly deflated. Then he took another stab at looking hopeful. "It's almost time for dinner. You think the old woman will cook for us? I'm starving."

"If she won't," Derek said, "I'm sure we can whip something up ourselves. We can't expect Mrs. Jupp to work when she's just lost her husband."

"Is she still in her room?" Tommy asked.

It was Jamie who answered. "As far as I know, she hasn't left it all day. Maybe we should be the ones to take some food up to her. She must be hungry as well."

Again Tommy asked, "Who was it who told you I was upstairs when Mr. Jupp was killed? I want to know."

Neither Derek nor Jamie answered.

A moment later, a scream tore through the house. It was so loud it penetrated not only the outer wall, but the storm as well, outvoicing the wind. The shrill cry bled out into the trees like a banshee's dwindling wail until the storm at last swallowed it whole.

CHAPTER NINE

DEREK, WITH Jamie and Tommy Stevens racing behind, barreled through the front door and into the foyer. Jamie slammed the door behind them, shutting out the storm. To their left, entering the foyer at the back, past the stairs and beyond the little door beneath it, they spotted Banyon rushing into the hall as well. He wore a dish towel tucked into the waistband of his trousers and clutched a large wooden spoon in his hand. He looked stunned, as if he carried inside himself a massive fear that was trying desperately to get the better of him.

"I was fixing dinner!" he cried, spotting the three men at the door. "Who was that? What's happened now?"

Derek opened his mouth to speak, when the scream suddenly repeated itself. It was a long, ululating howl of pure terror that sent goose bumps crawling up Derek's neck like a line of ants. The scream came from upstairs. All eyes flew to the landing above, but there was no one there.

"Oh shit," Tommy muttered under his breath. "This can't be good."

All four men raced to converge on the staircase at once, plowing into each other as they clambered up the steps. Jamie clutched at the back of Derek's shirt, and feeling him there, Derek reached around and clasped Jamie's hand, hoping to comfort him, wanting to keep him close. They stampeded up the stairs. The house came alive under the racket they made.

From the top of the steps, they had an unimpeded view along the second-floor hallway. Several doors down, almost lost in the gloaming light of a stormy evening, they spotted what looked like a body on the floor. It lay crumpled just outside the door leading into Mr. and Mrs. Jupps' suite of rooms. The door stood open, and a feeble yellow light flickered out into the hall. The warm light seemed to caress the woman on the floor.

For it was a woman, Derek suddenly realized, and more, from a glimpse of straw-colored hair, he knew it was Cleeta-Gayle Jones. She had to be the one who screamed. Then she must have passed out.

A haze of woodsmoke filled the hall. On it wafted the reek of tainted meat. And something else.

"Oh God," Derek mumbled as his nostrils flared. "What's that smell?"

Jamie turned bulging, frightened eyes in his direction. "I don't know."

Derek and the others moved warily now, uncertain how to proceed. Since it always seemed to fall to him anyway, Derek took the lead and proceeded cautiously down the hall. He kept expecting Mrs. Jupp to show herself at the door, but the only sounds he could hear now came from the storm. The lashing of rain on panes of glass. The driving wind whistling through the eaves. Somewhere off to his left, a loosened shutter banged against the side of the house. A flash of lightning strobed the hallway, bringing everything into sharp relief for the space of a single heartbeat. Then, as thunder grumbled in the distance, marking the lightning's end, the hallway fell into shadow once more.

At the last minute, Jamie edged past Derek and knelt beside the woman on the floor. He gently eased her head around to look at her face. Derek watched over Jamie's shoulder as Cleeta-Gayle's eyelashes flicked and her eyes slowly opened. A smile almost appeared on the woman's face, but then she seemed to remember where she was. And what she had seen. A sudden wrench of terror twisted her features.

Before she could speak, Tommy uttered the words everybody was afraid they'd hear. He stood at the door leading into the Jupps' suite and spoke in a hollow voice, as if all emotion had been stripped from his throat.

"We've got another one," Tommy said, his young face lit by firelight. His shoulders slumped, and he turned away from the door. To everyone's surprise, heaving a sob, he edged forward and pressed his face to Banyon's chest. Banyon, in turn, wrapped his arms around the boy and held him tight. Nevertheless, his gaze traveled to the open door.

The stench was stronger here, and it was Derek and Jamie, hand in hand, who finally moved toward the oblong of golden light spilling out into the hall. And closer to the source of the smell.

Cleeta-Gayle, tears spilling from her eyes now, reached out as if to stop them, but they were already out of reach. As if remembering what they were about to see, she uttered a muffled groan and folded herself back into a miserable ball on the hallway floor.

Derek, with Jamie at his side, poked his head around the frame of the door and beheld what lay inside. The room was gray with smoke. The acrid reek of singed hair lay so heavy on the air he could taste it on his tongue. Bile surged up his throat. He swallowed hard, trying not to gag.

For a moment, Derek had the sensation that his heart had suddenly ceased to pump life through his veins. It was as if a stillness—an *emptiness*—had settled over him like a cloak. The only movement before him was in the dance of the flames on the hearth. But it was not the flames that held the eye.

It was the savaged body of Mrs. Jupp that did that. Fully clothed, she lay sprawled on her back on the brick apron before the fireplace, her arms and legs splayed out into the room, while the ball of black cinder that was her head crisped merrily in the flames.

TO DEREK'S surprise, it was Jamie who acted first. He tore himself from Derek's grasp and raced toward the body. Grabbing the dead woman's feet, he yanked her from the fire. Her blackened head gave a muffled thump as it was pulled off the grate. Sparks rained down around it onto the floor.

In the mask of ash that had once been a human face, a few streaks of red could be seen where the flesh had split open in the heat. Her hair was gone, her ears burned to nothing. In the center of that horrible black ball of cindered meat and bone, the old woman's mouth stretched wide over flame-blackened teeth as if screaming a silent, anguished wail. But sounds no longer escaped from that awful black hole. All that escaped from there now was a tiny wisp of smoke that curled into the air and was instantly sucked upward, through the flue and ultimately into the stormy, pounding night outside.

As quickly as Jamie freed the old woman's head from the fire, he turned away. Like Tommy had done with Banyon, he buried his face in Derek's chest. Derek accepted him there, his own eyes riveted to the grotesque head still smoking and smoldering at the edge of the grate.

"Wait," Derek whispered into Jamie's hair, brushing him with a kiss while he was there. Easing Jamie out of his arms, he stepped forward to take up the little broom from the rack of fireplace tools and brushed it over the bodice of Mrs. Jupp's dress, where the fabric had erupted into tiny flames. When the fire on her clothing was extinguished, Derek tossed the tiny broom into the corner as if he couldn't bear to touch it any longer. He pulled Jamie toward him, wrapping him in his arms once more.

But for the cheerful crackling of the flames and the sizzle of the logs burning on the hearth, the room fell silent. Only the tumult of the storm outside and the gentle sobbing of Cleeta-Gayle trespassed on the scene.

That and the reek of charred flesh.

"I have to get out of here," Jamie half wept, his lips brushing the front of Derek's shirt.

Derek ducked his head and laid his cheek to Jamie's. "You go ahead," he whispered. And raising his voice, he added, "All of you. I'll bank the fire and cover the body. We need to close off this room before the smell permeates the house."

Cleeta-Gayle stood in the doorway. She could not seem to tear her anguished eyes from the body on the floor. "Why is her mouth stretched open like that?" she all but gasped. "Was she put in the fire alive?"

Banyon had the answer for that. "No. We would have heard her fighting, screaming. She must have already been dead when her head was put in the flames. Thank God. The heat made the muscles and tendons in her face contract. That's why her mouth is open."

"More information than I needed to know," Jamie mumbled, and without looking back, not at Derek or the body or *anyone*, he squeezed past Cleeta-Gayle and stumbled out into the hall. He was quickly followed by Banyon and Tommy.

Finding himself alone, Derek, for the second time that day, pulled his T-shirt up over his nose to mitigate the stench of violent death. He set about methodically sealing off the room. Not content to simply bank the fire, he filled a basin with water and doused the flames in the fireplace entirely. It made a bit of a mess and raised more smoke, but there was nothing he could do about that. Stripping a blanket from the bed in the adjoining room, he tucked it carefully around Mrs. Jupp's body. At the last moment, he checked the old woman's clothing once more to make sure no fabric was left smoldering. When all else was satisfactory, he blanketed her head, tucking the ends in securely. Leaving her body in front of the now-flameless hearth, he took a final inventory of the room to make sure he hadn't forgotten anything.

Backing into the hallway where the others waited, he surveyed the room one last time, then switched off the light and closed the door, abandoning the stench—and Mrs. Jupp's cooling corpse—to the darkness.

As Jamie returned to his place in Derek's outstretched arms, Derek leveled an unflinching gaze at everyone standing in the hall. Cleeta-Gayle Jones. Oliver Banyon. Tommy Stevens. And last of all Jamie. Before speaking, he laid his hand protectively over Jamie's stomach as if drawing strength from his presence.

"My lover and myself I know to be innocent," he said. "That leaves one of you three as the killer. Which means the other two are innocent. How do we weed out the murderer?"

"Nice," Tommy sneered, no longer in Banyon's arms but still standing close to his side. His previous display of emotion seemed to have dissipated. Now he was back to his usual cocky self. "I see you've neatly subtracted yourselves from the list of suspects. I'm not sure I agree with that theory."

"Nor do I," Banyon said.

"Or I," Cleeta-Gayle chimed in. She had pulled herself marginally together. Her hair and clothes were still a mess, but then they usually were. At least her face had a little more color in it, and she didn't look like she was on the verge of passing out anytime soon.

Derek watched them all. And as he stared, he pulled the T-shirt down from his nose to test the air. Thank heavens there was very little hint of burned flesh in the hall.

"Derek and I know we didn't do any of it," Jamie said. "But I guess we can't expect you to believe us. We probably wouldn't believe you either. So what are we going to do?"

Banyon glanced down at the wooden spoon he still held in his hand. As if noticing for the first time the dish towel tucked in his waistband, he plucked it out and wadded it up. "Before we do anything, we have to eat. It's been a long nerve-racking day, and none of us has eaten since this morning. Even murderers get hungry, I would presume, although I don't suppose anyone is in the mood for anything grilled on an open fire."

"Is that supposed to be funny?" Tommy asked. He wasn't smiling.

Banyon shrugged. "Sorry. A feeble attempt at levity." He turned his eyes to the others. "What do you say? Anybody else hungry? We can discuss what we're going to do over dinner. It's just stew, mind you. I threw a few cans of crap together. I'm not much of a cook, I'm afraid."

"That's all right," Derek said, a feeble smile twisting his mouth. "There's been enough cooking for one day."

Tommy cast a final glance at Mrs. Jupp's door. Derek studied him, wondering if he was reliving what had just happened inside. As if any of them would ever forget it.

Derek coaxed Jamie toward the stairs, following along behind the others. "Jamie and I will set the table in the dining room."

"I'll make some iced tea," Cleeta-Gayle added, glancing back, still wiping the tears from her face.

"Iced tea sounds good," Jamie muttered, following obediently along at Derek's heels.

"I'll stand guard," Tommy said, retrieving the knife from his pocket and holding it not quite casually at his side.

They all stopped to stare at the boy, then at the weapon he held. If anyone had a problem with what he'd said, or the fact that he had suddenly armed himself, they didn't voice it.

And who's going to watch the watcher? Derek idly wondered. But he didn't voice his opinion either. Instead he led Jamie down the staircase toward the dining room, astonished at himself for suddenly feeling as hungry as he did. After what they had just seen, he hadn't thought he would ever be hungry again.

Jamie tugged on Derek's sleeve, slowing their advance down the hall until the others had gone on ahead.

When they were alone, Jamie turned around to face him, resting his hands on Derek's chest. "I'm scared," he said. "I need you to tell me you love me." There was a tremor in his voice Derek had never heard there before.

With a lopsided grin, Derek gently pushed Jamie against the wall and smothered him with his body. "Funny you should ask," he mumbled with his lips on Jamie's throat. "I was about to say it anyway."

Derek was surprised to feel a shudder of desire rumble through him like thunder. Before he could act on it, Jamie froze in his arms.

"Wait! Listen," he breathed. "The storm. It's stopped!"

Jamie was right. Derek stood stock-still, taking in the sudden silence like a breath of fresh air. While he was at it, he basked in the familiar scent of Jamie's warm body.

"Thank God," he sighed. "We've had enough rain." Then he found Jamie's mouth with his own. And in the midst of that long, sweet kiss, he muttered the words Jamie had asked him to speak. And he said them from the heart.

"I do love you," he whispered. "You're mine now. I'm yours. We belong to each other."

Jamie seemed to melt in his arms. Derek liked that. What Jamie said next, he liked a little less.

"Promise me you'll get us out of this house alive."

Derek's continuing kiss was the only promise he gave. For deep down inside he knew, he *knew*, it was the only promise he *could* give.

"Just stay with me," he said in lieu of lying. "Never leave my side. If we do that, we can protect each other."

And with that, it was Jamie who made the promise. "I will," he said. "I promise, Derek. I won't let myself out of your sight."

FOR ALL their talk of hunger, their plates of beef stew were left barely tasted. A loaf of bread, still in the wrapper, had not been touched at all. None of them were in the mood for formal dining, so they hardly noticed that the candles weren't lit, the glassware was mismatched, and Banyon had set out a roll of paper towels to be used as napkins, since he couldn't find the real thing in the kitchen. The five of them sat around the table, avoiding each other's eyes. Their thoughts had turned inward. Even Jamie sank into despair after the horror of what he had seen upstairs. He cast a sidelong glance at Derek, wondering how he was coping with what they had witnessed. Under the table, he pressed his knee to Derek's leg, needing the contact. Banyon spoke first. He glanced around the table, at the food, at the people not eating it. "I'm sorry. I told you I wasn't a very good cook."

Cleeta-Gayle took up her napkin and patted a mouth that had not seen a single bite of dinner. "It's not your fault. It's this house." A flash of desperate hope appeared to light her eyes. She leaned her elbows on the table and eagerly gazed around from face to face. "How do we know the killer isn't hiding somewhere on the property? Maybe it isn't one of us at all?"

Banyon was quick with an answer. "Don't you think we would have heard someone else moving about? It's a big house, but it's not a rambling mansion. There are only so many places to hide." His eyes darted around the table, scanning each face. "Who could have got into

Mrs. Jupp's room earlier? She'd obviously been dead awhile. Who had access to her? Who was closest?"

Most eyes turned reluctantly to Cleeta-Gayle. Tommy was the only one who didn't look reluctant about it at all. He was also the one who voiced everyone's suspicion, even if they were too meek to voice it themselves. His gaze held no sympathy as he studied the woman in front of him.

"That's right, dear. Heads don't cook in a minute. This had to have happened hours ago. You were just across the hall from her. You both went upstairs after Mr. Jupp fell. None of us has seen either of you since. While we were all in other parts of the house, you had plenty of time to sneak across the hall, bash her in the head, and when she fell into the fire, you just left her there to sizzle." Banyon laid a hand on Tommy's arm to silence him, but Tommy shook it off. He continued to glare at the woman he had accused of murder.

Cleeta-Gayle stumbled to her feet. Her chair toppled over behind her, crashing to the floor, making everybody jump. Her eyes traveled to each of them in turn. "You think *I* killed Mrs. Jupp? You think *I* left that poor old woman to burn in the fire?"

Jamie was the only one who looked down, uneasy beneath her accusing gaze. "No," he said quietly. "I'm sure none of us really thinks that."

"Speak for yourself!" Tommy snapped. Then a nasty grin twisted his mouth as he studied Jamie instead. "Or maybe you and your boyfriend are the ones we should watch. You could be backing each other up with your alibis."

"Don't be stupid!" Derek barked. "We don't know any of you people. Why would we want to kill you?" Jamie watched as a light of understanding brightened Derek's eyes. "That's what we should be searching for, you know! We should be searching for what it is that brought us all together. There must be something we all have in common. An acquaintance, maybe. Something that made the killer decide to lure us all to this house together and pick us off one by one."

"But why would anyone want to kill *us*?" Jamie pleaded. "Who could hate us that much? And *why*?" Banyon fiddled with his glass of iced tea, using a fingertip to draw a smiley face in the condensation on the side. Iced tea still filled it to the brim. It had not been tasted.

"Do you think we haven't already been trying to figure that out? The only one of you people I know at all is Tommy. And we've only been acquainted personally for a couple of weeks."

Cleeta-Gayle shot a wary glance in his direction. "How do we really know that?" she asked, her voice as cold as the tea in her glass. Banyon was so surprised by the suspicion in her words, he sat mute. Tommy did not.

"I guess you'll just have to take our word for it!" he snapped at the woman. "Don't *you* start. It's bad enough we have to put up with nasty looks from the fucking help!"

"Not anymore we don't," Derek said, more to himself than to anyone at the table.

Jamie blinked, a sudden clarity suddenly invading his senses. He turned to stare at Tommy Stevens. "You're right," he said, eyes wide. "They hated us from the start." His mind was suddenly racing. He sifted through his thoughts, trying to make sense of it all. "Why did they hate us so much? Doesn't that seem a little strange?"

All eyes turned toward him, staring. "Jamie…," Derek mumbled, but he didn't finish his thought. A furrow formed between his eyebrows as he stared down at his plate, obviously considering what Jamie had said.

"But there's still no connection," Banyon interrupted. "There's still nothing to show why any of us were individually chosen." He leaned forward, his eyes flashing angrily. "*What the hell is the motive?* What is the common thread that brought us all here? And why would anyone hate us enough to destroy the cars so we can't leave? And trash the phones so we can't call out? And how the hell did they collapse the fucking bridge?"

Cleeta-Gayle was standing at the sideboard now. She had poured herself a glass of wine. It shook, untasted, in her hand. "Please stop swearing," she said softly.

All eyes swiveled to her. She looked so frightened, so beaten down, Jamie pushed himself to his feet, intending to go to her. To comfort her.

But it was Banyon who made the effort first. He rose from the table and approached the woman, coaxing her into a gentle hug. Jamie watched, entranced, as she closed her eyes and rested her head on his chest. Only then did she begin to quietly weep.

"I'm scared to death," she sobbed. "I don't want to die in this horrible house."

Tommy sat watching his lover comfort the woman. He was doe-eyed in wonder, as if he were as amazed by this development as he was by any of it. He finally tore his gaze away and turned to Jamie and Derek.

"The bridge had to be a fluke," he said, eyeing them closely for their reaction. "Nobody could have planned that. Still, it fit right into the killer's plans. He must have been thrilled."

"Maybe not," Jamie said. "If he had an escape plan, it must have been the road. Now he's trapped here too. Just like us."

A comforting hand stroked the back of his neck, and Jamie almost smiled at the familiar heat of Derek's touch. He tilted his head back and Derek's fingers slid into his hair.

While continuing to caress Jamie's scalp, Derek directed his words to the room, to anyone who cared to listen. "None of us wants to die here," he said. "I think we need to look at this like the cops would. We have to figure out the clues."

"What clues?" Jamie asked.

Derek offered him a patient smile. "It's like we talked about earlier," he said gently. "We need to figure out why the pictures are missing from the walls. That's the most obvious clue, and the one that's most puzzling to me. We were clearly brought here because of something we've all done, or something the killer *thinks* we've done. And the one who brought us here had a connection to this house. A close connection. In fact, the killer must have been a relative or friend to the old couple in the basement." Derek's eyes flashed impatiently at some of the obstinate looks he received. "Don't you understand? The killer's face was in those pictures, which meant he had to get rid of them so we wouldn't know. Why else would they be removed? Our resident madman needed this house to stage his little show, and he was willing to kill the old couple to make it happen. To keep his identity secret, he did away with all evidence of his own presence in this house and in the lives of the old couple who owned it."

Tommy tore his gaze from Banyon, who was still comforting the woman by the sideboard. He leveled his gaze at Derek. "That makes sense," he said. "But how do we prove it? That's the most important question."

"We have to find the pictures," Derek said. "We have to search the house!"

Cleeta-Gayle twisted herself free from Banyon's arms. She stared about the room through terror-filled eyes.

"No!" she cried, suddenly pushing Banyon farther away, causing him to stumble back and almost fall. She glared in turn at each and every face staring at her. Her fists clenched at her sides, and she trembled in fury. Suddenly it was there. In the line of her jaw. In the fire in her eyes. Anger. And mindless, undiluted panic.

"Don't you understand?" she screamed. "The storm is over. We have to run. Now! *We have to get away from this evil house before he kills us all.*"

Her haunted eyes flew from face to face, then from door to door, as she gauged every avenue of escape. She glanced at the wineglass in her hand and instantly flung it away. The crystal smashed against the stone fireplace, scattering tinkling shards of glass in every direction. Streaks of merlot stained the wall red, like blood spatters at a crime scene. Under the circumstances, an apt simile if there ever was one, Jamie thought.

Her gaze at last fell upon the door leading out to the hall.

Stumbling as if blinded by her own fear, she lurched across the room. Her ankle caught the overturned chair and sent it skidding across the floor. She almost fell but with a cry righted herself at the last moment.

"Stop her!" someone demanded.

Only Jamie answered the call.

He flung himself away from the table and pounded after her. A rush of cool air struck his face as she pulled the front door open, then hurled herself out into the waning daylight.

The rain had stopped, the skies at long last silent. But still angry clouds, like great balls of black silk, hovered overhead. In the air was a sense that it wasn't over yet. The storm, the killing, none of it.

Running as fast as she could, Cleeta-Gayle splashed through the mud toward the cars.

"The cars are useless. They're destroyed," Jamie called out, but she didn't stop. She didn't turn.

Jamie was surprised how quickly the woman could move. He bizarrely took the time to wonder if she was a jogger. Then before he knew it, she had passed the cars and disappeared among the trees at the edge of the property.

Jamie threw himself into the woods directly behind her. Here, the shadows were deeper. The gloom was almost tangible, as if you could actually reach your hand out and feel it on your fingertips. In the raw, damp air, he thought he could still smell the smoke from the second-floor fireplace, where Mrs. Jupp had lain crisping. It had to be his imagination, but the thought sent a chill through him anyway.

He wasn't wearing a coat, and when a limb caught his arm, it tore the skin. He cried out in pain but kept going. Glancing back, he saw Derek and Tommy and Banyon standing on the porch, watching him. Derek was pointing off to the side, and Jamie realized he was steering him toward the woman he was chasing.

Jamie shifted directions, and a moment later, there among the trees ahead, he saw a crumpled mass at the base of a tall, twisted pine. It was Cleeta-Gayle Jones. She was weeping, hugging the bole of the tree. She must have stumbled and fallen. Her legs were smeared with mud, and her cheek was scraped raw where she must have struck the trunk of the tree on the way down.

Ignoring the muddy ground, Jamie quickly dropped to his knees beside her and wrapped her in his arms. "It's all right," he cajoled. "Trust me. We won't let anything happen to you. You're safe."

She lifted her head to stare at him through frightened, tear-filled eyes. The scrape on her cheek looked nasty. A tiny rivulet of blood had already slipped along the planes of her neck to disappear inside her blouse. Jamie would have to treat the cut when they got back to the house.

She eyed him with what could only be described as profound sympathy. "You don't understand, do you?" she asked, as if speaking to a child. "We really are trapped. There's nowhere to go, no way to leave. We're already dead. All of us. You, me, your boyfriend, all of us. We were dead the minute we set foot inside that house."

Somehow the simple way she referred to Derek as his boyfriend bothered him. He smiled and spoke softly, as gently as he could. "Derek's not my boyfriend, he's my lover. And I'll keep him safe if it's the last thing I do."

"Is he worth dying for?" she asked. "Is your kind of love really strong enough for that?" Her eyes were wide, piercing, as if she really wanted to know. As if she truly needed to understand.

"Yes," Jamie said. "It's strong enough for that."

And reaching down, he clasped her muddy hand and pulled her to her feet.

At that moment, Derek came splashing through the muck and gathered them both in his arms.

"Let's go back to the house," he said calmly, as if it were the most normal thing in the world that they should be hanging on to each other in the middle of the woods, covered with mud. "Let's get the two of you cleaned up."

Jamie and Derek held tightly to Cleeta-Gayle as they stumbled a soggy path back through the trees toward the house. She almost fell once, but they braced her and kept her safe. Jamie cast a weary smile in Derek's direction as they approached the porch, and a second later, Derek shot him a wink in return.

As they steered the woman up the porch steps and into the house, Tommy snarled at the woman as she passed. "Stupid bitch."

Jamie withered him with a look of pure hatred. Fists clenched, Jamie moved to throw himself at the kid, but Derek tugged him back.

"Help me with her," Derek said. "Let's get her inside. This is more important than you punching that twat in the face."

Their eyes met, and Jamie smiled through tight lips. The mere sight of Derek's sweet face caused him to swallow his anger and refocus on the task at hand.

Cleeta-Gayle, propped between the two, lifted her eyes to first Derek, then Jamie.

"You boys are both kind. And you do love each other. I can see it now," she whispered softly. Resting her head on Jamie's shoulder, she let them steer her toward the door. By the time they ducked inside, she was once again softly crying.

"I'm sorry," she breathed as they led her up the stairs. And she kept saying it as she wept. "I'm sorry. I'm sorry. I'm sorry."

Jamie tutted her to silence and lowered her to a chair inside her room. "We'll let you clean yourself up," he said kindly.

He and Derek eased back out into the hall and quietly closed her door behind them.

CHAPTER TEN

"I LOVE the taste of you," Jamie murmured, his voice deep and husky, his lips traveling the still-moist length of Derek's softening cock.

Derek had to concentrate to unearth his voice. His body was still shaken by the explosive orgasm he had just experienced, thanks to Jamie and his extremely talented mouth.

He had been gently coaxed from a troubled sleep maybe fifteen minutes earlier. Jamie, he discovered then, had slipped beneath the covers and was oh so lovingly burrowing his way down Derek's torso, trailing kisses over his skin, seeking what Derek knew Jamie loved the most.

"Let me reciprocate," Derek breathed into the darkness. He made a move to roll Jamie onto his back, but Jamie unexpectedly pushed back.

With his lips still on Derek's tender skin below, Jamie whispered in a fragile voice, "Please don't move. I'm enjoying myself." And with that, he slipped Derek's glistening length into his eager, loving mouth yet again.

Derek shuddered blissfully. Grasping at Jamie's hair, holding him in place right where he knew Jamie wanted to be, he wrapped a leg over Jamie's back and trapped him close.

"Oh God, yes…," Jamie moaned, barely coherent since his mouth was full. "I love your fuzzy legs around me."

Derek giggled, but he tried to sound butch about it. He wasn't quite sure he succeeded.

Jamie's hands soothed him as they traveled over his body. Jamie's warm breath on his stomach felt wonderful. Jamie's lips and tongue, tickling a path through Derek's damp pubic hair, made Derek's breath catch in his throat, made his heart skip little beats now and then.

Derek twisted sideways in the bed, wrapping himself around Jamie and holding him as close as he could. Together they created a bundle of satin flesh, welcoming, worshipping, sleep-warm. Arms, legs, chests. When Jamie squirmed higher in the bed, their mouths came together in a long, devouring kiss.

Jamie tasted deliciously of Derek's juices. Jamie's breath lay hot on Derek's face as they pulled gently apart in the cocoon of darkness beneath the covers.

Together, they pulled the blankets down and peeked out into the room, like two animal peering from the safety of their lair.

The house lay buried in late-night shadow, the darkened sky outside still oddly silent. The storm had not returned. Not yet. But was it Derek's imagination, or did the postmidnight air smell of ozone once again? Was another storm drawing near, creeping over the horizon perhaps? Not that it mattered. They couldn't be trapped here in this damnable old house any more than they already were. If the weather cleared they might be able escape through the trees, he supposed. But if they did, who would they choose to travel with them? Who did they trust?

It was bizarre the way Jamie often deciphered Derek's thoughts. Sometimes even before Derek could.

"You want to leave," Jamie said softly. "If we do, we'll have to go alone. I don't trust anyone enough to take them along." He was under the covers again. He had burrowed back down to lay his cheek to the soft fuzz on Derek's stomach. When he spoke, his lips and hot breath caressed Derek's skin. It was such an erotic sensation, Derek felt his cock begin to lengthen again in increments.

Jamie must have felt it too. He purred and snuggled closer.

Derek wrapped Jamie's head in his arms, holding him tightly against him. Down below, their hairy legs bristled together, and at his back, Jamie's warm hands traced the line of his hips, massaging gently.

"We can't abandon everyone," Derek said, his mouth in Jamie's hair. "There are three other people here, and as far as we know, two of them are innocent. Do we really want to leave them behind?"

Jamie lay still for a moment. Finally, he circled Derek's lengthening cock in his warm fingers and laid the shaft lovingly against his cheek. Derek felt Jamie's tongue slip out and lick away a drop of Derek's juices left over from the orgasm before. Or was it a prelude to the next explosive eruption? Derek smiled in the dark at the casual way Jamie laid claim to his secretions.

"Then we'll have to stay," Jamie breathed, his lips moving once again to Derek's stomach.

As if a thought had suddenly occurred to him, Jamie rolled away from Derek's embrace and sat up in the bed. The night was so lightless and the sky outside so wreathed in the residue of the storm that had come before, and the new one moving in now, that Derek could not discern even Jamie's outline in the dark.

By feel, Derek doubled over and planted a kiss on Jamie's knee. Jamie responded by stroking Derek's ear with just a lazy tweak of his fingertips, as if he was too busy thinking things through to really respond. "We have to search the house," Jamie said. "We need to find those pictures, but every time we've talked about it, something happens to distract us. We can't let it go again."

"Yes," Derek agreed. "You're right. Tomorrow we'll search the house. And if it's not storming, we'll check out the grounds as well."

They both fell silent when they heard the sound of sobbing coming from down the hall yet again. It was Cleeta-Gayle, the only woman left among them.

"Poor thing has been crying all night," Jamie muttered. "She's terrified."

Derek gave an unsympathetic grunt. "Aren't we all."

The sobbing stilled. The house grew silent once more. Jamie settled down under the covers again and pulled Derek into his arms.

"I like this," Derek crooned, laying his cheek to Jamie's chest.

"Me too."

Beyond the windowpane next to the bed, Derek heard the soft twitter of night birds somewhere off in the trees. He wondered if they were mourning the fact that another storm was moving in.

"Have you ever been in love like this before?" Derek asked quietly. "I mean, we've both had infatuations with people over the years. Crushes with one hunk or another. Sometimes both of us slobbering over the very same guy, ha-ha. But has it ever felt like *this* before? Has it ever felt so... *exactly right*?"

Jamie brushed a kiss through the hair on Derek's chest. "Never," he breathed. "Not once."

"So we really do love each other, then," Derek said on a sigh. He sounded faintly amazed, as if the truth of it had only this minute belted him between the eyes.

"Yes" was all Jamie said. As if he knew deep down in his heart it was all he *needed* to say.

"You were my friend before, and now you're my lover," Derek whispered. "Yet somehow I never noticed when it happened. It's like you gradually melted into me. I'm glad you're with me, you know. I'm glad you're here."

Jamie laughed. "You mean you're glad I'm here with you in this house of death with a murderer lurking behind every potted plant? Thanks a lot. I'm glad you're here too."

Derek yanked Jamie closer, playfully setting his teeth into the curve of his neck. He gnawed at Jamie like a dog with a bone. Through a grin, he said, "You know what I mean."

Jamie laughed and tried to squirm away.

They quieted when in the distance they heard an ominous rumble. The faintest flash of silver light stabbed a path through the shadows around them. A flurry of raindrops, fat and quick, spattered the window by their heads.

"Crap," Jamie said, his body tense in Derek's arms. "It's starting up again."

"Atmosphere," Derek groaned. "A cheesy plot device. Who writes this shit, anyway?"

Jamie laughed softly. "It's not a story, precious. It's real life. And I'm afraid we're stuck in the middle of it."

"Don't remind me," Derek groused. Tugging the covers over their heads, he pulled Jamie close, losing himself in the joy of their melded warmth.

The last words Derek remembered hearing before sleep overtook him was Jamie muttering softly in his ear, "I love you so much. I love you. So. Much."

And even in sleep, their embrace lived on. Derek awoke at dawn, still clutching Jamie tight.

As Jamie snored softly in his arms, Derek, eager and hard, slid downward in the bed, his cheek gliding smoothly across Jamie's hip. Time for a little tit for tat.

THE NEW storm had not reached its peak yet when Jamie, feeling feisty and sexually drained, which he thought was an excellent way to start the day, opened the bedroom door and ushered Derek into the hall. "You go first," he said, executing a sarcastic little salami-salami-baloney bow, "in case the killer is out there waiting with a hammer. We don't want the brains of the outfit to be bumped off first."

Derek slipped past him with a good-natured scowl. "You're right. The butch one *should* go first."

For show, Jamie tried to look stricken. "That's not exactly what I meant."

Chuckling, they descended the stairs and headed straight for the front door. The house was silent. As they passed the dining room, Jamie peered inside, but there was no one there. Perhaps no one else was up yet.

Stepping out onto the porch, again with Derek going first, they were met with a gusting, dew-laden morning that sent goose bumps creeping and crawling up Jamie's back. It must have dropped twenty degrees during the night. An icy wind stirred the hair around his face. He edged closer to Derek and peered out over his shoulder.

"The storm is definitely coming back this way," Derek said, scanning the sky. "If you close your eyes and listen, you can almost hear it building overhead."

"Then, if we're going to search the grounds," Jamie observed, "we'd better do it now."

Derek studied his face. Jamie stood patiently while he did, loving those warm brown eyes on him. Loving the way Derek let a tiny smile slip onto his features as he stared. Loving the way he remembered waking up that morning with Derek's mouth engulfing him, ravishing him as dawn slipped into the room.

Derek finally released him from his gaze. Taking Jamie's hand, he led him down the porch steps and onto the unkempt lawn. There was no grass underfoot. There never had been. They crunched over brittle plant life, weeds and bracken mostly, all of it long dead from lack of care. Beneath the dead stems, the ground was muddy from yesterday's rain.

Still clutching Jamie's hand, Derek steered them around the corner of the house. At one point they stepped over a green shutter that had succumbed to the storm. Wedges of roofing shingles, ancient and bleached pale from years of sun, were scattered about, torn from the roof in the gale.

"If this weather keeps up," Jamie said, "the house will fall down around our ears."

"Let's hope not," Derek answered. He stopped and pointed up ahead. "Look! There's a shed back there. Let's check it out."

Jamie let himself be led toward an old clapboard building that had once been a garage, but was now clearly used for storage. They knew this by all the discarded junk piled in front of the broad front door. Peeking around the side of the building, they found a simple storm door, the glass in it filthy with age and embroidered with cobwebs.

Derek reached out and tested the door handle. To Jamie's surprise, it turned easily. Cautiously, they pulled the door open and stepped inside, again with Derek leading the way. Jamie followed close behind, his fingers hooked in Derek's back pocket. Not because he was afraid, he told himself, but because he wanted to be near if Derek should suddenly need protecting.

Yeah, right.

They took two steps inside before stopping to study the interior. The place was packed with junk. Boxes, old furniture, bags of trash. An old riding lawn mower stood in the corner, splotchy with rust. Perhaps it had been used before the tenants grew too old to continue to care for the property. A battered bicycle, equally rusty, stood propped against the wall, the once colorful plastic streamers trailing from the handlebars now faded to gray. The tires were flat. It didn't look like it had been touched in a decade.

They heard some sort of small animal chittering back among the boxes.

"What the hell is that?" Jamie hissed, knowing he was biting off the words in nervous little clips but not really caring. The great thing about love was that Derek had already seen him at his worst. There was nothing more Jamie needed to hide. At least he hoped there wasn't.

"Probably a squirrel," Derek answered, and the moment he spoke, the chittering stopped.

When Derek tensed beside him, Jamie jumped. "*What?*"

"Look there," Derek said, maddeningly calm. He pointed to a window on the far side of the old garage. The window was half-covered with the remnants of a torn shower curtain, brittle and faded with age. Beyond the curtain, Jamie saw the trees in the distance, and closer in, an old steel barrel, blackened and eaten away with rust at the top.

"They burned their trash!" Derek said. "Let's check it out."

Not quite absorbing the gist of what Derek was getting at, Jamie relinquished his lead yet again, giving Derek the helm. Derek claimed it by tugging at his hand and pulling him back out onto the muddy yard through the filthy storm door.

Taking broad strides on his long legs, Derek led him around the corner of the dilapidated garage. There, between the garage and the edge of the forest perhaps fifty yards away, was a burned circle of ground with the rusty, charcoal-encrusted metal drum standing upright in the middle of it. The ground was littered with partially scorched pieces of junk and wood. Tatters of half-burned paper, drenched from the previous storms, lay sodden on the ground. The stench of melted plastic and watery ashes lay heavy on the air. Jamie scrunched up his nose at the reek.

"Isn't burning your trash illegal?" he asked.

Derek snorted back a laugh. "Anywhere else, maybe. Out here in the boondocks, it's probably standard practice. And they were old. Let's cut them a little slack, shall we?"

"You mean the old couple in the basement?" Jamie asked.

"Yes," Derek said, his eyes growing pensive, as if the thought of them lying down there among the cobwebs and the coal dust still saddened him. "The old couple in the basement."

He stepped forward, and Jamie stayed close to his side. As one, they peeked over the rim of the barrel and peered inside.

Jamie barked out a laugh.

"Well, I'll be damned!" he cried, slapping Derek on the back hard enough to rattle his teeth. "Are you the bomb, or what?"

OLIVER BANYON, Tommy Stevens, and Cleeta-Gayle Jones all looked up when they strode into the dining room. Before they could speak, Derek walked up and dropped three cell phones on the dining room table. The cell phones were melted into twisted clumps of metal and plastic. Smeared with mud and ash, they lay like dead things on the pristine tablecloth. Banyon leaned in close. With a shaky hand, he tapped one particular blob of plastic with the tip of his butter knife. "I think that one's mine," he said, his eyes round and sad.

"And the other two are ours," Derek said. "Jamie's and mine."

Banyon found his way to his feet then, his napkin forgotten, still tucked in the vee of his shirt front. "What does this mean?" he asked.

"It means we're in deep doo-doo, but then we knew that already," Jamie answered. "And while we're on the subject," he added, "here's another piece of the puzzle." He tossed a charred piece of wood onto the table next to the ruined phones. The wood was perhaps eight inches long, and the part that was not burned to a crisp was ornately carved.

"What's that?" Tommy asked, checking out the charred wood.

"It's part of a picture frame," Derek said, watching Tommy closely. Watching them all closely, in fact. Well aware that one of the three at the table must have had something to do with this. "It's probably part of one of the picture frames that were taken from the walls to be destroyed. The flames didn't quite do their job on this one. If you want to go out back and sift through the ashes, you might find a few more fragments, but I doubt if they'll tell us anything more than what we've got already."

"Did you find any pieces of the pictures themselves?" Tommy asked, his young face bright with hope. "Anything that could lead us to the killer?"

Derek shook his head, still staring down at the charred clues. "No."

Lifting his eyes, he scanned the faces in front of him. Cleeta-Gayle, as always, looked terrified. Tommy seemed curious. Banyon appeared angry. Jamie alone seemed sad. When Derek's gaze touched him, he turned his forest-green eyes right back at him. They were so beautiful and so *hurt*, Derek's breath almost caught in his throat.

"We should eat," Derek softly said, and Jamie nodded. With the thought of food, some of Jamie's inner turmoil seemed to slip away. Jamie lifted his eyes and stared in turn at every face around the table. His usually lush lips were now a thin slit carved across his face. Suddenly his angst appeared to be doing battle with pure anger.

"Which one of you is doing this?" he asked, his voice taut, his hands clenched at his side.

All eyes glared back at him as if offended by the question. All eyes but Derek's. He couldn't bear to see such anger suddenly spilling from the man he loved. Rather than witness it, he stared down at his own hands, only realizing at that moment how dirty and smudged with soot they were from digging through the burned trash.

Without looking up into Jamie's face, he eased his hand along the table and gently grasped Jamie's hand. Only then did he raise his eyes, and as he watched, the anger and distrust on Jamie's face appeared to melt away, replaced by a feeble smile as Jamie squeezed his fingers.

Silently, Jamie mouthed the words "Thank you." And at that precise moment, the peace and the calm of the morning exploded.

An almost physical chill spilled through the air. An ugly darkness claimed the sky. The house dimmed. With the roar of an avalanche, a great wash of rain peppered the grounds outside and slapped the roof above their heads. A whipcrack of lightning sizzled through the house, followed by an immediate crash of thunder that jarred the knickknacks on the mantle. One statue fell and crashed onto the brick apron below. Shards of porcelain sprinkled the fire. In the wake of the thunder came a sudden pall of unearthly silence that only comes with the loss of electricity.

All heads turned to the window looking out onto the yard in front. A spray of sparks showered down through the rain, and a moment later a horrendous explosion jarred the house, sending more trinkets crashing onto the floor. The floor shifted beneath Derek's feet, and in the same second of time, Jamie swept to his side and clutched at his arm, holding on for dear life.

An awful creaking sound set Derek's teeth on edge. And just as he was about to ask what on earth that sound could be, the storm answered his question for him.

The house heaved sideways as the light pole outside split like kindling and the entire length of it crashed down onto the porch roof, sending timber and shingles scattering across the yard. The window they were staring through exploded inward. Wind and rain and razor-sharp wedges of glass swept into the room. Burning embers blew up from the grate, scattering flecks of fire across the floor. Everyone wheeled away, running toward the back of the room to escape the encroaching storm.

They came to rest along the back wall—Jamie in Derek's arms. Tommy in Banyon's. The only one alone, Cleeta-Gayle clung to the doorframe leading out to the old servants' quarters. The wind swept through the house with such wanton strength that she had to clutch her skirt to keep herself covered. From her lips emitted a continuous wail of heart-wrenching terror. Her eyes were the eyes of a creature. Hunted. Facing death. Helpless to flee but afraid to stand its ground.

Still clutching Jamie to his side, Derek rushed toward her, and the two of them, Jamie and Derek both, wrapped her safely in their arms.

As one, they stared through the gaping maw of the shattered window, while outside, the storm continued to batter the house.

Derek alone lifted his eyes to the powerless light fixtures overhead. Darkness would be here soon, he knew. *Without electricity, what the hell would happen when the sun went down?*

CHAPTER ELEVEN

"I'VE FOUND more candles," Jamie declared, dumping them on the dining room table. "At least we won't be totally in the dark when night comes."

He stood perfectly still, head cocked to the side, listening as if reaffirming the fact that the power was still out. It was, of course. With the light pole splintered across the front porch and all the damage the storm had wreaked on the house, there was no way it could *not* be.

"Don't panic," Derek said. "We'll have the fireplaces too. They will afford some light if we keep the fires burning." He turned to the broken window where Tommy and Banyon were nailing planks across the opening to keep out the elements. They were both soaked by the rain still pelting in, driven by that ceaseless wind that was a major component of this latest storm, which had descended on them with a vengeance.

Outside, the storm still howled like a wounded, furious beast. There seemed to be no end to it. The trees beyond the perimeter of the yard were being thrashed to within an inch of their lives. Branches stripped away and hurled through the air landed now and then against the side of the house with a horrendous crash. Only minutes before, somewhere over their heads, in the attic perhaps, they had heard another window shatter, but none of them had the heart to check it out. Their hands were already full resecuring the windows on the ground floor.

Earlier, as a group, they had surveyed the damage done to the front porch. The light pole that fell had a large metal transformer attached to the top of it, which landed on the house like the head of a club. It had not only taken out the electricity, it had taken out the front porch as well. Little remained of it now but kindling and shingles, with that awful great light pole speared through the middle of it. Even the porch floorboards had been crushed. They could still leave through the front door if they wished, but they would have to be careful doing so. The floor was littered with sharp spears of wood and vicious long nails, ancient and rusty, that tore up into the light as if gleefully waiting for someone to come along and step on them, driving them deep into tender flesh.

Jamie and the others had quickly ducked back inside to escape the storm's wrath.

Cleeta-Gayle stood in front of the fireplace now, staring down into the flames. The scattered embers had been extinguished earlier and a safer fire relit on the grate. She was hugging it for the warmth it offered, for with the latest storm had come a vicious cold that still whipped through the broken window.

"Can't you hurry?" she called out to Banyon and Tommy. Patiently, Banyon told her they were working as fast as they could, while Tommy muttered something a little less charitable.

Banyon nailed the last plank across the shattered window and stepped back, drenched in rainwater, wiping it from his eyes. It puddled at his feet. Tommy stepped back too, shaking himself off like a wet dog. Derek noticed he had rather an amused expression on his face, but his eyes were cold. And they were aimed directly at the only woman in the room.

"Thanks for all your assistance," he said, running his filthy hands through his wet hair to get it out of his eyes. "I can't tell you how much your constant nagging and bitching helped."

Banyon laid a calming hand on Tommy's shoulder. "Don't be mean," he said quietly, turning his back to the group and facing Tommy alone. "We're all nervous and frightened. Don't make it worse than it is."

Tommy glared down at the hammer in his hand, then with a sigh and a god-awful clatter, he tossed it in the corner. "Sorry," he mumbled to no one in particular.

Banyon smiled and reached out to brush a dribble of water from Tommy's cheek. In that moment, Jamie thought he saw what it was that attracted Banyon to the boy. Aside from the fact that he was gorgeous. In that snippet of time, there was almost a fatherly light in Banyon's benign expression as he gazed on the boy. Jamie wondered how quickly that fatherly gaze could turn into something else when they were alone and naked in their four-poster bed upstairs.

Jamie turned away to give them some privacy. Cleeta-Gayle, too, turned back to the flames at her feet. Derek sat at the dining room table, his feet propped up on a second chair. He had removed his wet shoes and socks, and his bare feet were pointed toward the fire. His eyes, however, were on the pile of charred cell phones on the table in front of him.

Jamie moved up behind him. Massaging his shoulders, he looked down as Derek tilted his head back and gazed up into his eyes.

"Listen to that," Derek said on a tremulous breath.

In unison, the two turned toward the boarded-up window, where outside the storm was pounding the house like a wild animal trying to get in.

"It can't last forever," Jamie said.

"Let's hope not. I don't know how much longer the house can stand up against it."

They fell silent as Oliver Banyon and Tommy Stevens slipped past, shoulder to shoulder, whispering and nodding embarrassed excuses to the others in the room. Jamie heard a conspiratorial laugh as they climbed the staircase out in the hall, obviously headed back to their room.

"I think I know what they're gonna do," Jamie smirked. But Derek wasn't listening. He was studying the charred and mangled cell phones again.

"Whoever is doing this," Derek said, his voice low, as if sharing his thoughts with Jamie alone, "they had it all planned out. Whatever they have against us, it must be important enough to make the killer seriously crazy." Derek twisted his head around to stare up at Jamie again. "What the hell did we do to warrant such hatred? Who did we hurt? Who did we make mad? Who do we both know who is insane enough to be behind all this?"

Jamie stepped around and knelt by the side of the chair. He rested his chin on Derek's knee. Absentmindedly stroking Derek's bare toes, he stared at the phones on the table. Outside, the storm had lessened a bit, but Jamie didn't get his hopes up about that. It was only a momentary lull. The storm had quieted now and then before, but it always cranked up its fury again when they least expected it.

He was beginning to think the storm would be with them forever. All the way to the end of whatever fate they were being led toward.

"It wasn't part of the plan," Jamie said, as if realizing the truth for the first time. "The storm. It couldn't have been part of the plan. Neither could the collapse of the bridge. I suppose that *might* have been planned, although for the life of me I'm not sure how. No." Jamie burrowed his chin into Derek's leg, excited now by his own ponderings. "Disabling the cars would have been enough to keep us here. The bridge, the storm, stabbing the front porch with the light pole, that's all gravy for the killer. He's probably loving every minute of the fucking drama."

"But who is it?" Derek whispered, his voice so low now that even Jamie could barely hear it.

They both turned simultaneously to study Cleeta-Gayle in front of the fire. Her hair was a mess, as usual. Her clothes were rumpled and damp. She wore no stockings under her dress, and her legs looked veined and anemic, as if they never saw the sun.

"It can't be her," Derek said, again his voice as soft as a breath of air. "She hasn't got the strength to do all this. And look at her. She's terrified."

Jamie slipped his fingers under the cuff of Derek's slacks to caress the brush of hair above his bare ankle. Even such an innocent touch caused his cock to stir. "It's either Banyon or Tommy," he said, his chin digging into Derek's knee again. "One of them has to be the killer."

"How do you suggest we prove that?" Derek asked, smiling now at Jamie staring up at him. He was clearly enjoying Jamie's fingers on his leg, and Jamie smiled back to let him know he knew.

Despite the battering of the storm, Jamie felt a weary peace settle down between them. He glanced at his wristwatch. A lot of the day had slipped past already. The storm, repairing the window, examining the shattered front porch, exploring the grounds—it had all taken time. Before long, night would fall.

And since they no longer had electricity, it would be the first night they would all share the house in darkness.

As before, Derek proved their thoughts were often mutual. "We'll have to lock ourselves in our rooms tonight," Derek said. "All of us. We can't be roaming around in the dark. It's too dangerous."

"I'll be safe as long as I'm with you," Jamie said. "I always feel safe when I'm with you. Even before we got trapped here with a crazyass murderer, I knew I was always safe as long as you were around."

Derek slid a fingertip across Jamie's mouth as if drawn to the texture of his lips. The light in his eyes was as soft as cotton. "You're right. You will be safe. I won't let anything happen to you. We need to hunker down, survive the storm, avoid the madman trying to kill us, and either find a way to contact the police or simply sit back and wait for them to contact us. Someone is bound to start worrying about the old couple who lived here. It's just a matter of time. My only job in the meantime is to keep you safe."

Jamie kissed the fingertip at his mouth while continuing to run his own fingers through the hair on Derek's shin.

"You really love me," he said softly.

At that, Derek finally smiled. "Yes, dipshit. I really love you."

They were both surprised when Cleeta-Gayle came up quietly behind them. She cleared her throat awkwardly, as if apologizing for interrupting.

Stubbornly, Jamie refused to remove his hand from beneath the cuff of Derek's trousers. He merely continued to kneel there, waiting for her to speak.

Derek had tilted his head back to look at her. His face was kind. "Yes?" he asked.

She laid a hand to Derek's shoulder, then just as quickly removed it, as if thinking she might have gone too far. "I'm going to go into the kitchen and try to prepare us all something to eat. You must be hungry. I know I am. When I get the food together, we can call the others." She cast an embarrassed glance toward the ceiling, as if knowing full well what Banyon and Tommy were doing upstairs. "And then we can all have dinner together. We should probably stay in the same room as much as we can from here on out, at least during the day," she finished quickly, taking a step back, giving them their space.

"We were just talking about that," Derek answered. "After dinner, we should lock ourselves in our own rooms."

"Yes," she said. It was all she needed to say. But then, just as quickly, she looked unsure of herself. Fear lit her eyes once again. "I guess I'll go see what I can find in the kitchen for us to eat."

Jamie smiled up at her, more than aware of the terror she was trying to hide. "Maybe we should all go," he said. "We can help you carry everything out."

The relief on her face was as evident as the flames on the grate. "Thank you," she said. "I'd like that."

"So would we," Derek kindly said, and ruffling Jamie's hair, he pulled himself to his feet, then hoisted Jamie up as well.

"Thank you," she said again as they headed toward the kitchen single file.

OLIVER BANYON looked like he'd been dragged behind a horse. His hair was sticking straight up off the top of his head, his usually impeccable clothes were somehow hanging askew on his body, and his chin was chafed as if he had been kissing a wolverine.

Or quite possibly a young student named Tommy Stevens, who hadn't shaved that morning. The tinge of dark stubble on his cheeks was evidence of that.

Dinner was a disheartening affair of cold soup, apples, and tinned meat. The old couple who owned the house must have adhered to a simple diet. They found nothing in the larders that required extensive preparation, which was just as well since the power was out anyway. During the meal, Derek kept casting proud glances in Jamie's direction. Through this whole horrible ordeal, Jamie had shown a hidden strength that pretty much amazed Derek. But Derek also knew it wasn't easy for Jamie. Jamie was scared, as was he. As were they all. Still, Jamie was trying hard to hold it together, and Derek was proud of him for that.

He nudged Jamie's foot under the table and smiled when Jamie shot a surreptitious grin in his direction.

Tearing his eyes from Jamie, he set about slicing an apple into quarters while speaking to the group as a whole.

"Did any of you leave word where you would be? That you had answered an invitation to a house party and where they could find you if an emergency came up?"

Tommy snorted back a laugh. "You mean leave a note on the door that we were off being murdered in the backcountry? No, it must have slipped my mind."

"You know what I meant," Derek said, narrowing his eyes. He turned to Cleeta-Gayle. "Did you warn anyone that you'd be out of town?"

She laid her fork across the edge of her plate and placed her hands in her lap. A blush rose to her cheeks, as if the question somehow embarrassed her. "There was no one to tell. I live alone. My friends are… few. No one would have cared if I left town or not."

"I'm sorry," Derek sighed. "I don't mean to ask personal questions. I'm just trying to figure out if anyone will be coming to look for us." He turned his gaze on Banyon, sitting next to Tommy. "How about you?" Derek asked. Banyon still looked like he had just tumbled out of bed, which of course he had. Derek shot a quick glance at Jamie, knowing that if he and Derek hadn't been an item, Banyon would have been the exact sort of man Jamie would be salivating over. Derek was pleased to see that Jamie's eyes were only on him, and he nudged Jamie's foot again beneath the table to let him know he liked it.

Banyon cleared his throat. With his tousled hair and a drop of soup on his chin even Derek was tempted to lean across the table and lick away, Banyon seemed totally unaware of how handsome he was. He also seemed surprised by the question being aimed his way. He glanced quickly at Cleeta-Gayle before answering. Then his eyes drifted to Tommy for a second before settling on Derek at the end of the table.

"I don't have a lot of friends either," he said cautiously. "I thought I would only be gone for the weekend, but that seems unlikely now, doesn't it? There will be hell to pay when I don't show up for my classes tomorrow, but there's nothing to be done about it. When the truth comes out, I suppose the school will make allowances for my truancy."

He blinked as if suddenly hearing his own words. Collapsing back into his chair, he dropped his spoon in his bowl of soup and laughed. "Jesus! How pompous do I sound? We're fighting for our lives here, and I'm worried about my job." He reached out and took Tommy's hand, redirecting his attention back to Derek. "The only person who knew I was coming here was Tommy."

Jamie leaned forward, his elbows on the table. He stared at Banyon and Tommy as if trying to figure them out. "Didn't you guys think it strange that you both received the same invitation from the same anonymous person when you had never really socialized together before? It's not like you had any mutual friends, right? It's not like you even really knew each other very well."

Tommy answered. "We only knew each other from the classroom. We had nothing but a teacher-student relationship until I decided to get into the good professor's pants."

Cleeta-Gayle blushed but then quickly forced herself to listen anyway. She eyed everyone around the table in turn before her gaze slid back to Tommy.

Tommy stonily returned her stare as if daring her to start moralizing on what he'd said. When she didn't, he turned back to Derek.

"We talked about it, of course, Ollie and me. But we couldn't figure it out. That's what made the invitation intriguing enough to accept. It seemed like a cool mystery. Plus it afforded us some extra time together where I could worm my way into those pants I referred to earlier."

This time Banyon was the one who blushed, although he didn't deny Tommy's version of things. "And you two?" he asked Derek. "You didn't have any idea who might have sent the invitations either?"

"No," Derek said. "Of course not. We would have already mentioned it if we knew."

A silence settled over the table, a silence only interrupted by the storm still battering the house outside. Shadows were already deepening as dusk approached. The flames on the grate painted wavering shadows on the dining room walls. The air was growing chillier as well. It would be a cold night.

Gradually, the tinkle of cutlery continued as everyone resumed their dinner. Only Cleeta-Gayle sat motionless, her fork still resting at the edge of her plate. She lifted her eyes from her lap and gazed around the table. Derek noticed there were tears shimmering in her eyes. Her expression was so empty of hope, Derek's heart ached to see it.

"We're all going to die here, aren't we?" she asked.

The only answer was a streak of lightning that seared the sky and erased the shadows from the room in a blinding flash of light. A moment later, a bark of thunder shook the house around their heads.

Chapter Twelve

Was it Jamie's imagination, or on the way to their room that night, did they scurry a little quicker past the door to the suite belonging to the late Mr. and Mrs. Jupp? And was it any surprise if they did, considering the condition of the charbroiled woman who lay inside?

Their bedroom had no fireplace. And with the power out, the minute they closed the door behind them, they were swallowed in icy darkness. But for intermittent flashes of lightning streaking past the two windows from outside, it was like standing in a tomb.

"Should have brought a candle," Jamie muttered.

They pushed the curtains back, staring out at the storm.

"This thing has to blow itself out sooner or later," Derek said. "The minute it does, we'll leave."

"And go where?" Jamie asked, seeking Derek's hand in the dark and twining their fingers together.

"Into the trees, Jamie. No matter what happens out there in the woods, it has to be better than what will happen to us if we stay here."

"In which direction will we go?"

"In any direction but the one we came in. We'll stay off the lane. We can't get past the collapsed bridge or the swollen stream that way."

"So you really mean for us to go into the woods?"

"Yes. We're not in the Amazon rain forest, for God's sake. The trees have to end somewhere. And sooner or later we're bound to run into a house or a highway or some other splotch of civilization where we can call the cops."

"Do we take anyone with us?"

Jamie stood quietly while Derek hesitated. The grumble of thunder replaced their voices in the shadows. Derek's silence lasted longer than Jamie expected. He finally asked again. "Derek? Do we take anyone with us?"

In a particularly bright strobe of lightning that slashed across the sky like a flash of gunfire, Derek's troubled eyes continued to stare past

Jamie out at the storm. When Derek's gaze shifted around to touch his face, the sadness was still there.

"Dammit," he said. "We can't leave them, can we? It's the same as it was before. Two of those people are innocent. Since we have no idea which two it is, we can't leave them to their fate. Either we take them all, which might play right into the killer's hands, or we have to stay. Maybe we can keep them safe until help comes."

"That could be days," Jamie said. "And that's if help comes at all. I'm not entirely sure that anyone on the face of the planet actually knows we're here. Or cares."

"Wait here," Derek whispered, and slipping from Jamie's side, he treaded lightly toward the door and quickly yanked it open. Despite instructions to the contrary, Jamie had stayed with him every step of the way. Now they both poked their heads out into the hall and scoped it out in both directions. Amid the lightning flashes, which were coming a little less frequently now, they were able to see with reasonable certainty there was no one there.

"I thought I heard something," Derek said.

"You're scaring me," Jamie answered.

At that, Derek gently latched the door, pulled a spindly legged chair from the corner, and propped it under the doorknob.

"There," Derek said. "If anyone tries to get in, they'll have to work at it."

With the door secured, Derek walked into Jamie's arms. "You're shivering," he said.

Jamie nodded, resting his chin on Derek's shoulder. "It's cold. I miss the fire. I miss the light."

Rain lashed the windows. Somewhere off in the distance, that same damned shutter started banging against the side of the house with renewed frenzy. Jamie wished the wind would rip the fucker off and get it over with. He was tired of listening to the racket.

Derek gripped his shoulders and pushed him to arm's length. "You're right. It's too cold to stay here. Let's go down to the dining room and make a bed in front of the fireplace. Grab the blankets and pillows off the bed."

Jamie didn't have to be asked twice. He immediately hustled across the room, pulled all the bedding from the mattress, and stuffed it under his arms. Derek grabbed the pillows, and together, they kicked the chair from under the doorknob and slipped out into the hall.

They quietly descended the stairs. But for the fury of the storm, the house was quiet around them. Someone had banked the fire in the dining room for the night, and now only the glow of a few embers showed it was still lit at all. It was a matter of moments before Derek restacked firewood onto the grate and, leaning close, blew the embers back into flames. The fire snapped and caught at the firewood, and the light and the heat drew them closer. Together, they spread their blankets on the hearth. Still fully dressed, they slipped beneath them, fluffing the pillows under their heads.

Derek immediately pulled Jamie into a hug.

"Better?"

Jamie nodded, pressing his lips into the vee of warm flesh at the base of Derek's throat. "This is *much* better," he murmured, his arms at Derek's back, their stockinged feet playing toesies near the fire. "If it wasn't for the weather and the serial killer and the fact that we haven't had a decent meal in two days, it would be perfect."

"Gripe, gripe, gripe," Derek tsked. "Why is it you never look on the bright side?"

Jamie reared back and glowered. "There's a bright side?"

Derek laughed. "Well, maybe it's not exactly *bright*."

In the light of the fire, Jamie snuggled deeper into Derek's arms. Together they stared into the flames and listened to the storm batter the world outside the dining room windows. A cold wind slipped in through the planks that covered the one broken window, but the flames kept the chill away for now.

When Derek began to speak, he did it so quietly Jamie had to hold his breath to listen. Derek's voice was as warm and heartening as the flames that caressed their skin. Derek's fingertips touched his cheek; they were a perfect accompaniment, Jamie thought, to the romantic light in Derek's eyes, to the romantic timbre in his voice.

"I can't believe how easy it was to fall in love with you. I can't believe how simple it was to take that one little step."

"What step?" Jamie asked, breathless, entranced by the loving lilt in Derek's words.

"The step from friendship to love, Jamie. It's like love was always there in front of us, but neither of us ever saw it coming until it knocked us on our butts."

Jamie slipped his fingers under Derek's shirt and caressed the soft matting of hair on his chest. Beneath his hand he imagined Derek's heart pumping away like a piston engine. Pumping out love. Pumping out truth.

"It just happened," Jamie whispered. "Isn't that right? In spite of everything we did, or in spite of not doing *anything*, it just happened."

"Yes." Jamie could hear the wonder in Derek's voice when he said it. "It was like an invisible force plowing forward under its own steam. Our love didn't wait for us to figure it out, it didn't wait for us to see it for what it was, it settled over us anyway. Sort of like the warmth coming off that fire. Like the waves of rain washing over the house. It was an outside force that we never purposely created at all. It just happened. It swept around us and through us and tossed us together like two sticks of driftwood on a beach."

Jamie closed his eyes. "Two sticks of driftwood on a beach. I like that picture."

"And now," Derek said, his voice darkening, "a tsunami is threatening to wash it all away."

Reluctantly, Jamie opened his eyes. "You mean the killer."

"Yes. The killer. We have to stop him. We can't leave, Jamie. We have to stay here and stop him."

"I know."

"If we don't, we'll never be together, and I can't let that happen."

"I *know*."

"I love you too much."

A lump formed in Jamie's throat. Once again he nestled his lips into the satin softness at Derek's throat. The heat there comforted him. The teeny pulse he could feel against his chin, Derek's pulse, made him happy. Made him feel connected.

"I know," Jamie murmured. "I know you love me. I can feel it in you right now. I can taste it on your skin."

Derek relaxed in his arms, as if Jamie's words had somehow soothed him. He spoke no more. Together they lay close to the fire, absorbing the heat, listening to the storm outside the windows, hearing the firewood snap and pop as it was eaten by the flames.

Six feet away from the grate, the darkness lay waiting like some sort of stalking, lightless beast. Jamie could feel it lurking, slipping a little closer every time the flames flickered, then pulling back again when the fire took hold once more to shed a splash of light across the room.

Above their heads Jamie heard footsteps. Someone moving around inside one of the bedrooms. Either Tommy or Banyon or Cleeta-Gayle, for other than themselves, those were the only souls still living inside the house.

Jamie wondered sadly how many would still be living at this time tomorrow.

Pulling Derek closer, he stared into the fire until sleep took him down into a dreamless pit.

When he awoke two hours later, something was wrong.

Derek lay tense at his side. Jamie knew instinctively that Derek sensed danger too.

It took them long seconds to finally realize what it was.

"THE FRONT door is open!" Derek whispered.

"Why is it open?" Jamie hissed.

"I don't know, but the storm is blowing in. We have to close it."

Jamie clutched his arm. "No, Derek. Don't go out in the hall. Don't move away from the fire, away from the light. Maybe that's what someone wants you to do."

"You mean the killer."

"Yes."

"Then I guess we'd better find out for sure," Derek sighed. With a grunt of stiffness, he eased himself from Jamie's grasp, flung the blankets aside, and stumbled to his feet. He didn't have to wait for Jamie to join him. Jamie rose the same moment he did.

"Stay close," Derek whispered.

"Well, duh," Jamie groused, as if he had already made that decision for himself and sure as hell didn't need reminding. He hooked a finger through one of the back belt loops on Derek's pants, latching himself to him like a barnacle.

"Close enough." Derek almost smiled as they tiptoed out into the hall.

They didn't have their coats, and when they stood at the front door, carefully peeking past the shattered front porch to the storm beyond, the cold air bit into their skin like acid. Jamie pushed himself closer to Derek's back, and Derek reached around to take a fistful of Jamie's shirt to hold him there.

They froze, listening. Somewhere out in the storm, in the darkness, in the rain, Derek heard a voice on the wind. A human voice. It wove in and out amid the storm's fury, riding along on the gales one moment, then lost among the thrashing of the trees the next. In one brief lull, when the storm seemed to retreat and the wind and thunder fell hushed for the space of a heartbeat, Derek heard a single angry word screamed out among the trees.

"Murderer!"

And on the heels of that one angry bellow, barely audible in the distance, the lightning and thunder awoke, and the wind once again almost knocked Derek off his feet. He tugged Jamie back away from the doorway to escape the cold and wet, but he still cocked his head, trying to hear that voice again.

"It sounded like Tommy," Jamie whispered. "I think Banyon's with him in the woods."

"But why?" Derek asked. "Why would he be?"

In unison, they turned and tilted their heads back, staring up the staircase toward the second floor.

Derek's breath caught when he spotted Cleeta-Gayle staring back down at them from the shadows on the second floor landing. She wore a long white nightgown, the sort an older woman might have worn. In the light of the burning candle she held in her hand, her eyes were as big as silver dollars, her face slack with fear. At the exact moment when she opened her mouth to speak, to scream out her fears, perhaps, the wind twisted the flame on her candle. It sputtered weakly, then winked out, leaving them all in the darkness once more. A flash of lightning illuminated her gliding quickly down the stairs toward them, one clawlike hand clutching the railing at her side. She sobbed softly as she descended.

Halfway down the stairs, she swayed, as if it were all suddenly too much for her. Derek rushed forward to catch her before she fell. Together, Jamie and Derek half carried her toward the dining room and the comforting light and heat from the fire. As soon as she had a grip on the mantle and Derek knew she wouldn't fall flat on her face, he rushed back into the hall and slammed the front door, blocking out the storm. For a brief moment before he closed the door, he listened for that same bellowing voice in the night. He heard only thunder and wind and the pelting of rain. If it really was Tommy out there, he had moved too far away to be heard, or either the storm or the killer had silenced him for good.

Derek waited behind the closed door, his hand on the knob. What he was waiting for, he wasn't quite sure. He rested his forehead against the wood and absorbed the vibrations of the storm as it rattled the house around him. Goose bumps rose at the back of his neck. He blinked in amazement as the truth finally struck him.

Oliver Banyon must be the killer! At least Tommy must think so. He hadn't been screaming at any of the others—him, Jamie, or Cleeta-Gayle. They were all still inside the house. That left only Banyon for Tommy to be calling a murderer out there in the storm. Or was it the other way around? Maybe it was really Banyon Derek had heard yelling in the dark.

Making sure the front door was only latched, not locked, Derek rushed back into the dining room. There he found Jamie muttering soothing words to Cleeta-Gayle in front of the fire. As he spoke, she cried softly and clutched her nightgown in bunches at her chest. Unknown to both her and Jamie, backlit by the fire as she was, she might as well have been naked. Her thin silhouette, as shapeless as a boy's, showed clearly through the flimsy fabric of her gown. Derek snagged a blanket off the floor and wrapped it around her. She accepted it gratefully, but more for the heat than to protect her modesty.

"Did you see him?" Jamie asked, studying Derek closely. "Did you see Tommy?"

Derek shook his head. "He'll come back when he can."

They both turned to Cleeta-Gayle. She twisted away and stared down into the fire. There was a tremor in her voice when she spoke.

"They were fighting," she said. "I could hear them across the hall." Her eyes darted shyly to Derek, then to Jamie. "You didn't hear them?"

Jamie was the quickest to answer. "We were already downstairs. Our room was too cold, so we came down here to sleep by the fire."

A clap of thunder made her gasp. She tried to shake off the terror by brushing at the blanket around her, mindlessly smoothing out the wrinkles as if she were about to be presented to the queen and she didn't know how she had got herself so rumpled. When her eyes returned to Derek's face, there were tears shining in them again.

"Tommy was screaming at Oliver to leave him alone. He said he was hurting him. I thought they must be joking, or—or playing a sex game, but then I heard a fist striking flesh. And after that, Tommy crying." She bit at her lower lip as if attempting to stifle her own weeping.

Jamie turned to Derek. "Who's chasing who out there in the storm? Was it really Tommy we heard?"

Derek had been thinking about that. "I think so. Yes. Banyon's voice is deeper. I would have recognized it." He shifted his attention to the one unbroken dining room window. The instant he peered at it, lightning lit the raindrops chasing each other down the pane like little round globules of light. "We have to go out there and help Tommy," he said.

Jamie paled in the firelight. "You're not going out there. I won't let you."

Cleeta-Gayle reached out and touched Derek's arm. "Jamie's right. You can't go out there. It's too dangerous. We—we need you here."

Derek knew she was right. And so was Jamie. He couldn't leave them alone. But if he didn't, how could he help Tommy?

Again, he let his eyes drift toward a silver flash of lightning outside the dining room window, and there, in the mist and rain, stood the outline of a man peering in.

In the next flash of lightning, the figure was gone.

Derek turned to see if the others had seen it just as Jamie bit back a cry.

"Who was that?" Jamie hissed.

"I'm not sure."

Cleeta-Gayle buried her face in Jamie's chest. "It was Oliver," she sobbed. "He's killed Tommy. I know he has. Now he's coming after us."

Derek laid a comforting hand to her shoulder. Her thin body shivered beneath his touch. "We don't know that. It could have been either one of them."

"No," Jamie said, "It must have been the killer."

They spun toward a chorus of sounds out in the hall. There was a clatter of footsteps. The patter of water striking the floor. The swish of soaked fabric. The squeak of a wet shoe.

A figure solidified in the shadows.

"No," said a voice from the doorway. "It wasn't the killer. It was me."

CHAPTER THIRTEEN

TOMMY STEVENS looked like he had been run through one of those ringer washing machines. He was dripping wet, his face muddied. One trouser leg was torn from hip to ankle. His hair lay squeegeed flat to his head, and incongruously, on his face he wore a beaming great smile. Tommy's white teeth flashed in the shadows, catching the light from the fire at Jamie's back. The kid looked like a fucking jack-o'-lantern.

Derek stared at that weird, muddy smile and opened his mouth to speak, to ask what the hell had happened, but Jamie got there first.

"Is he dead?" Jamie demanded, his eyes serious, his face somber.

Tommy continued to grin his outlandish grin. "No. He almost had me a couple of times, but I finally lost him in the trees. Maybe he'll lose himself as well."

With that, Tommy shivered and clutched at his chest. He dragged his wet clothes around him. The smile on his face faded, and a weary frown replaced it. He lurched as if pulled by an invisible rope toward the fire, toward the heat.

Not looking at any of them directly, his eyes focused solely on the welcoming flames. Almost nonchalantly as he reached the fire and put his hands out to soak up the heat, he said, "He has a gun. Ollie. He has a handgun." He touched a bruise at the side of his face, which until that moment Jamie had not noticed. "I woke up in the middle of the night, and he was sitting there beside me pointing the barrel directly at my head. Before he could fire, I tried to snatch the gun out of his hand. He wrenched it from me and hit me with it." Tommy's eyes grew wide with hurt, as if he still couldn't believe what had happened. "I know we were mainly together for the sex. But still, I thought he actually cared."

"I'm sorry," Derek said.

Tommy blinked as if preventing the fall of tears, but his eyes did not shimmer in the firelight. They were dry. A look of resolve crossed his face. He gazed at each of them in turn. "Glass won't stop a bullet, so we'll have to stay away from the windows."

"So it's really Banyon," Derek whispered, more to himself than to anyone in the room. As soon as he muttered the words, he turned to the one remaining dining room window that offered a glimpse of the storm outside—and consequently, if one stood on the outside looking in, offered a glimpse of them as well. He moved quickly toward the window and pulled the drapes shut, sealing out the night and whatever dangers might be out there lurking—for instance, an unexpected pistol shot squeezed off by a maniac.

Cleeta-Gayle pulled the blanket from her shoulders and wrapped it around Tommy instead. He glanced at her with eyebrows raised, and she looked down as if embarrassed by her own act of kindness.

Derek watched this interaction between the two. Meanwhile his heart thudded like a tom-tom inside his chest. Fear? Dread? An approaching aneurysm?

He turned to Jamie to see how he was coping.

With his features lit by firelight, Jamie stared back and asked simply, "What do we do now, kemo sabe?"

Derek studied Jamie for a long moment while the flames crackled on the hearth and that same damn window shutter clattered in the wind. Then he shifted his attention to Tommy Stevens. Tommy's lips, once blue with the cold, had reacquired their normal color. He had dried his hair as best he could with a hand towel Jamie had given him from the sidebar. The kid's clothes were still wet, but he wasn't shivering as much. The heat of the fire was bringing him back.

Jamie contemplated Tommy's torn pant leg. He pointed at it. "How did you do that?"

Tommy followed Jamie's eyes. He reached down to slip a hand through the rent in the fabric and stroked his bare leg as if it still hurt. "I fell into a bush. Oliver was chasing me. I had to rip myself free and keep running."

"Are you hurt anywhere besides that bruise on your face?"

Tommy seemed reluctant to answer. "No, I'm fine. A few scratches is all."

"You need to change," Derek said. "You have to get out of those wet clothes."

Tommy nodded. "I know. I'll go up to the room in a minute."

"No. You stay here. I'll go get some of your clothes," Jamie said. "Banyon's still outside, so it should be safe enough for a while."

"You don't know anything of the kind!" Derek snapped. He grabbed the cast iron poker from beside the fire and hefted it for a moment to get the feel of it in his hand. "I don't want any of you to leave this room. I'll go."

Tommy slipped the blanket from across his shoulders and let it fall to the floor. "I said I'll go. I don't want any of you guys rummaging through my stuff."

Jamie's jaw dropped. "What the hell is that supposed to mean?"

Tommy wouldn't meet his gaze. "It doesn't mean anything. But I'll get my own stuff."

Without giving anyone a chance to argue, he strode off in his wet, squelching shoes, headed toward the hall.

Jamie moved to follow, but Derek grabbed his sleeve and held him in place. "No. Let him go. We'll wait here," he said. "You were right. He should be safe enough for a while."

The blanket Tommy had dropped to the floor lay too close to the flames. Derek kicked it away from the hearth. It was too wet for anyone else to use anyway.

Cleeta-Gayle watched the boy as he disappeared into the shadows. "I always thought *Tommy* was the killer," she said under her breath. She lifted her eyes to each of them in turn. "Why would Oliver Banyon want to kill me? I didn't know him."

"But you didn't know Tommy either," Jamie said.

"No," she said hesitantly, as if all the suppositions about guilt and innocence were starting to addle her mind. "I didn't. I don't. You are all strangers to me. Every one of you."

Derek watched as Jamie stared at her for a long second, then shook his head. He gave one of his patented shrugs. It was the shrug he always employed when he didn't quite understand what was going on. Derek almost smiled. Jamie was trying to hold it together. He had to give him that. If he was frightened, he didn't let on. Derek was proud of him for that. Derek finally responded to Cleeta-Gayle's comment. "And before you ask, we didn't know any of you either," he said. His eyes moved to the pristine patch of wallpaper above the fireplace where a large picture once hung. Once again he silently bemoaned the fact that the answer could have been right there in front of him. If they only had one of the missing pictures, they could figure this out pronto. Was Banyon related to the old couple in the basement? Had he killed them for the sole purpose of using their secluded house to play his sadistic little game of cat and mouse?

But that still didn't explain what it had to do with him and Jamie!

Footsteps echoed above their heads. Tommy moving around. Jamie edged closer to Derek's side. Derek smiled at him and reached out to ruffle his hair. He gave Jamie's cheek a pinch because he knew Jamie hated it. The wind picked up outside with a roar, and a windowpane rattled in its sill behind the curtains Derek had closed. He ached to look outside and see what he could see, but if the killer was out there with a gun, it would be stupid to offer such a tempting target.

"We have to lock up the house," he said. "Every door that leads inside needs to be made impenetrable."

"How do we do that?" Jamie asked.

"I don't know. Nail 'em shut. You got a better plan?"

Jamie frowned. "No."

"Then let's do it."

The hammer still lay on the floor where Tommy had tossed it after securing the broken window. There were nails there too, a little box of them gleaned earlier from among the flotsam in the basement. Derek grabbed both items and headed for the front door.

With Jamie offering moral support—and little else since it was pretty much a one-man job—it took Derek less than a minute to hammer three strategic nails in place that would prevent anyone from opening the door without a crowbar.

The back door off the kitchen didn't require any nails at all. It was equipped with an old-timey metal bar that fell across it and lay inside two brackets attached to the doorjamb on either side. With the bar down, no one could gain access without a battering ram.

The last door Derek secured was the small door high on the basement wall that led into the coal bin, where the two old people lay side by side in death. It didn't take either Derek or Jamie long to realize the old couple were not preserving well. The stench of rotten meat lay heavy on the air. Coupled with the wailing of the storm outside and the cobwebs on the ceiling, Derek figured he had never been in a more depressing place in his life than that reeking, filthy basement.

Jamie had his hands over his nose. "Please hurry," he mumbled.

So Derek hurried. It took less than two minutes for them to be in and out. But when they left, the coal-bin door was nailed tightly shut.

The basement was cold and damp, and with the smell of death surrounding them, they both craved warmth and light and cleaner air. After clattering quickly up the basement steps and slamming the basement door closed behind them, they hurried back to the dining room and the welcoming fire. As they passed along the staircase in the hall, they heard Tommy Stevens's shower running on the second floor. The kid was cleaning up after his adventure in the woods.

They rushed into the dining room a little too quickly and startled Cleeta-Gayle so badly she almost passed out from fright. That brought a small laugh from the three of them. Then, pulling dining chairs around the fire, they spoke quietly among themselves while waiting for Tommy to return.

"Anyone want a drink?" Jamie asked, eyeing the bottles lined up on the cabinet used as a bar.

Derek gave Jamie a gentle chuck on the arm. "I don't think we'd better drink. We need to keep our wits about us."

Jamie frowned but didn't argue. Neither did Cleeta-Gayle. An odd silence settled around them, interrupted only by the continuing sounds of wind and rain battering the house.

Finally Cleeta-Gayle shyly cleared her throat and glanced at each of them in turn. "You boys live in the city?" she asked. "I mean, together?"

"No, but we will be when we get back," Derek answered.

He shot a sidelong glance at Jamie to see how he had reacted. The look of love that beamed out of Jamie's eyes straight in his direction was everything he might have hoped for.

"We're lovers now," Jamie added, still staring deep into Derek's eyes. "We've known each other since the fifth grade, but suddenly we're lovers. We take our time about things. No sense being in a rush about stuff like that."

Derek grinned, and even Cleeta-Gayle smiled, although faintly.

"I've never really understood gay people," she said quietly. "I never allowed myself to, I suppose."

"Because of your religion?" Jamie asked with no sarcasm in his voice. He seemed to really want to understand.

Cleeta-Gayle glanced up at him as if surprised by the question, then quickly lowered her gaze to the fire. "No," she said, her voice so weak as to be almost soundless. "No," she repeated, but she didn't attempt to explain. Perhaps, Derek thought, she couldn't have explained if she wanted to.

"I'm sorry about your son," Jamie said. He was watching her closely. "Had he been ill? Is that why he—"

She looked up, startled. Her lips parted ever so slightly as she studied Jamie's face. "Why he left me, you mean?" she said softly.

Jamie blushed but nodded. "Yes. Why he died."

Derek sat back, studying Jamie, wondering what Jamie was getting at and wondering, too, how Cleeta-Gayle would respond to such personal questions, since she was usually pretty tight-lipped about herself.

She appeared disconcerted by the last word Jamie uttered. *Died.* But in the end, she merely trained her eyes on the fire and left them there, staring into the flames. Color rose in her cheeks. "I—I didn't know him well."

Derek tore his eyes from Jamie and turned to her instead. He leaned forward in his chair. "He was your son. How could you not have known him well?"

Her cheeks flushed even redder than they had before. She locked her gaze on the flames harder now, as if it were the only place she felt safe. "We weren't together very long."

"How'd you manage that?" Jamie asked, but Derek touched his sleeve to silence him. Cleeta-Gayle caught the movement and slipped a grateful glance in Derek's direction. She pulled herself to her feet, and once again, with the flames behind her, her naked outline showed clearly through the folds of her nightgown.

"I'm going upstairs to get my robe," she said, averting her eyes. A shiver coursed through her body as if the cold had finally reached her. "Tommy's up there now, so I'll be safe enough on my own."

Derek hesitated. "If you're sure."

She seemed suddenly desperate to escape the conversation, the questions. She clutched at her flimsy nightgown, wadding the bodice into a ball at her throat. Derek noticed tears on her cheeks that hadn't been there a minute ago.

"I'll be right back," she said. "Don't fret about me."

She didn't wait for an answer. Five seconds later she was gone from the room, leaving nothing behind but the swish of cotton fabric and her padded footfalls on the stairs.

"Should I go with her anyway?" Jamie quietly asked.

Instead of answering, Derek stood and pulled Jamie up into his arms. The storm outside had quieted a bit, but not by much. The house was still being sledgehammered from all angles by wind and rain. Derek wondered how Banyon was faring out among the trees. Or had he hunkered down inside one of the cars to escape the rain and cold? Or better yet, had he kept going so far into the trees that he was now hopelessly lost and would never in a month of Sundays find his way back to the house no matter how hard he tried? Like they should be so lucky.

"It's after midnight," Derek said, nuzzling Jamie's ear.

"I know," Jamie answered. "The witching hour. I hate this bloody darkness."

"At least we're safe inside the house."

Jamie reared back with an ironic leer that held very little humor. Acidly, he asked, "I wonder if all the dead people in the house used that argument as well."

Derek offered him a lopsided grin. "You're a glass-half-empty sort of guy, aren't you?"

"No," Jamie grinned right back, "I'm as cheerful as a woodpecker. I'm just able to recognize reality when I see it, unlike some people I know."

Derek studied Jamie's soft mouth. It was still turned up in a smile that Derek ached to kiss. And he ached to do more than that. "I miss making love to you," he said.

Jamie's smile widened. "It hasn't been that long ago."

Derek puckered his chin and offered a phony pout. "Even two minutes is too long."

Jamie dropped his head to Derek's chest and laughed. "Your recuperative powers aren't *that* good."

"No," Derek said, "but yours are."

Jamie snorted. "True."

At the sound of approaching footsteps, they peeled themselves out of each other's arms and spun toward the door.

Tommy stood there gazing at them. He was wearing sweatpants and a sweatshirt over tennis shoes, like he was about to go jogging or something. Maybe he chose them because they were the warmest clothes he had.

"Lovebirds," Tommy muttered sarcastically. He whirled and headed for the bar. "I think I need a drink."

"Go easy on that," Jamie said.

But Tommy ignored him, pouring a deep dollop of bourbon into a large wineglass, then dumping a couple of ice cubes into the amber liquid.

A moment later, they were joined by Cleeta-Gayle. She wore a flannel robe over her nightgown. Tartan. Well-worn. Unflattering. She glanced uncomfortably at Tommy, still at the bar, then even more uncomfortably at Derek and Jamie standing in each other's arms by the fireplace.

Tucking her hands deep in her robe pockets, she moved toward the fire.

As if pleased as punch that everyone was together again, the storm decided to batter the house a little harder. To keep things interesting. The wind fairly howled through the eaves outside, and the windowpanes rattled under a sudden onslaught of hail. It sounded like a dump truck full of gravel was being poured over the house.

"That's new," Derek commented on the hail, but no one responded.

Jamie sighed longingly, staring at Tommy's drink. Seeing the look, Derek frowned and gave his head a shake.

BY THE time Tommy was on his second wineglass of bourbon, Jamie was ready to wring his neck. Jealousy and thirst will do that. He turned beseeching eyes on Derek, but Derek said flat out, "No. We shouldn't drink."

Jamie clapped his mouth shut and wondered, in a life-and-death situation such as this one, how churlish it would be to actually whimper. He stuffed a cookie from a plate on the sideboard into his mouth instead.

Moments later, Tommy banged his empty wineglass down on the sideboard, not quite hard enough to break the stem. In a slurred voice, he announced he was going to bed. Without waiting for a response, he quickly left the room, not quite steady on his feet, but not exactly reeling either.

Cleeta-Gayle watched him go, then equally quickly announced she would go to bed as well.

"Lock your door," Derek reminded her. "Don't let anyone in if they're alone."

"No," she said, avoiding his gaze. "I won't."

Jamie watched her disappear into the gloom, carrying a candle with her to light her way. When she was gone, he turned and stared, hypnotized, as the flickering firelight shifted soft streaks of shadow and light over the planes of his lover's face. In Derek's dark eyes, the flames on the grate were transformed into golden specks of light that wavered and flared in the shadows. Jamie slid his thumb over Derek's brow, smoothing out the worry lines he saw there.

"We're all right," Jamie said. "We're still together. We're still alive."

Derek gave a sarcastic grunt. "For the moment," he grumbled, before tilting his head back and kissing Jamie's hand.

Jamie's lips twisted into a grin. "So you're a glass-half-empty sort of guy."

"Oh shut up."

In unison they tore their eyes from each other and stared into the fire for a change. Derek took the opportunity to toss another log onto the grate. Sparks shot up the chimney. They lowered themselves to the floor before the fire and crossed their legs, getting comfortable. The heat felt heavenly to Jamie. And having Derek there beside him to share it was even more heavenly.

"You can still have a dog," Derek said out of the blue.

Jamie shared a secret smile only with himself. "I would have got one anyway. With or without your permission. You know that, right?"

Derek sighed. "Yeah. That's why I said it."

Their eyes met, and they both laughed. Minutes of silence followed.

"A big dog," Jamie reminded him, killing the quiet.

Derek groaned but didn't say anything. A sharp crack of thunder split the sky above the house, but after two days of storm, they hardly noticed.

Jamie laid a hand on Derek's knee and dropped his head to Derek's shoulder. His eyes seemed to be trying to close up shop whether he wanted them to or not.

"I don't care if our room is cold," he said quietly, suppressing a yawn, "I think we'd better go upstairs and go to bed. I need sleep, and I'm pretty sure you do too."

Derek nodded, twisting his head to plant a kiss in Jamie's hair. "You're right. We're not accomplishing anything down here. And we both need rest. If we lock ourselves in, we should be okay."

"What about Banyon?" Jamie asked, keeping his eyes on the fire, refusing to turn to the menacing shadows surrounding them, shadows that could be hiding anything. Or anyone. "What if he gets into the house?"

Derek cupped Jamie's face and coaxed it toward him. Locking gazes, he said, "Then we'll deal with him when he does."

Jamie tried to absorb some of the bravery he saw staring back at him from Derek's eyes, but he failed miserably. In truth, he had never felt more chickenhearted in his life. "He has a gun, don't forget."

"I know."

"Tommy's lucky to be alive."

Derek blinked, interrupting the golden sparks reflecting from his eyes. "I know that too."

They stared at each other for a long, quiet moment, listening to the fire crackle at their feet.

"I wish I knew why he chose us," Jamie said.

"When I see him, I'll ask him," Derek said, and unfolding himself like a pocketknife, he rose to his feet, pulling Jamie up as well.

Jamie eyed the fire one last time to assure himself it was well laid and wouldn't burn down the house. Burrowing under Derek's outstretched arm, he let himself be steered from the room. But for the wailing and the clatter of the storm, and an occasional flash of lightning through the foyer windows, the house lay dark and silent around them.

Wearily, they staggered up the stairs, still arm in arm.

At the landing, they gazed down the long hallway, buried deep in shadow. Only one light shone. It was a flickering stream of candlelight that spilled from a doorway farther down. It was Cleeta-Gayle's door. And it was standing wide open.

A piercing cold stabbed Jamie's chest. A wash of pure terror splashed over him. At the same moment, Derek tensed beside him. He must have seen it too.

No, Jamie thought. *Not now. Not yet.*

With not a breath stirring between them and their hearts hammering with sudden dread, they approached the block of light that poured out into the hall.

Before they reached the lighted doorway, they stopped. But for the storm, the silence was profound. A chill traveled up Jamie's spine and made the little hairs on the back of his neck stand up.

Then he saw it. A bloody handprint on the jamb of the door. And on the floor, peeking into the hall, a splash of tartan fabric, also steeped in glistening red. It was the hem of the woman's robe.

"Oh no!" Jamie gasped, this time out loud. His vision darkened, and he swayed on his feet. Afraid he would fall, he clutched at Derek's arm. Together, they stepped forward on shaky legs.

The coppery reek of fresh blood wafted out to greet them.

Chapter Fourteen

DEREK HISSED in pain as Jamie's fingers dug into his arm. *Too tight. Too tight.* "Easy," he whispered, and Jamie's grip relaxed.

Derek stared down at the floor, at that slip of tartan bathrobe soaked in blood. Creeping closer, he and Jamie peered around the doorjamb together. From the corner of his eye, he saw Jamie instantly look away. With Jamie's hand still on his arm, Derek forced himself to finish the journey, and he stepped forward, planting himself directly and firmly in front of the open door.

The scene inside was heartbreaking. And horrific.

Lit by a candle burning in a saucer on a small table by the door, Cleeta-Gayle Jones lay at the foot of her bed, her arms and legs thrust out in agonized angles across the blood-soaked carpet. Her head, eyes open, mouth peeled wide in a silent scream of terror, lay twisted to the right. Her hips, bent sharply at the waist, pointed left. One bloody slipper had fallen from her foot and was nowhere to be seen. Derek suspected it was under the bed.

In the flickering candlelight, her throat was an open gash, a gaping wound that exposed parts of the human anatomy never intended to see the light of day. Bone. Sinew. A severed tendon. Great gouts of blood pooled among the damaged tissue. More blood had spilled out across her body, puddling around her, seeping into the carpet, drenching her clothes and hair. Blood spatter had sliced through the air all the way to the wall, more than six feet away. There, it etched sharp lines of color across the faded wallpaper, and when its momentum was spent, sent crimson droplets slipping down toward the floor, forming little puddles by the baseboard.

Untouched by the spray of blood, her open eyes, unseeing, stared out at a world she could no longer claim as her own. Derek gazed into those empty eyes, expecting to see the residue of pain there, the residue of fear. But he saw nothing. Her eyes were expressionless orbs. No humanity remained inside them at all. None of the horror of her final moments had survived. Maybe that was a good thing.

The room smelled like a slaughterhouse. That wasn't a good thing at all.

Derek felt Jamie's chin at his back. Jamie's words fell weak and shattered on his ear. "Her throat's been cut."

"Yes," Derek muttered. "And we didn't hear a thing."

He turned to study the open door. "She didn't have time to lock herself in. She must have died the minute she walked inside. He was waiting for her."

Suddenly Derek stiffened. Surprised by the sudden movement, Jamie jumped.

Derek grabbed at him, mumbled an insincere "sorry," then raced out into the hall.

"What?" Jamie cried. "What is it? What's wrong?"

"Tommy!" Derek hissed. "Where is he?"

Jamie blinked back fresh terror. "Oh my God."

They raced deeper into the shadowy hallway. Tommy and Banyon's room had been the last one on the right, two doors down from theirs.

Derek slid to a stop outside the door, which was closed. He reached out and tried to twist the doorknob. It wouldn't turn.

"Maybe he's asleep," Derek whispered. "The door's still locked."

He looked down at his hand and realized he was clutching the knife he had swiped from the kitchen hours ago. For the life of him, he couldn't remember pulling it from his pocket. When Jamie saw what he was looking at, he retrieved his own knife as well.

Jamie pressed his ear to Tommy's door. "I don't hear anything," he whispered.

"Then we'd better knock," Derek said, and stepping forward, he brushed Jamie to the side none too gently and started pounding on Tommy's door.

A bellow of fury rose up from the other side of the door, and the next thing Derek knew, the door flew open in front of him. Caught by surprise, Jamie stumbled back and almost fell.

Not sure who would be coming through Tommy's door, Derek braced himself and held his knife out in front of him. It was a stupid little knife, and it didn't give him much confidence. But happily, there wasn't much time to worry about it.

Before he could plan or anticipate anything, Tommy Stevens hurled himself through the door and confronted them in the hall. He was bleary-eyed from too much booze and too little sleep. He stood naked in front of them. His hair, damp with perspiration, stuck up off the top of his head like weeds. His features were torn between fury at being wakened and fear that something horrible had happened. In the long run, it was his fear that seemed to win the war.

"What is it?" Tommy cried, concern etched deep in his voice. His eyes darted about like frightened mice. He tried to rub the sleep from his face. "What the hell is wrong? What's happened now?"

Derek studied him closely. He made a concerted effort to keep his eyes trained on Tommy's face, although even in the midst of all the drama, he had to admit it was tempting to glance down and survey the naked rest of him. He doubted if Jamie had managed to resist the temptation so easily.

"It's Miss Jones," Derek said. "She's dead."

Somehow, in Derek's opinion, that simple statement didn't do justice to the facts. In fact, it was the understatement of the century. Cleeta-Gayle wasn't just dead, she was fucking annihilated. Apparently, Jamie agreed.

"Banyon cut her throat!" Jamie cried, his voice far too loud. Even he seemed to know it. When he sputtered "she—she's dead" all over again, he did it more gently, more calmly. And with considerably reduced volume. The minute the words were out, Derek watched a tear spill from his eye.

Tommy's eyes were fixed on Jamie too. Still blinking back sleep, his expression grew somber. Almost detached. "Show me," he demanded quietly.

Derek and Jamie stepped aside and let their eyes travel back along the shadowy hallway to the candlelit doorway, beyond which chaos lay. Tommy blinked, seeing the light.

Before stepping away from his doorway, he reached back into the room, snagged a pair of blue jeans off the floor, and slipped them on. Carefully dragging the zipper over his unprotected dick, he stepped out into the hall and headed for the light.

With Jamie still at his back, Derek followed Tommy down the darkened hall. When he reached the candlelit doorway, Tommy stopped and stared inside. Derek heard no intake of breath, no muttered curse, nor any show of horror whatsoever. Tommy simply stood there—not moving, not breathing, taking it all in clinically.

"Did you hear anything?" Jamie asked. When Tommy didn't answer, he tried again. "Tommy? Did you hear anything?"

Derek watched from the back as Tommy shook his head. "I was asleep. I drank too much, I think. I sort of passed out." He cocked his head and fell silent for a moment, listening. "It's still storming," he said.

Jamie nodded. "Yes. It's still storming. It hasn't stopped. I don't think it ever *will* stop. Not the storm. Not the killing. None of it. It's all just going to go on and on and on."

Derek slipped his arm over Jamie's shoulder and pulled him close. "Shush," he breathed, his lips in Jamie's hair. Jamie was crying. His tears spilled onto Derek's cheek as Jamie nestled against him, trembling in his arms. "Cry if you want," he whispered. "Somebody should be crying. It might as well be you."

Derek stood comforting Jamie, and as he did, Tommy turned away from the horrors inside the room and watched them. There was no sadness in his own eyes. Only a sudden, wary anger.

His words bubbled out of him, like a seething, rising froth. "He's in here with us, isn't he." It wasn't a question; it was a furious statement of fact. "Oliver's inside the house."

Derek stared back at Tommy over the top of Jamie's head. "He must be," he said quietly. "But how did he get in without us knowing?"

Jamie lifted his head from Derek's shoulder. He turned and, palming the tears from his eyes, stared past Tommy to the blood-drenched body on the floor.

A steely look entered Jamie's eyes. His body tensed. "We have to go," he announced, as if he'd thought it through and there was nothing else to do. "We have to leave. We have to run. We have to get out of here as soon as we can. Now. Tonight. Right this minute."

"No," Tommy said. "There's no protection for us outside. We have to stay here."

Derek watched the two, purposely preventing his eyes from traveling past Tommy to fall even one more time on the blood-splashed body behind him. He had seen enough of Cleeta-Gayle in death. He didn't need to see her anymore.

Stepping past Tommy, he reached into the room. He lifted the saucer holding the burning candle from the table by the door and carried it back out into the hall. Behind him, as the light from the candle moved away, the room slipped back into darkness, hiding the body in shadow.

In the hallway once again, Derek pulled the door closed behind him, sealing the horror inside.

With the candle's flame illuminating their faces, Derek studied each of the other two in turn. Finally, he rested his eyes on Jamie. "Tommy's right, I think. We have to stay in the house."

"And do what?" Jamie asked, fear and growing anger once again rising in his eyes.

"We have to find Oliver," Tommy quietly answered. "Find him and kill him. Before he kills the three of us."

The candle flickered between them, and beyond its light, the silent house waited. Slowly all three men turned to face the shadows and whatever awaited them in its depths.

WHILE TOMMY dressed, Jamie and Derek raced downstairs to test the front door. It was still nailed shut. No one could have entered that way.

Without a word between them, Jamie followed Derek across the foyer. One after the other, they ducked through the little trapezoidal door under the stairs.

"The boy who lived," Jamie muttered to himself.

Derek ignored Jamie's comment, not that Jamie could much blame him. He held a candle out in front of them to push back the darkness. They were halfway down the rickety basement steps when the candle flame flickered, then blew out entirely. Jamie gasped as darkness fell over them like a quilt. Continuing downward, moving slower now and groping their way through the dark, it was suddenly clear to Jamie, and probably to Derek, that they had found what they were seeking.

The first clue was that cold, damp wind tearing up the stairs from the basement floor. Jamie shuddered and edged closer to Derek to shield himself from it. On the wind, buried in among the ozone and the damp reek of rain-soaked loam and pine, he breathed in once again the meaty stench of death and rot.

"Oh God," Jamie mumbled, pulling his shirt over his nose.

Derek reached behind him and took a fistful of Jamie's belt. "Don't worry," he murmured. "We'll be all right." Then he pointed forward and exclaimed, "There! In the corner!"

Reluctantly, Jamie peered through the shadows to where Derek pointed.

Proceeding cautiously, they left the stairs and stepped onto the basement floor. In the coal bin where the old couple lay side by side, they spotted a square of blue darkness in which shapes were moving. It was like a TV screen showing the storm-tossed trees in the distance, flailing in the wind. Those trees came into sharp contrast a moment later when a streak of lightning illuminated the world outside—and illuminated the world *inside* as well.

The coal-bin door had been flung wide open! Faintly, they could hear it squeaking in the wind as it rocked back and forth on its ancient hinges.

"But I secured it," Derek fumed. "I nailed it shut!"

Derek stepped closer, and since he still held tight to Jamie's belt, Jamie followed. That was okay with Jamie since he had no intention of letting Derek out of his reach anyway.

Casting wary glances in a dozen directions at once, because he didn't like these shadows *at all*, Jamie stayed glued to Derek's side as he was led into the coal bin where the bodies lay. The respect they'd afforded the old couple earlier, when they wrapped them securely and laid them respectfully side by side, seemed like a wasted effort now. They were soaked, lying in inky, foul puddles, the filthy water blackened with coal dust. The blankets they were wrapped in were sodden with rain. Under the relentlessly prodding fingers of the wind, one of the blankets had peeled away from the old man's torso. He stared up at them now, his horrible, mummy-like face glistening with damp and rot, his cadaverous mouth open, his tongue as black as the dark water beneath his head. That tongue, horrible and bulging, protruded from his lips like the head of a snake.

"Don't look!" Derek snapped, roughly pushing Jamie back.

He quickly knelt and tucked the sodden blanket once again around the old man's head in a vain attempt to protect Jamie from the wretched sight, no doubt knowing it was already too late.

"Thank you," Jamie said, helping Derek to his feet and purposely looking away as Derek had begged him to, even though there was little point. He had seen everything there was to see.

Together they turned to study the coal-bin door, shivering in the wind blasting through it. Hoping to prove he wasn't totally worthless in survival situations, Jamie reached out and pushed the little door closed. Since the clasp was broken, he had to hold it there, bracing it against the wind.

While Jamie did that, Derek relit the candle.

"Look," Derek said, pointing. At the edges of the wooden door where Derek had driven the nails to keep it closed, the wood was shattered and splintered.

"Banyon pried it open," Jamie said, studying the ragged edges.

Derek shook his head. "No. He must have kicked it open from the outside. The wood is old. It wasn't strong enough to keep him out. The planks just peeled away from the nails."

Jamie edged closer until his lips were next to Derek's cheek. His heart pounded against the solid wall of Derek's chest. With his voice barely a flutter in the darkness, he whispered, "He's still here, then. Banyon. He's still inside the house like Tommy said."

Derek gazed into his eyes in the candlelight. Jamie wondered if he could see in their depths how frightened and how *furious* he was. Derek spoke evenly, all the while caressing Jamie's cheek with his hand. "I don't know, baby. I don't know."

Jamie spent a precious moment losing himself in Derek's eyes. Finally he swallowed and stepped away. "We'll be all right," he said. "I know we will. It's three against one, right?"

Offering a weak smile in return, Derek said, "Right." Derek gazed down at the tiny knife in his hand. Following suit, Jamie stared at the puny little knife in his hand too.

"We need to be better armed," Derek said, and before Jamie could answer, he crossed the basement to the work area in the corner. The old man who owned the property, presumably the same poor guy who now lay moldering with his wife in the coal bin, must have been handy around the house. He had everything by way of tools that a homeowner could ever want.

In the glow of the candle and the intermittent flashes of lightning that still streaked across the sky every few seconds, Jamie and Derek stood scanning all the crap the old guy had: hammers, hacksaws, a plethora of screwdrivers and wrenches, axes, hoes, posthole diggers propped against the wall, one bigass sledgehammer that looked like it weighed a ton, and in boxes along the floor, rasps and jacks and paintbrushes and awls and countless bins filled with screws and nails and bolts and washers. Even more tools hung on hooks on the wall behind a battered workbench.

Jamie blinked at all the stuff; then he blinked at Derek. Uncertainly, he asked, "So what are we doing, then?"

"We're arming ourselves," Derek said.

"We are?"

"Yes." And without explaining further, Derek grabbed a machete, the blade of which was locked in place between the wall and the back of the workbench. Derek hefted the machete in his hand as if weighing exactly how useful it would be in chopping off a murderer's fucking head.

Jamie got the picture pretty fast. Scanning the tools himself, he reached out for a clunky gardener's pick approximately the size of a hammer. Its rusty, fat blade was sharp on one side like a miner's pick, and flat on the other as if for digging trenches. The pick seemed butch, if Jamie could characterize it as such. And as an extension of his arm, it made him feel butch too. Sort of.

Weapons in hand, they squared off with each other. Jamie hitched up his pants with what he hoped was unwavering purpose. "You ready to go upstairs and kick some butt?" he glowered. He then proceeded to hawk up a ball of phlegm the size of a marble and spit it into the dark, dribbling more on his chin than he got on the floor.

Derek stared at him, mouth agape, then honked out a blast of laughter. Looking apologetic and trying to catch his breath at the same time, he quickly gave up and bent over with his hands on his knees, laughing like a hyena. It took a minute, but he finally managed to pull himself together. "I wish you could have seen yourself," he gasped. And before he could say anything else, he started laughing again, with happy fat tears rolling down his cheeks and dribbling off his chin.

Jamie glared at him, entirely unamused.

Still chuckling, Derek scooped Jamie into a bone-crushing hug, being careful not to slice off any body parts with his machete as he did.

"Come on, Rambo," he said, tears still streaming. "Let's kill this fucker and get your butch ass home."

Still not entirely appeased, Jamie muttered through clenched teeth, "Yes, let's." With his pick dangling at his side like a purse, he followed Derek up the basement stairs.

"Asshole," he mouthed at the back of Derek's neck, and Derek started laughing again.

TOMMY EYED Jamie's gardener's pick and Derek's machete. He seemed to find their newfound weaponry fairly amusing. "Well, you guys are certainly armed to the teeth. Anything happen that I should know about?"

Derek stared down at the machete in his hand, then back at Tommy. "No. Just being prudent."

"Yeah. Prudent." Jamie scowled, going for butch again. This time Derek decided to let him keep his dignity, so he didn't laugh.

Tommy did. "Spooky," he said. "An armed hairdresser."

"Stylist," Jamie corrected, taking a swipe through the air with the tool, which caused everybody to jump back out of the way.

When Jamie spoke, Derek was surprised to see his breath billowing out of his mouth like steam escaping a Crock-Pot. Not until that moment did he realize how cold the house had become. Jamie and Tommy seemed to suddenly notice it too. They were standing in the dining room, and they all turned to the fireplace to see that the fire was dying. Alongside the grate, the wood box stood empty.

"We're running out of firewood," Tommy said. "I saw a pile of it stacked under an overhang beside the back door. I'll go get a load."

"I'll go with you," Derek said.

Tommy gave him a sidelong glance with enough sarcasm in it to get his point across. He also pulled a large butcher knife from the back of his belt loop where he had it stowed under the tail of his shirt. "I swiped this from the kitchen," he said, waving the shiny steel blade around like a Ronin warrior flashing his samurai sword. "I think I'll be safe enough on my own."

Jamie looked doubtful. "Well, be careful then. Banyon's out there somewhere."

"Gotcha." Tommy grinned and slipped through the darkened doorway leading out into the foyer like a ghost melting through a wall.

Once they were alone, Derek turned to Jamie to grab his attention. "We have to search the house. You understand that, right? If Banyon's here, we need to know it."

Jamie nodded, although he didn't look too pleased about it. "I know," he said. Jamie stood trembling in the light of the dying fire. Once again Derek picked up the cartoon clatter of teeth clacking together. Jamie was clearly freezing to death, but being in butch mode he was trying not to let on.

Somehow that made Derek love him all the more.

Derek gave a shudder of his own when he felt a brush of cold air on the back of his neck. Still, he was more concerned with Jamie's comfort. He reached out and stroked Jamie's arms, trying to get the blood moving.

"You've got goose bumps on top of goose bumps," he said. "Let's go upstairs and get our coats."

Jamie wrapped his arms around himself to ward off the cold, like that was going to help. He gave the few embers still burning on the grate a baleful look. "G-good. I'm freezing."

"We can search the bedrooms while we're up there."

Jamie stared off into the shadows. His tongue came out to give his lips a nervous lick. "What do we do if we find him?" he asked quietly.

Derek shot him a wink, which he hoped would be heartening. "Wing it," he said, holding up his machete with a comic-book leer in his eyes. "Wing it *butchly*."

With a little less bravado, Jamie lifted his gardener's pick and looked at it dolefully. "Shouldn't we wait for Tommy?"

Derek turned in the direction Tommy had gone. Holding his breath, he listened carefully for any sounds of footsteps or slamming doors. Nothing.

"You're right," he said. "We'd better find him and make sure he's okay."

Taking Jamie's hand, he led him from the dining room and along the foyer toward the door at the back of the hall that opened onto the kitchen. Once there, they stopped in the shadows and listened again.

Here the sounds of the storm were much louder, the winds that whipped through the house stronger and colder. It wasn't hard to figure out why.

The door leading out the back was wide open, swinging idly in the wind. The kitchen floor was already soaked with rain and leaves swept in by the storm.

Jamie and Derek rushed toward the opening and squinted into the downpour. The back steps descended directly from the door to the muddy ground below. There was no porch to speak of.

"Wait here," Derek hissed, and letting his machete lead the way, he stepped out into the night. He gasped when the wind and rain hit him full force. Out here the air was arctic, whipping through the trees and over the dead lawn before plowing into the house like a Mack truck. It lifted Derek's shirttail and sprinkled his belly with ice-cold rain that *really* made him cry out.

"Tommy!" he bellowed into the wind. Before he could yell again, he glanced down and saw a bunch of firewood, soaked now and unburnable, scattered in the mud. Amid the muddy firewood rested Tommy's butcher knife, its blade flashing silver beneath a sudden stroke of lightning that made Derek stumble back in surprise.

Cowering against the storm, he looked first at the knife and the firewood, then up and down along the side of the house. In the intermediate flashes of lightning, he could see that the backyard was cluttered with branches torn from surrounding trees. An old circular well stood about twenty feet from the house. Before Derek really knew what his own intentions were, he hooked his arm over his face to shield himself from the rain and headed straight for it.

Ignoring Jamie frantically calling to him from the doorway, he reached the well and peered down into the shadowy depths. Knowing it was foolish, he called out Tommy's name. Then he called again. The only answering cry came from the storm. It roared like a dying beast from every direction at once. If he didn't know better, he could swear it was laughing at him.

Streaming now with rainwater and damn near freezing to death, he wondered what the hell had possessed him to wander halfway across the yard in the storm. Furious with himself, he whirled and sloshed his way back through the mud toward the house.

Jamie stood waiting for him at the door. "Where's Tommy?" he cried, grabbing Derek and pulling him into the kitchen to escape the rain.

Derek stood drenched and shivering in Jamie's arms. "He-he's not out there," he stammered. "I found the firewood and his knife lying in the mud."

Jamie bent to get a more direct line of sight on Derek's eyes, as if better trying to figure out what he was trying to say.

"You think he's dead?" he finally asked. "Do you think Banyon killed him?"

"I don't know, Jamie. But if he's still out there, he's not armed anymore. And he's being awfully quiet."

They eyed each other morosely.

"So we're on our own, then," Jamie whispered. "It's just us and him. Banyon. The host of this murderous little soiree."

Because he didn't know how to respond, Derek offered a pathetic shrug, which was the best he could come up with on the spur of the moment. Then, suddenly filled with rage, he turned and slammed the back door closed, shutting out the storm.

Jamie pawed at Derek's dripping shirt. He splayed his fingers over Derek's chest, as if to comfort himself. But as far as Derek was concerned, reassurance was the one thing he was out of.

He whirled and lifted his head, screaming into the silent house. "Banyon! Enough of this sneaking around shit. Come out and face us like a man."

He and Jamie froze as, in the shadows, rooms away, somewhere over their head, they heard a faint chuckle.

"That was upstairs!" Jamie gasped, eyes wide. "I think I'm going to faint."

"Let's kill him first. *Then* you can faint."

Jamie swallowed with an audible gurgle. "Oh. Okay. We'll do *that*, then."

They shared a glance. Derek straightened his shoulders and took a firmer grip on the weapon in his hand. Jamie did the same. His pick. Derek's machete.

In tandem, sucking in long shuddering breaths, they turned wary eyes skyward. With Jamie still clinging to his shirttail, Derek moved cautiously toward the stairs.

DEREK HAD stripped off his wet shirt because he said he was warmer without it. Clutching the waistband of Derek's pants instead, Jamie tried not to be distracted by the warm fuzzy rise of Derek's lovely ass against the back of his fingertips. They were tiptoeing along the foyer toward the stairs. If they weren't murdered along the way, their first stop would be their room where they would grab their coats before setting off to search the house for a killer.

Jamie gripped the gardener's pick so tightly his hand was beginning to cramp. If he'd had his druthers, he would have preferred wielding a shotgun. A big one. He was pretty sure Derek felt the same about his stupid machete.

As they passed the dining room, he saw that the darkness inside had grown since the last time they were there. Clearly, the fire was almost out, and without more firewood, it was apt to stay that way unless they started breaking up furniture. A clap of thunder made Jamie cringe and edge closer to Derek's back. Derek reached around behind him and patted Jamie's hand. He made little shushing noises to ease Jamie's fear. It didn't work, but Jamie loved him for it anyway.

Warily, at turtle speed, they crept up the long staircase, their eyes never leaving the black hole of shadow awaiting them at the top. The wailing storm outside covered the few bumps and scrapes of their footsteps as they climbed. At least Jamie hoped it did.

"Remember what Tommy said?" Jamie asked in a squeaky voice. He didn't like that he sounded so scared, but there wasn't much he could do about it. He was terrified.

"What's that?" Derek softly asked. "What did he say?"

"He said Banyon had a gun."

"I remember." There was a beat of silence before Derek answered further. "I also remember Jamie said they fought in the bedroom after Banyon *pulled* the gun. When Tommy told us about their chase through the woods, he never mentioned the gun again."

"And…?"

Derek stopped and turned, gazing down at Jamie on the step below. "And I was hoping the gun might still be in their room."

Jamie swallowed again. It felt like he had a rolled-up pair of socks stuck in his throat. "You think it's really there?"

Derek shrugged, a wicked grin lighting his face in a sudden flash of far-off lightning. "It's worth a look."

Jamie couldn't resist. He laid his hand flat to the furry expanse of hair that circled Derek's belly button, wishing he had time to poke his tongue in there too. Derek gave a little jump at his touch, probably because his hand was cold.

"If it's still there," Jamie said, "I'll let you keep the gun. I've never shot one in my life."

Derek's grin faded. "Actually neither have I."

Jamie groaned. "Great."

They turned, and with his fingers now brushing Derek's ass again, they proceed up the stairs.

The scattered lightning strikes were coming fewer and further between, as if the storm might be moving away. The hallway on the second floor was as dark and cold as a cave. They felt their way along the wall to the door of their room and, moving as quietly as they could, twisted the knob and slipped inside.

Derek didn't bother with a shirt. He simply grabbed his coat off the back of a chair and slipped it around his naked back. Jamie grabbed his own coat and pulled it on as well. He gazed longingly at the bed, wishing he had a naked Derek there, nestled under the covers, wrapped tightly in his arms. He spotted Derek watching him as if he knew exactly what he was thinking.

Jamie offered a guilty smile, and Derek answered it with one of his own. He stepped close and laid a kiss to Jamie's mouth, but before Jamie could get serious and add some tongue to the kiss, Derek stepped away and tugged him toward the door.

"Let's check out their room," he whispered.

"Whose room?"

"Tommy and Banyon's."

"Oh, okay."

"Stay close," Derek admonished.

"Well, duh," Jamie muttered, wondering if Derek could hear his eyeballs rolling up into his skull.

Back out in the hall, they listened for a moment to make sure they were alone. Hearing nothing, they moved deeper through the shadows to the rooms at the back of the hall. Jamie started shaking when they passed Cleeta-Gayle's room, remembering what lay there behind the door. Derek must have felt his tremor.

"It's okay, Jamie. Just keep moving. Stay with me."

So Jamie did. The rumble of thunder and the scattered flashes of lightning, carried on the wings of the storm, followed them deeper along the hall. Sometimes the lightning showed them the way. Other times it left them breathless and shivering in the dark.

"Here," Derek whispered, and feeling along the wall, Jamie touched the molding of the door leading to Banyon and Tommy's room. The door was ajar.

Praying to God the room was empty, Jamie followed Derek as they ducked inside and quietly latched the door behind them.

"There's a candle in my pocket," Derek whispered. A second later, a match flared as Derek lit the wick. Soft golden light fanned out across the room.

Jamie looked around. The room was remarkably similar to their own. An unmade bed, mussed by sex. A night table on either side. Dusty curtains framing the two windows. A door off to the side led into the bathroom. A huge chifforobe, with drawers on one side and a door on the other that would open up to afford hanging space for clothing, stood in the corner like a looming giant waiting to lunge.

Taking the candle with him, Derek stepped away and peered into the bathroom. Jamie moved straight to the bed and began ruffling through the bedclothes, hoping to find the gun. It wasn't there. He bent and peeked under the bed.

"Light!" he hissed, and Derek came quickly to his side, thrusting the candle under the bed so Jamie could see. There was nothing there but a lot of dust balls and a used condom.

"Yuk," they said in unison.

Standing, they dusted themselves off. While Derek quietly drew open the drawers on the right side of the chifforobe, Jamie swung open the closet-sized door on the left.

The eyes that peered back at him startled him so that he cried out and stumbled backward. Tripping, he landed flat on the bed, his mouth wide with terror, his pick falling from his hand and clattering across the floor.

Derek gawked at him, then turned his attention to where Jamie had most recently been looking. Inside the chifforobe. And there, with his head squeezed in among the empty hangers, sat Oliver Banyon, barely visible in the shadows, his arms and legs folded tight in the confined space. His throat had been cut like Cleeta-Gayle's. His eyes were open like hers had been as well. The bloody handle of a knife still protruded from the awful wound in his throat.

"No," Derek muttered, almost dropping the candle. "It can't be."

To Jamie's horror, Derek reached out and pressed a fingertip to the hardening lava flow of blood that had spilled down Banyon's chest and puddled in his lap. When Derek pulled his hand away, his fingertip was clean.

"The blood is coagulated," he said.

Jamie blinked. "What does that mean?"

Derek turned to study his face. "Don't you understand? It means Banyon was killed hours ago."

Jamie's eyes narrowed. He was still confused. When Derek stared at the corpse again, Jamie stared at it too. He let the candlelight illuminate Banyon's still body, and this time he tried not to look away. He struggled desperately to understand what Derek was attempting to explain. He thought back through everything that had happened, trying to trace a chronological order of the events that had brought him and Derek to this very moment.

Then it hit him. Jamie finally understood. "His clothes are dry."

"Yes," Derek said. "And so is the blood. Like I said, he's been dead for hours."

"But Tommy said—"

"I know what Tommy said."

Jamie tried to remember Tommy's story. Every word of it. The truth finally dawned on him like a rising sun creeping over the edge of a hill.

"He lied," Jamie said. "Banyon never chased him through the woods, did he?"

"No," Derek said, extending the candle to study the body again. The hard, clotted blood, the dry clothing. "He couldn't have. Banyon was dead by then. He must have been right here where we see him now. Everything Tommy told us was a lie. He made it all up."

Jamie remembered something else. "It's also why he didn't want us to come up to his room after he came in out of the rain. It wasn't because he didn't want us rummaging through his things. It was because he didn't want us to find the body."

Their eyes met before they both turned back to the corpse.

Something about the boyish clump of hair hanging over Banyon's still forehead sent a spasm of sorrow shooting through Jamie that almost ripped his breath away.

Before he could speak, a footfall shuffled over the hardwood floor behind them. A floorboard creaked. Jamie jumped, and Derek whirled around so quickly the candle went out. Darkness fell like a hammer. A heartbeat later, a blaze of excruciating light, as sharp as glass, poured over them both. Just as quickly, the light was replaced by an exploding flash of pain at the side of Jamie's head. With considerable surprise, he watched the floor fly up to meet him. When it struck, a different kind of darkness enveloped him. Before his brain shut down completely, he heard a wail of fury tear from Derek's throat.

Jamie raised his head and tried to shake away the pain, but he couldn't move. His strength seemed to have evaporated with the light. Derek's horrified face swam away from him in the encroaching gloom.

Somewhere in the darkness, somewhere *close at hand*, Jamie heard the sound of flesh striking flesh. Then he heard a duller sound, like the thudding of wood clubbing bone. Derek cried out in agony, but his cry was quickly cut off. A moment later, the floor under Jamie shook as Derek's body struck the floor beside him.

Then came a most horrible silence.

A voiceless scream of loss rang out, the sound alive only inside Jamie's head. With a deep, eternal sadness, Jamie bowed before the closing darkness. His cheek landed hard against the cold wood floor, and with a last jarring burst of pain, he knew no more.

CHAPTER FIFTEEN

JAMIE AWOKE in darkness to the sound of quiet laughter. The moment consciousness hit him, his thoughts started spinning around inside his head, rattling senselessly, tumbling over each other. His mind was a thrumming hive of questions, impressions, and hazy, confused snippets, none of which made any sense at all.

What the hell happened? Where the hell am I?

In response to a sticky warmth on his neck, he reached with trembling fingers and found a thick smear of blood. He knew full well what it was by the viscous heat of it on his skin.

Cold wood lay beneath him, and he knew he was on the floor somewhere inside the house. But in which room? The air smelled musky and rank, like a long-unused animal lair. Over his head, the storm sounded closer. Inches away. It felt like he could reach out and touch the wind and the rain. Like he could grab a handful of cold, stormy air as it whipped past, stirring the cobwebs in the eaves. From the corner of his eye, he saw the shape of a tricycle parked against the wall.

The attic! He was in the attic. Where the playroom had been. Where the old, unused toys were stored. Where the implements of a forgotten child's life had been left to molder and gather dust. Unremembered. Unmourned. Where rats, perhaps, or squirrels had built nests inside the walls. All gone now but for the pestilent, musky reek they left behind.

Jamie's tongue found a gap in his gumline that shouldn't have been there. One of his lower front teeth was broken. As soon as his mind began to clear, he could taste the blood. Tiny shards of tooth enamel dusted his tongue. He tried to spit them out, but his mouth didn't seem to be working properly. That was because his lips were split and swollen, he suddenly realized. Probably from the blow that cracked the tooth, although he didn't remember it. A switch clicked, and a bright spear of light stabbed into his eyes. He gasped and tried to turn away. When he moved, an overriding ache touched him in places he didn't know he had. Everything hurt. His head thumped. Bones creaked. A sharp arrow of agony pierced his hand, and he looked down, squinting against the light, to see that one of his fingers was bent in a way that it never should have been bent. It was the index finger on his left hand. It was clearly broken, and peering closer, he saw that not only was the bone shattered between the first and second knuckle, but the fingernail had been torn away. That was where most of the pain came from.

Jamie bit back a sob, staring at it. Then he sensed a human presence close to him in the room.

It took every ounce of concentration he possessed to gather up the strength to speak, and when he did, his voice sounded alien to his ears. Like the choked plaint of a trapped animal, barely alive, desperate, hopeless. Even the simple act of forming words on his tongue caused him to shrink into himself in pain.

"Derek?" he wept softly. "Are you there?"

When no answer came, he squinted past the light, trying to see around it. The bright bulb was so close he could feel the heat of it on his face. It must have been a gazillion fucking watts.

He remembered the quiet laughter he had woken to. Somewhere past the glare of that damnable light, aimed directly at his aching eyes, he caught the merest susurration of sound. The smallest noise in the world, it seemed. And easily recognizable. It was the inhalation of a single human breath. It wasn't his, he knew, and he was pretty sure it didn't belong to Derek either. He didn't know how he could possibly know that, but he did.

The sudden pain in his throat that came with the utterance of words caused a spate of tears to well in his eyes. He tasted grit from his broken tooth again. Wouldn't his dentist be thrilled! What did crowns go for these days? Fifteen hundred bucks? Of course, if he didn't get out of this alive, he supposed he wouldn't have to worry about it.

"Move the light," he rasped. "Please. Where's Derek? What have you done with him?"

"I'm not sure," came a voice from behind the light. "The last time I saw him, he was sprawled out like a dead thing. Bleeding like a stuck pig, I think they call it. Head wounds are so messy."

Jamie cried, "No!" and the split in his lip tore farther. The pain of it caused him to cry out again, and that wail of misery caused his tender mouth to split even more. He bit down on his tongue to keep from bellowing yet again.

His voice was stronger now, but still every syllable tore at his throat. "Help him," he sobbed. "Don't let him die." And after a pause, he added, "Please, Tommy. Don't take Derek from me."

The same chuckle he had woken to came again—a carefree little chortle that brought a rising surge of fury crashing through him.

"So you figured it out," Tommy Stevens said, his voice still chipper, like he was having a spot of tea and conversing about the weather.

"Y-yes," Jamie said, biting back his anger. "We found Banyon's body. It was you who killed him. It had to be. Just like you killed the others."

The chuckle died, lost in the cries of the storm overhead. "Hmm. Do I detect a rebuke?"

Not waiting for an answer, Tommy commenced humming an atonal little tune. He sounded like someone passing the time, casually waiting for something interesting to happen.

Jamie licked his lips and tasted blood. The first spasms of pain from his shattered tooth began to sharpen itself on his senses. It dug through his head like the blade of a knife scraping across a whetstone. His broken finger ached, the empty nail bed burning like fire. His other injuries—a few bruises and contusions—were minor compared to the tooth and the finger. And even those two miseries were as nothing compared to the hatred that swelled inside his heart and head.

"Help Derek," he screamed. "Don't let him die! Where is he? Let me go to him!"

The light rolled away from in front of him. The absence of glare gave Jamie strength. He tried to sit up. And as he pulled his legs beneath him and pushed himself to a sitting position, the pick he had carried earlier came down in a flash of steel and wood and embedded itself in the floor inches away from his left knee. Shattered wood chips flew, stinging across the skin of his hand. The echo of the blow made Jamie fall backward, raising his arms to shield his face.

Tommy laughed out loud. "You're a jumpy little faggot."

And with that simple insult, Jamie's courage and fury flared yet again. "Fuck you," he spat. "Why are you doing this? Why did you kill all these innocent people? Why did you hurt Derek?"

Jamie could see now. With the flashlight no longer aimed directly into his eyes, he realized he had been correct earlier. They *were* in the attic, where all the old toys were stored. The flashlight had rolled to a stop at the base of the wall. It illuminated nothing now but the dusty old baseboard inside this room that hadn't been used in years. But in the flashlight's ambient glow Jamie could now see the features of the room. He could see, in fact, everything. Toys, furniture, the lot.

Including Tommy Stevens, the little prick, standing in front of him, glaring down. Tommy's hair was sopping wet and plastered to his forehead. He was shivering, either with cold or hatred, or maybe a little of both. Insanity seemed to be writhing around behind his eyeballs too, and that scared Jamie more than anything else.

Tommy's face was so filled with hate it almost stripped Jamie's breath away. Awkwardly, Jamie murmured through his injuries, through his swollen, damaged mouth. "Why, Tommy? Why did you do it? This has to be a mistake. Derek and I don't know you. We don't know *any* of these people! What did we ever do to you? What did we ever do to *anybody* inside this house?"

Tommy's hands clenched at his sides. As quick as a snake, Tommy reached down and grabbed a fistful of Jamie's hair. With his head wrenched back, Jamie cried out again. He stared upward to see Tommy glaring down at him with such icy disgust that Jamie cringed before it. A flash of lightning strobed through the attic window, and in the explosive play of shadow and light, Tommy's young features were momentarily transformed into the face of a demon. Deadly. Mad. His mouth, tight and thin, smiled down at Jamie with such malevolence, Jamie could feel the fury of it digging into his skin like needles.

Again, Jamie rasped, "Why? What did we do to you?"

"*Nothing*," Tommy snarled, the two simple syllables writhing through the air like snakes spilling from a hole. "Don't you understand that yet? I'm not the reason you're here. I'm not the one you hurt. It's someone else you have to answer for. Not me. I'm just here to exact revenge." Leaning closer, he chortled again. "Yes. That's me. I'm the taxman. Collecting the debts."

Jamie shrank away, but still he battled to clear his addled brain, trying to understand. "Debts for what? Debts for who?" he asked, wincing again as Tommy yanked at his hair, twisting Jamie's face up to point to his own. "Who did we hurt? Revenge for *what*?"

"For Jerod," Tommy softly answered.

A silence settled between them, broken only by the pounding of Jamie's pulse and from the creak in his neck from having his head twisted back at such an impossible angle. He bumped his broken finger against the floor and almost screamed.

"*Who?*" he finally stammered. "*Who* did you say?"

To Jamie's amazement, tears slid from Tommy's eyes and spilled out onto his cheeks. Beneath the tears, Tommy offered a curiously cold smile as he released his grip on Jamie's hair. He bent over to wrench the pick from the floor, ripping it away in a flurry of splinters. Hefting the tool in his hand, he slid his eyes to the attic window. As if Jamie were almost forgotten now, he stared out into the night. His gaze left the window and traveled around the room, almost casually, brushing over the forgotten toys one by one, studying all the rest of the dusty items. The small, childish bed. The chest of drawers with a stack of comic books on the top, draped in spiderwebs. The baseball bat leaning against the wall in the corner. While the storm wailed outside, Tommy's eyes, glowing like embers burning in shadow, gradually wandered back to Jamie's face.

By the time they did, Tommy's wounded, pensive gaze had once again begun to seethe with hate. And with utter disbelief.

"You don't even know his name," Tommy whispered sadly, biting off each individual word and spitting them into the air. "*You don't even know what your lover did.*"

It was the voices drifting down from above that pulled Derek awake. Jamie's voice in particular. In his first conscious thought, Derek breathed a sigh of relief knowing Jamie still lived. Then with a grunt of pain, he took stock of himself. He tried to move his limbs, all of which seemed suddenly to be made of Jell-O for some reason. Focusing on his own predicament, rather than worrying about Jamie's for the moment, Derek realized he might be in a wee spot of trouble here.

First of all, peering through blood-drenched eyes, Derek tried to understand where he was. It took him a moment to remember; then he knew. He was in Tommy and Banyon's bedroom. He and Jamie had been staring at the corpse they had discovered in the chifforobe. Oliver Banyon's corpse.

Derek twisted his head and found the chifforobe in front of him, right where it was supposed to be. Banyon's body, too, was still there. Crammed into the space where clothes should have hung. The knife still protruded from his throat. Eyes open. As silent and still—and dead—as stone.

Derek quickly turned away, squeezing his eyes shut, not because of the horror of what he was seeing, but because of the blood seeping over his face. He tried to wipe it away with his coat sleeve, but the blood continued to flow. It was blinding him. Burning his eyes. Delicately, easing his fingers through his hair, he found the wound, a long cut just below the crown of his head. Blood oozed from it, flowing over his fingertips.

He stumbled to his knees. Gave his head a shake, trying to clear his thoughts, his vision. A splash of blood spattered the floor in front of him. Kneeling there with the room whirling around like a manic carousel, he wondered how much blood he had lost, or if he had suffered a concussion. Was this how a head wound made you feel? He didn't know what he had been hit with, but he knew it had been hard and unforgiving. Far more unforgiving than his poor aching skull.

Dropping back to the floor with his legs curled under him, he reached up and dragged a pillow from the bed. Stripping the pillowcase away, he wrapped it around his head and tied it in a big clunky knot over his left ear. At least it would stop the blood from flowing into his eyes.

The clink of metal caught his attention, and he looked down at the floor behind him. His foot had come to rest against the machete, rattling it against the floor. He quickly snatched it up and hugged it to his chest. He was armed!

His gaze shot toward the ceiling, where voices once again drifted down, settling over him like fallen leaves. The terror in Jamie's voice sent a stab of anguish coursing through him. Derek clutched his chest, his fear for Jamie's safety like a knife piercing his heart.

The rush of emotion caused Derek's vision to fade. Blackness once again began to close in. Afraid he would pass out entirely, he leaned sideways, resting his forehead against the mattress until the darkness passed. Desperately, he reached out and grabbed on to a chair. Praying he wouldn't fall flat on his face, he waited for his head to stop spinning. Falling on his noggin was the last thing he needed. One more head injury would probably do him in. Wryly, he wondered what the hell was wrong with him that he could make a joke at a time like this. Or was it really a joke at all?

Before he could think about it very long, a stream of bile rose in his throat. He gagged and doubled over, emptying his stomach onto the floor. After that, he felt better. Marginally. Dragging the bare pillow once again off the bed, he wiped his mouth with it and flung it across the room.

Groaning with the effort, he pulled himself to his feet, using the chair as a crutch, and turned to face the door. The candle still burned where they had left it on the nightstand earlier, but he ignored it. If he was going to save Jamie, he couldn't be walking through the house with a fucking torch in his hand. He'd have to be stealthier than that. He'd have to be sneaky.

As the fuzz in his brain continued to clear, he slowly faced reality. He knew now beyond any doubt who the killer really was. It was a matter of simple subtraction, after all. Outside of Jamie and himself, there was only one human left alive on the property. And that was Tommy Stevens. He didn't have the vaguest idea what Tommy's motive for all this was, and at this point, Derek didn't much care. He just wanted the fucker stopped.

And he wanted Jamie safe in his arms.

He carefully edged his way through the door and into the hall. The only touches of light that illuminated his path were the scattered streaks of lightning slicing across the heavens. And they weren't coming as often as they had before. Perhaps the storm was at long last moving away.

Derek froze and, tilting his head upward, listened. There it was again. The murmur of voices.

He toed off his shoes and trod silently along the hallway. He dragged his hand along the wall to keep from toppling over and to better steer himself in the right direction through the blinding darkness. The cut on his scalp burned like fire, but the pillowcase prevented the still-seeping blood from running into his eyes. His limbs were wobbly, and he wondered if he really had the strength to do what he was setting out to do.

To kill Tommy. It was the only way he could save Jamie, and he knew it. Tommy had to die.

He gripped the machete and, moving more slowly now, more carefully, followed the bend in the hallway around to where it met the narrow staircase leading up to the attic. Here, with no windows near, the darkness was a solid, breathing presence. Above, he heard Tommy speaking again, his voice cold and threatening. Derek wondered if he was even aware of all the lives he had taken. Of the innocent people he had killed.

But most of all, Derek wondered what he and Jamie had to do with it all. Why the hell had *they* been brought into this mess?

The first step on the attic staircase creaked beneath his foot. Derek froze, listening. Tommy was still talking. He apparently hadn't heard.

Carefully, Derek proceeded up the narrow stairs, one agonizingly slow step at a time, the machete gripped tightly in his hand. Tommy's words, Tommy's *explanation* for it all, drifting down toward him as he climbed.

JAMIE TREMBLED and shrank away. Tommy's face was inches from his. Tommy's breath was sour and reeked of hate.

"He let me fuck him, you know," Tommy was saying. "Ollie. He had a nice ass. He let Jerod fuck him too. That was before he dumped him, of course, and broke his heart."

Jamie forced himself to turn toward the voice. "I don't understand," he said. "Who was Jerod? What did he have to do with everyone inside this house?"

A trickle of blood spilled from the corner of Tommy's mouth, and Jamie wondered if in his rabid fury, he had bitten himself. Jesus, was he really *that* nuts?

"Jerod grew up in this house," Tommy leered, his eyes burning into Jamie's. "He played in this very room when he was little. We both did."

"The old couple in the basement…," Jamie began, but Tommy waved him to silence.

"Yes. They were Jerod's adopted parents."

"A-and you knew them?" Jamie stammered.

Tommy's mouth tightened. His eyes narrowed. His voice turned colder. "Yes. I knew them."

A sudden understanding sparked in Jamie's mind. "That's why the pictures were removed. You were in them."

"Yes. A few of them. Jerod and I were friends. I visited all the time. Naturally, I found my way into a few of their family pictures. But mostly they were pictures of Jerod."

"So you were friends," Jamie whispered, trying to understand.

"Yes!" Tommy snapped, anger lighting his eyes again. "Of course we were friends. We were inseparable. I spent a lot of my childhood inside this house with my best friend. With Jerod." Tommy's eyes drifted to a photo on a desk by the window. The picture was small and faded to sepia, a cheap snapshot tucked neatly into a little wooden frame. It showed an elderly couple standing arm in arm. They were unsmiling. There were no children in the photo. There was only them. Jamie recognized the couple immediately. The last time he had seen them, they were lying sprawled in the coal room downstairs, beaten to death with a shovel.

Tommy stared at the picture with such contempt in his eyes that Jamie almost sobbed in terror, waiting for that fury to fall on him.

"What happened?" Jamie whispered, ignoring the tremble in his own voice. "Why did you kill them if they were good to you?"

Tommy's gaze drifted back to Jamie's face. For a moment, he looked almost surprised to find him there. Once again, there were tears shimmering in his eyes. Tears, Jamie suspected, of both grief and madness. On Tommy's young face, it was a terrifying combination.

"We were close. Jerod and I. We loved each other," Tommy calmly recited, as if he had told himself the same thing over and over again. His eyes drifted back to the picture on the desk. The muscles in his jaw tightened. "They caught us. We were seventeen."

"They caught you… having sex?" Jamie murmured, his eyes riveted to the knife he suddenly spotted in Tommy's hand.

Tommy sniffed and returned his gaze to Jamie's face. "Yes. They caught us having sex. They threw me out of the house and told me never to come back. Jerod never came back to school, and I didn't learn until later what had happened to him."

"Why? What happened?"

Jamie watched as Tommy's eyes softened. "Jerod was beautiful. The most beautiful young man I've ever seen in my life."

"I understand," Jamie said kindly, and to his own dismay, he found himself reaching out and touching Tommy's arm to show he really did care. But Jamie needed answers too. And it seemed like the perfect time to acquire them. "But I still don't understand what it has to do with everyone in this house. I assume you invited us all here for a reason. But what did it have to do with Jerod. I didn't know him, Tommy. Why am I here? Why is Derek here, and all the others. Explain it to me. Please."

Tommy's eyes went vacant, as if his brain waves had suddenly ceased to carry thought. He leveled an empty gaze on Jamie's face, and licked another drop of blood from the corner of his mouth.

"Explain it to you…," he said, his voice as empty as his eyes.

He lifted the knife in his hand and stared at it. He tested the edge of the blade on his thumb. Behind him, Jamie heard the scrape of a footstep on the stairs. Tommy didn't seem to notice.

"Tell me," Jamie said again, his voice stronger now. Louder. A sudden burst of hope welled through him, caused by that one tiny noise he heard coming through the attic door. Was it Derek? Was he alive after all? "Tell me why everyone is here, Tommy. Tell me why you murdered them." After a heartbeat, he added, "And tell me why you want to kill me too."

THREE STEPS down from the attic door, an avalanche of pain stopped Derek cold. A roar of agony exploded inside his damaged head. As a chilling weakness flooded through him, his vision began to fade again. The blackness closed in. As carefully and as quietly as he could, he lowered himself to his knees and tried to fight the urge to simply close up shop and let the darkness win. He squeezed his eyes shut, striving with all the strength he still possessed to stay alert. But the darkness claimed him anyway.

When he opened his eyes, he knew that time had passed, but he didn't know how much. Tommy Stevens was still blabbering behind the attic door, so Derek figured Jamie was alive, and that's all he really cared about.

He lifted his aching head from the floor, reknotted the blood-soaked pillowcase to make it more secure, then tried to concentrate on what Tommy was saying. Time had definitely passed, he quickly realized, for the conversation had moved on to Cleeta-Gayle Jones.

And her relationship to the mysterious Jerod. Whoever the hell that was.

Derek reached out and flattened his trembling hand against the attic door, as if that would help him absorb Tommy's words more clearly. As if that might help Derek understand.

JAMIE WATCHED Tommy lay the knife aside and lift the pick again. Slowly he raised his eyes to the level of Jamie's face.

"She was his mother, you know."

Jamie found himself stuttering. "C-Cleeta-Gayle Jones was Jerod's mother?"

"Yes. Although she never claimed him."

"What do you mean, she never claimed him?"

In an explosion of anger, Tommy drove the pick into the floor again. Jamie almost passed out from fright. But Tommy wasn't watching Jamie. He was staring once again at the old couple's snapshot atop the desk.

"She gave him up at birth. Never saw him again after that. Never *cared* enough to see him again. I heard her tell you she never knew him well. A bit of an understatement there. How can you know someone if you throw them to the wolves when they're two minutes out of the womb?"

Jamie tore his eyes from the pick and the shattered floor at his feet. He thought of Cleeta-Gayle Jones. He remembered the shame on her face when she spoke of her son. "Then how did you know who she was?"

"After Jerod died, I found her. It took me a year." He returned his gaze to Jamie. "She had to be killed, of course. She was the root cause of everything. She started it all."

"Did she know her birth son had committed suicide?" Jamie quietly asked.

"Only at the moment of her death."

"You... told her," Jamie sighed.

"Yes. I told her." Tommy almost smiled, but the smile turned to a sneer at the last moment. His voice rose in a scream. *"He was only nineteen when he killed himself. Hell, yes, she had to know."*

Jamie swallowed hard. His eyes kept shifting toward the baseball bat in the corner. He wondered how long it would take him to reach it and if his muscles were strong enough yet to attempt it.

To kill a little time, Jamie asked, "What about Banyon? How did he warrant an invitation to your little party? And what happened to his gun?"

Tommy smiled at that. A kid caught with his hand in the cookie jar. "There never was a gun. I lied." Just as quickly, his face sobered. He shifted his gaze to the attic window when a grumble of thunder rolled across the heavens outside, but he immediately turned to Jamie once more. "Jerod was sent away. To separate him from me, I suppose. They turned him against me, you see. He finished high school in another city. Came back to enroll in college in San Diego. Boarded with some relatives of the old couple, I later learned."

"And Banyon?"

Tommy sighed. "Banyon was the last straw for Jerod. His last hope at a gay life. He fell under Banyon's eye shortly after he started college. Naturally, Jerod fell head over heels in love with him. His sexy little history professor. After a few discreet blowjobs, no doubt, and a flurry of *illegal* fucks, since Jerod was a student *and* damn near a minor, Banyon dumped him. It broke Jerod's heart." Tommy's expression turned cruel, his eyes as cold as Jamie had ever seen them. Once again he tore the pick out of the floor and hefted it in his hand like he was gauging its weight. He turned back to Jamie. His gaze was dead now. Emotionless.

"I discovered the school he went to, and I listened to all the gossip. That's what turned my attention to Banyon. And my reason for stabbing the fucker in the throat. It was also the reason I contacted Mr. and Mrs. Jupp. After Banyon, they were Jerod's next stop. His one final chance to lead a normal life. Or so he thought." With barely disguised fury, Tommy added in a trembling voice, "They were the ones who truly killed him."

Chapter Sixteen

SITTING ON the top step, Derek stroked the attic door in front of him. The cool wood against his fingertips somehow calmed him. His head was starting to clear, his vision opening up as much as the darkness would allow. He didn't feel like he was going to faint any longer. He might even be getting his strength back. A portion of it anyway. Enough to function. Enough to launch an attempt to rescue Jamie.

Sucking in a great gulp of oxygen, hoping that would clear his head a little more, he wiped at his face where the dried blood was starting to itch. On the other side of the door, Tommy was talking again. Orating, the little fucker. Enjoying himself.

Carefully, Derek pulled the machete from between his hip and the floor. It made a scraping noise, but Tommy's diatribe—whatever it was he was raving about—didn't slow for a moment. He sounded angry now, though, and that scared the bejesus out of Derek. He could imagine Jamie's terror, trapped in there with Tommy screaming at him like a maniac. Was he hurt? Derek didn't know exactly what had beaned him in the head back in Banyon and Tommy's room. All he knew was that it was Tommy who swung the weapon. Did he strike Jamie too? Was Jamie even now sitting on the other side of this door slowly bleeding out? Maybe dying?

When that thought hit him, Derek's breath was almost stripped away. Another chill raged through him.

He slid his hand from the attic door and curled his fingers around the doorknob. His heart started hammering like crazy. Fear. He knew it well. Fear had become second nature to him now. Fear for his own life. Fear for Jamie's. Fear for everything the two of them had only begun to share. Love. Each other. A future together.

Derek squeezed his eyes shut, focusing his attention, gathering his courage, summoning his strength.

Releasing the doorknob so it wouldn't rattle, he pulled himself to his feet, biting back a groan. He had to get his head on straight before he attempted any sort of attack on Tommy. Otherwise he might get him and Jamie *both* killed.

He forced himself to stand there, slow down, breathe in, breathe out. He listened to the storm for a minute, let the damp night air flow over him. It felt good, that air. It refreshed him, as much as he could *be* refreshed.

Derek rolled his head around, trying to loosen up the muscles in his neck. Trying to get nimble enough to launch a rescue. Trying to think how best to go about it. And as he stood there thinking, pulling himself together, he listened to Tommy blathering on like a madman. He was screaming now. Furious. Derek could imagine him leaning over, bellowing in Jamie's face. Spit flying. Threatening. Accusing. Terrifying.

Once again, he reached out and wrapped his fingers around the doorknob.

Then the words coming through the door caught his attention. He leaned in closer, his ear to the door. *Jerod.* This time when he heard the name, he made a connection. Memories snapped into place with almost mechanical precision. A young face, a smooth, inexperienced body. Stolen moments driven by lust. An awkward ending to an affair that never should have started.

And suddenly Derek knew why he was here.

He knew why Tommy wanted to kill him. And why, perhaps, he thought he already had. Otherwise, Tommy would have finished him off back in that room. Left him bleeding alongside poor dead Oliver Banyon, stuffed inside that ridiculous chifforobe like forgotten luggage with a kitchen knife stuck in his throat.

He reached up and touched his injured head. The pillowcase was soaked, but still kept the blood that continued to seep from his wound from running into his eyes. He had certainly bled enough all over the floor back in that room for Tommy to think he was dead.

He shook thoughts of himself away and let his memory carry him back to another time. Remembering the boy Tommy was ranting about on the other side of the door. Recalling their brief love affair. Simply an extended bout of tricking, in Derek's eyes. But to Jerod so much more. He had been handsome and young and troubled. Derek remembered how the young man wept when Derek ended their relationship. How Jerod had pleaded with Derek to love him.

And how Derek had turned his back and walked away. Damn near ran, in fact.

Months later, Derek heard the boy had committed suicide. He was so ashamed to think it might have been partly because of him, that he never mentioned Jerod to anyone. Not even Jamie knew.

Was that why the pictures inside the house were gone? Did Jerod grow up here? That must be it. Derek knew now how the others were connected to Jerod by what Tommy had been screaming about on the other side of this door. And while they might have all been involved with Jerod too, none of them knew about each other. Derek had never seen the old couple who owned the house. Oliver Banyon, Cleeta-Gayle Jones, and Mr. and Mrs. Jupp were all complete strangers to him. And none of them had ever seen each other, apparently, or someone would have said so. Removing the pictures with Jerod's face in them cleverly kept them all in the dark as to why they had been brought to this place.

To be slaughtered.

And now Tommy thought he was down to his last victim. Jamie. Since he had nothing to fear from the rest of them, he was taking his time with this one. Taunting Jamie. Explaining it all to him. To Jamie. To the one person who never had anything to do with Jerod at all.

Derek knew, Derek *knew*, that if anything happened to Jamie it would be entirely his fault.

Derek's trembling fingers tightened on the knob. Slowly, quietly, it began to turn.

JAMIE SCOOTED his ass an inch or two to the right. Not enough to capture Tommy's attention, but enough to edge him closer to the baseball bat propped in the corner. It was about five feet away. He couldn't just reach out and grab it. He'd have to stand. He'd have to lunge forward. And Jamie wasn't entirely sure he had the strength to do that.

Then Tommy uttered Derek's name, and the baseball bat was momentarily forgotten.

"Before Banyon, Jerod fell in love with your boyfriend. I'll bet you didn't know that."

Jamie tried to think. He and Derek had both bedded lots of men, sometimes they even shared them. Not at the same time, of course, but individually. Had Tommy's Jerod been one of those faceless tricks that every gay man has buried in his past, the kind of trick that might have been fun for a while but wasn't memorable enough to survive the test of time?

"For a while," Tommy said, his eyes mean, his voice sad, "when Jerod was just starting college in San Diego, he almost came to grips with his homosexuality. After he got away from the fuckers who raised him. He tried to live his life as he really was. He tried to be himself. He dated Derek for a while, but Derek broke his heart. Later he survived an affair with good old Ollie, the professor from hell. Or I should say he *tried* to survive it. But he never really did. Banyon was the last person Jerod tried to find happiness with. When it fell apart, he gave up. People who knew him told me. If I had known where he was living at the time, I might have helped him. But it was only after his death that I started digging around."

"After his death…," Jamie pondered, trying to understand. Trying to put the pieces together.

Anger ignited in Tommy's eyes. "Yes! And nobody mourned him. Nobody cared. I was the only one. *The only fucking one.*"

"I—I'm sorry," Jamie stammered, cowering in the face of Tommy's rage. And cowering, too, under the constant onslaught of his own injuries, his own pain.

His broken finger throbbed endlessly now. The agony had become excruciating. Before waiting for Tommy to acknowledge what he said, before even taking the time to think about what he was going to do next, he gripped his finger in his good hand and snapped the broken bone into place. The pain was so exquisitely sharp, he screamed out. He swallowed bile and stared down at the finger. At least now it was sort of straight. Unfortunately, there was nothing he could do about the missing fingernail.

Tommy watched him like an entomologist studying a new kind of bug. There was a newfound respect burning briefly in his eyes. But there was a smirk on his face as well. "Maybe you're not so faggoty after all. That took some guts."

"Fuck you," Jamie snarled, edging another millimeter closer to the bat in the corner. "Tell me about Derek. Tell me about Derek and your friend."

But Tommy ignored the request. He eyed him coolly, then picked up his narrative where he'd left off.

"I was talking about the Jupps. Don't interrupt me again." The muscles in his jaws flexed, and a spot of spittle formed in the corner of his mouth.

Jesus, Jamie thought, *he's going rabid on me. This fucker's really crazy.*

Calmly, Tommy resumed his tale as if there had been no interruption at all.

"The Jupps weren't exactly party people, so I lured them here under the pretense of work. I knew they'd be desperate to earn some money, since their finances had taken a hit lately, what with the old man's prison sentence and all."

He smiled down, waiting for Jamie to respond, so Jamie did. "The newspaper clipping."

Tommy made a noise somewhere between a snarl and a gurgle of laughter. The hatred that suddenly flowered in his eyes made Jamie cower before it.

"Yes. The newspaper clipping. Old man Jupp spent two years in prison for operating a gay conversion clinic. I don't know why his skinnyass wife didn't do time too, but she didn't. Jerod went to them on his own, you see. They promised to cure him of his homosexual desires. Make him straight. Make him *normal*. After three months in their clutches, Jerod killed himself. He took a gun to his head and blew his brains out. And nobody cared! They didn't even mention the name of the second suicide in the newspaper when Jupp was sentenced. Jerod was simply forgotten. Lost in the shuffle."

Tommy was so furious, he was shaking. A rope of snot slid from his nose, dampening his upper lip. Tears of rage filled his eyes. His face was almost purple with anger.

"Two years!" he screamed. "That's the sentence they gave old man Jupp. For beating two young men down so badly they couldn't face living life another day, they gave him *two lousy years*."

Jamie bit back his own sob. Even with his life hanging in the balance, the story of Jerod's sad existence had touched him somehow. Still, he had his own safety to worry about now. His and Derek's. For who else could be making those little noises outside the attic door? Derek wasn't dead. Even if Tommy thought he was.

"And Derek," he said, trying once again to draw Tommy's attention away from those scurrying noises outside the door. "Tell me about him."

Tommy turned his back on Jamie and strode toward the attic window, still clutching the pick in his hand. He stared out at the storm, at the gray of an approaching dawn peeping through the rain. While his attention was centered on the sky, Jamie edged closer to the bat in the corner.

Tommy's voice wafted across the room, blending with the cries of the wind outside, the rumble of distant thunder. "Derek was just another man who broke Jerod's heart. All those hurts were accumulating inside his head, I think. He fell in love with Derek, and Derek turned his back on him. Refused to even see him again. I heard about it from some of your friends, who don't mind spilling their guts if somebody buys them a drink. Apparently you were the only one of Derek's friends who *didn't* know about it. Anyway, Jerod was running out of places to turn, of people to reach out to. After Derek, he gave himself to Banyon, who used him and threw him away. Jerod once again found himself alone."

Jamie cleared his throat. He tucked his injured hand against his chest, trying to control the pain. "You still haven't told me why *I'm* here. Like you said, I didn't know Jerod. I never met him."

Tommy turned from the window and stared back at him. A streak of lightning fizzed across the sky behind his head, illuminating the surprised expression on his face. Once again, a grumble of thunder stuttered through the air. The rain continued to lash across the window pane at Tommy's back.

"Would Derek have come without you?" Tommy asked as if it was the simplest thing in the world to figure out. "Would he have left you behind for a long weekend? I don't think so. I guess that leaves you as collateral damage, my friend, as they say in military circles. I needed you here, see. As bait. And maybe so you could do what you're doing now. Provide me with the last person I can explain it all to."

"To ease your own guilt," Jamie said.

At that, Tommy faltered, but only for a second. "No," he said, straightening his shoulders. "To clarify my motives. There was nothing else I could do, you see. Everyone who brought about Jerod's death had to pay. Surely you understand that."

Not waiting for an answer, Tommy turned again and pressed his face to the attic window, gazing out at the storm.

A strange thought suddenly entered Jamie's head, yet he knew immediately it was the truth. He also knew that by saying it, he might hasten his own death. But it was worth the risk.

First, while Tommy was turned away, he inched closer to the baseball bat. It was so close now, he could almost reach out and touch it. One quick lunge and it would be his. But could he move fast enough? And would he still have the strength to wield it as a weapon?

"Look at me," Jamie said, all but commanding. Tommy wheeled around, an inquisitive look on his face.

Jamie stared back, trying to act fearless. Trying to show he wasn't afraid. He spoke loudly so Derek could hear his words on the other side of the attic door. If Derek was really there at all.

"You said you couldn't find Jerod. You didn't know where he was living. Not until after he died. That doesn't explain why Jerod didn't come searching for *you*. You said you were lovers. You said he meant everything to you before Jerod's adopted parents sent him away. Why didn't he try to find *you*? Why didn't he run away from his life and come to *you* for help?"

Fire lit Tommy's eyes, a fire as bright as the lightning flashing through the sky behind his head. He gripped the gardener's pick so tightly his knuckles went white. Hatred flared in those burning eyes, but Jamie refused to cower beneath them this time. This time he faced the hate head-on.

He raised his voice, hoping his words would carry out onto the stairs. "It's because he didn't love you, isn't it, Tommy? He didn't care about you the way you cared about him. Did he?" Jamie leaned forward, matching Tommy's hate with contempt of his own. Unshrinking. Refusing to back down. "Do you think he saw how insane you were even then? Huh, Tommy? Is that what you think happened? Did his folks really send him away because the two of you were having sex, or was it because they saw how crazy you were, the same as Jerod did? Which was it, Tommy? Explain it to me. If he loved you so much, why didn't he come looking for *you*?"

A bolt of lightning struck the roof over their heads. The immediate clap of thunder was so loud that both Jamie and Tommy cowered beneath the blow. The dusty room was suddenly lit by fingers of orange flame that sprang to life, reaching through the latticework where the attic wall met the eaves above the window. The blast from the lightning shattered the glass. Wind swept in through the opening, fanning the flames the lightning ignited.

In the flickering orange light, at that very same moment, Jamie cried out, "Derek! Now!"

Praying he was right about Derek being there at all, Jamie lunged toward the bat. He deftly snatched it from against the wall as he rolled past. Hurling himself to his feet, he whirled to face Tommy before Tommy could take a single step in his direction.

With a scream of pure rage, Tommy ignored it all—the fire, the wind, the rain blowing in. The fucking baseball bat. He barreled across the room, the pick held high in his hand, his eyes and the blade of the tool aimed directly at Jamie's heart.

In that same moment, as Tommy's bellow of outrage flooded through the house, Jamie saw Derek batter his way through the attic door, the machete raised high above his head.

Derek tore into the room, his eyes as mad as Tommy's. Tommy staggered in surprise, whirling to face the bloody figure barreling down on him from behind.

At that very moment, Jamie launched his own attack.

With a strength born of malice and his own madness, Tommy flung himself at them both.

DEREK CRASHED through the door and the first thing he saw was the flames eating into the corner of the ceiling. The storm was pouring through the broken window, and Jamie was clambering to his feet, a baseball bat clutched in his one good hand. Derek realized quickly that Jamie was injured, his other hand tucked away for safekeeping against his chest.

But the injury didn't seem to slow him down much.

The moment Derek stormed inside, Jamie hurled himself forward, swinging the bat wildly, aiming for Tommy's head, clearly intending to knock it right out of the park. Instead, the blow caught Tommy on the shoulder, but it caught him hard. Tommy roared in pain. With the pick still raised high in his other hand, he dove at Jamie like a wild animal focused on its prey, wailing out his fury as he lunged.

Derek ran forward to intercept Tommy's attack. Sweeping the machete through the air before him, he felt the impact of the keen blade as it sliced easily through the knuckles of Tommy's clenched fist. A look of horror crossed Tommy's face when a sprinkle of something dropped to the floor at his feet. At the same moment, the pick tumbled from his hand and struck the floor behind him.

Tommy stumbled to a stop and stared down in horror at the three bloody fingers scattered across the floor. He wailed in pain as the blood from his injured hand splattered across his face.

Derek was so shocked by what he had done, he almost tripped. He stumbled to a stop, letting the bloody machete fall to his side.

Jamie, however, saw the opening for what it was and, racing forward, swung the baseball bat one last time.

It struck Tommy above the left ear and sent him hurtling backward across the room. Tommy reached out blindly, grabbing the sill of the broken attic window with his bloody stump of a hand. Battered by wind and rain, he turned to glare at them one last time, a look of hurt and horror etched across his young face. A trail of blood leaked from his ear, staining the collar of his shirt. He clutched his mangled hand to his throat, the blood from it spilling out onto his chest. He gave his head a shake as if to clear it, and blood from his head wound spattered across the floor.

With an anguished cry of either pain or confusion, and before either Derek or Jamie could take a step to stop him, Tommy squeezed himself over the windowsill and hurled himself into the approaching dawn.

If he screamed at all as he fell three floors to the ground, the sound was lost in the cries of the storm.

Jamie and Derek, stunned, collapsed where they were standing. Only when they were seated on the floor and no longer had to worry about falling flat on their faces, did they lift their eyes to each other. Their smiles were weak and rattled, but they were there. Barely.

"I knew you'd come," Jamie muttered.

"Always," Derek answered.

And crawling, because that was all they had the strength to do, they met in the middle of the room. There, they clung to each other for far too short a time.

With his face buried in the heat of Jamie's neck, Derek whispered, "I know how Tommy was planning to get away."

"How?" Jamie asked.

"In the basement," Derek answered, his eyes bright. "Remember what we saw in the basement."

Jamie blinked. "What? What did we see?"

Derek's smile widened. He laid a hand to Jamie's cheek. "I'll show you." The smoke billowing down on top of them and the fire spreading relentlessly above their heads finally tore them apart. Derek knew they had only one way back to the city, and they'd better hop to it before the house burned down around their ears, otherwise the opportunity would be lost.

Caught somewhere between inane giggles and tears of relief, they stumbled away from the flames on the ceiling. They clattered down the rickety attic staircase, ran hand in hand along the turn in the hallway to the other set of stairs, then through the Harry Potter door into the basement below.

Where the motorcycle still stood. *Tommy's* motorcycle. Buried under the tarp. Just as Derek knew it would be.

EPILOGUE

THEIR NEW apartment was a mess. Boxes everywhere. Nothing unpacked. Jamie wasn't entirely sure everything would fit when it *was* unpacked. He stared down at his injured hand. The cast was off and the skin was all itchy and flaky from being bound up in plaster for six weeks. His finger worked, albeit creakily, but the missing fingernail was still a horror to look at. He couldn't wait for it to grow back.

"How's your finger?" Derek asked, sitting across the kitchen table and sipping his morning coffee, watching him.

"Fine," Jamie answered by rote. "How's your head?"

They had pretty much run this comedy routine into the ground by now, but that didn't stop Derek. "No complaints yet!" he announced grandly, and they both smiled, if somewhat wearily.

In truth, the stitches on Derek's scalp from the blow he received from Tommy that night still bothered him. He had headaches now and then, which he never used to have before. But the pain was slowly ebbing. His hair was growing over the scar at an incredibly slow rate, which irked him no end, but one day he felt certain the damn thing would be well hidden, and that was good, because frankly he was tired of looking at it.

The doctors had told them both they'd be right as rain in a few more weeks.

Tommy's motorcycle, which Tommy had planned to use for his own escape, had carried the two of them through the trees that night instead. As far away from the house as they could get. And as quickly. It was a long, miserable night for both. Injured, wet and cold, weak from blood loss, it was only out of sheer stubbornness that Derek steered the motorcycle onward through the forest for almost eight miles before they finally ran across a gravel road. They followed it for three miles more until it landed them in the backcountry town of Spangle, California, where they eventually located the sheriff's office between a laundromat and a hardware store. After imparting their tale of woe to the gaping patrolman on duty, every cop on the Spangle police force was summoned, a total of three. They were dispatched immediately to the murder scene by helicopter. Since the bridge was still out, and since the storm was still coughing up rain and spitting lightning, it was the only way they could get there. Jamie and Derek both got the distinct impression this was the most exciting thing that ever happened to the Spangle Police Department, and in their opinion, the cops were having way too much fun considering the circumstances.

As it happened, the house did not burn down. Apparently, either the rain or the wind doused the flames from the lightning strike before they could eat up enough wood to burn the ancient structure to the ground, along with the evidence and bodies it contained.

Of which there were plenty.

Jamie was glad Tommy had died in the fall (or jump) from the attic window. It saved Derek and him from attending a trial as star witnesses. As it was, there would be no trial at all. They were interviewed by numerous law enforcement agencies, but that was the extent of their participation. They ignored requests for interviews by the local press, and eventually the whole thing died down as they had hoped it would.

Now they were getting on with their lives. Together.

Derek passed an envelope over the table and placed it in Jamie's hand. "The mail came. This is for the both of us, but I'll let you answer it."

Jamie grinned. "Hey, thanks! Our first joint mail. How romantic is that?"

He tore open the colored envelope and extracted a card. He read it twice, then tossed it across the kitchen, nailing the wastebasket dead center. If he'd been playing basketball, it would have scored two points.

Derek watched the card sail through the air, then turned his eyes back to Jamie, looking a little confused.

"Nice shot. What *was* that?"

Jamie dug through a bag of cookies that rested on the table. He popped an Oreo in his mouth. "It was an invitation from my sister Lainie."

"An invitation to what?" Derek asked.

"A party."

Derek stared at him. He glanced through the kitchen window. It was nice to see sunshine for a change. Then his eyes traveled back to Jamie. "A party," he said again. The word plopped out of his mouth like a wad of stale gum.

"Yes," Jamie sighed. "A party. And I don't know about you, but I think maybe our days of accepting party invitations are over. We went to one party, and look how *that* turned out."

"You're right," Derek said. "It was the worst party ever. Why risk fate by going to another?"

An odd silence settled over them.

"Why didn't you ever tell me about Jerod?" Jamie asked. He averted his gaze, staring out the window, not at Derek. He had waited weeks to ask. Now, he knew, the time had come.

Derek, too, had known the question was coming. Inside his head, he had rehearsed his answer a hundred times, but still, now that it was time to speak the words, he hesitated to say them.

"I think… I was ashamed. Then later, after I heard about his death, I think I purposely forgot the time I spent with Jerod. It was as if I pushed it out of my mind."

Jamie's eyes found their way back. "You knew you hurt him?"

"Yes," Derek said. "I knew. But I never thought…."

Jamie finished the words for him. "You never thought he would kill himself."

Derek squeezed his eyes shut. Suddenly the sunshine pouring through the window seemed too bright. Too unforgiving. "No. I never dreamed he would do that."

Jamie's hand snaked out across the table and landed atop his own. Jamie's voice was gentle. Derek could hear the love in it. It was there. Like a kiss on the ear.

"It's not your fault, you know. Jerod's sadness was built-in, I think. It had more to do with his own weaknesses and his own upbringing than it had to do with you."

Derek felt a burning at the back of his throat. "I hope so."

They stared at each other for a long moment. Then, simultaneously, the sadness began to evaporate from their faces.

With his free hand, Derek reached across the table and snagged a cookie of his own. A moment later they were grinning at each other, their front teeth blacked out by Oreos, which made them grin even more.

"About that dog you promised me," Jamie said, far too casually.

With a groan, accompanied by an exaggerated eye roll this time, Derek snatched another cookie and sat there methodically chewing it to mush.

"What about it?" he finally asked.

"It has to be a big one," Jamie said. "I don't want some nellyass Chihuahua. You promised."

Derek narrowed his eyes. "You extracted that promise while I was in fear for my life. And your life too, I might add."

Jamie's left eyebrow shot up into a suspicious little arch. "And your point is?"

Derek sighed. He scooted his chair back and rose to his feet, leaned over the table, and planted a virginal kiss on Jamie's forehead. "I'll get the car keys," he said.

"Where are we going?"

"My baby wants a dog. We're going to the Humane Society. Where else?"

"Really?"

"Really."

Jamie's eyes misted up. "I love you, you know."

"I know," Derek said. "I'm a loveable guy." After a moment of reflection, he added, "Bring the stupid cookies."

JOHN INMAN is a Lambda Literary Award finalist and the author of over thirty novels, everything from outrageous comedies to tales of ghosts and monsters and heart-stopping romances. He has been writing fiction since he was old enough to hold a pencil. He and his partner live in beautiful San Diego, California, and together, they share a passion for theater, books, hiking, and biking along the trails and canyons of San Diego or, if the mood strikes, simply kicking back with a beer and a movie.

John's advice for anyone who wishes to be a writer? "Set time aside to write every day and do it. Don't be afraid to share what you've written. Feedback is important. When a rejection slip comes in, just tear it up and try again. Keep mailing stuff out. Keep writing and rewriting and then rewrite one more time. Every minute of the struggle is worth it in the end, so don't give up. Ever. Remember that publishers are a lot like lovers. Sometimes you have to look a long time to find the one that's right for you."

Email: john492@att.net
Facebook: www.facebook.com/john.inman.79
Website: www.johninmanauthor.com

THE HIKE

JOHN INMAN

Ashley James and Tucker Lee have been friends for years. They are city boys but long for life on the open trail. During a three-hundred-mile hike from the Southern California desert to the mountains around Big Bear Lake, they make some pretty amazing discoveries.

One of those discoveries is love. A love that has been bubbling below the surface for a very long time.

But love isn't all they find. They also stumble upon a war—a war being waged by Mother Nature and fought tooth and claw around an epidemic of microbes and fury.

With every creature in sight turning against them, can they survive this battle and still hold on to each other? Or will the most horrifying virus known to man lay waste to more than just wildlife this time?

Will it destroy Ash and Tucker too?

www.dreamspinnerpress.com

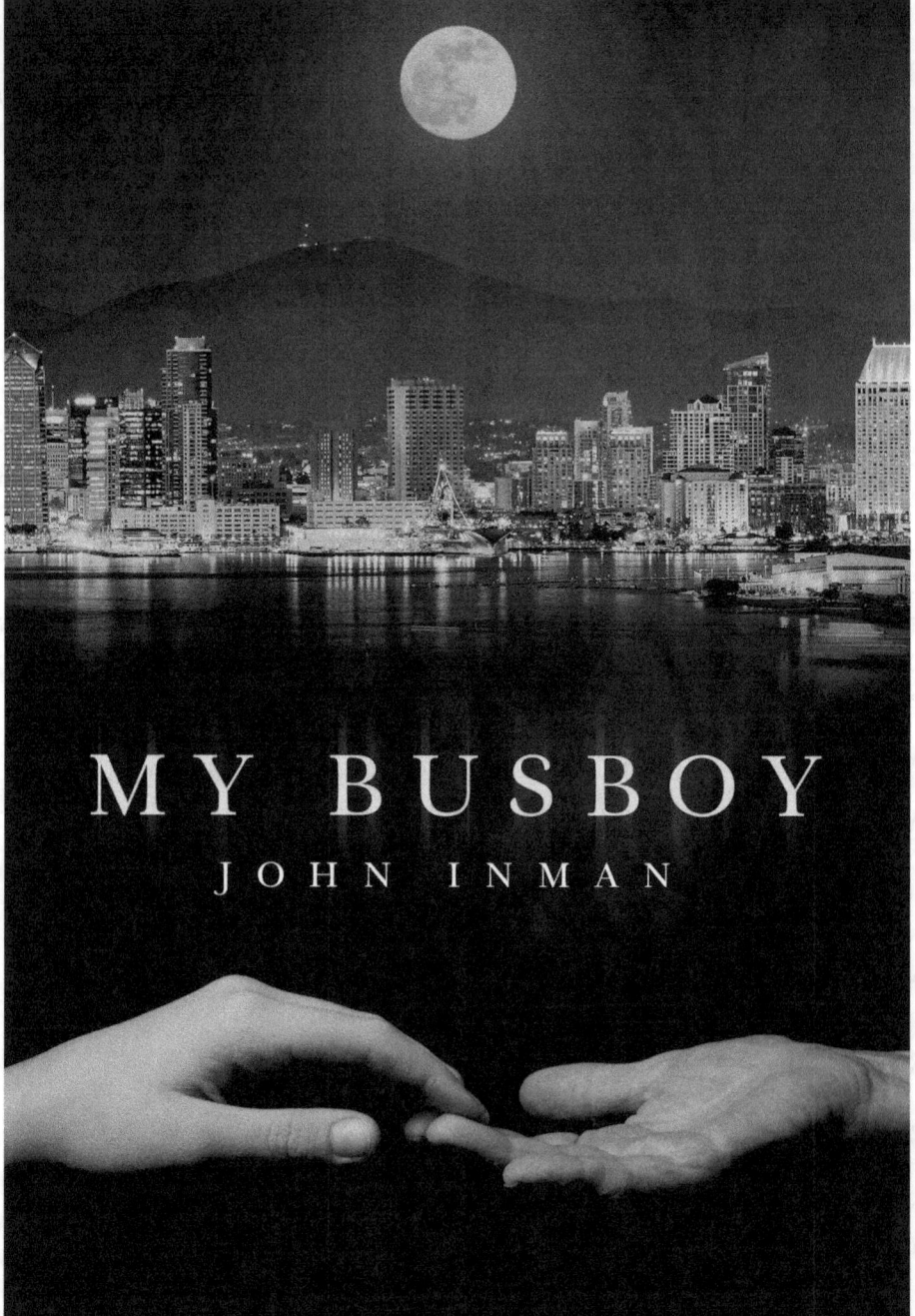

MY BUSBOY

JOHN INMAN

Robert Johnny just turned thirty, and his life is pretty much in the toilet. His writing career is on the skids. His love life is nonexistent. A stalker is driving him crazy. And his cat is a pain in the ass.

Then Robert orders a chimichanga platter at a neighborhood restaurant, and his life changes—just like that.

Dario Martinez isn't having such a great existence either. He needs money for college. His shoes are falling apart. His boyfriend's a dick. And he has a crap job as a busboy.

Then a stranger orders a chimichanga platter, and suddenly life isn't quite as depressing.

But it's the book in the busboy's back pocket that really gets the ball rolling. For both our heroes. That and the black eye and the forgotten bowl of guacamole. Who knew true love could be so easily ignited or that the flames would spread so quickly?

But when Robert's stalker gets dangerous, our two heroes find a lot more to occupy their time than falling in love. Staying alive might become the new game plan.

www.dreamspinnerpress.com

MY DRAGON, MY KNIGHT
John Inman

Danny Sims is in over his head, torn between his abusive lover, Joshua, and Jay Holtsclaw, the bartender up the street, who offers Danny the one thing he never gets at home: understanding.

When Joshua threatens to get rid of Danny's terrier, Danny knows he has to act fast. Afraid of what Joshua will do to the dog and afraid of what Joshua will do to *him* if he tries to leave, Danny does the only thing he can do.

He runs.

But Danny isn't a complete fool. He has enough sense to run into the arms of the man who actually cares for him—the man he's beginning to trust.

Just as their lives together are starting to fall into place, Danny and Jay learn how vengeful Joshua can be.

And how dangerous.

www.dreamspinnerpress.com

JOHN INMAN

NIGHTFALL

Joe Chase and Ned Bowden are damaged men. They each bear scars from surviving the world they were born in. Deep scars, both physical and emotional.

When fate offers its first kind act by bringing the two together, suddenly their scars don't seem so bad, and their lives don't feel so empty.

Yet that kindness comes at a price.

Just as Joe and Ned begin to experience true happiness for the very first time, the world turns on them again.

But this time it turns on everyone.

www.dreamspinnerpress.com

JOHN INMAN

TWO
PET
DICKS

Old friends and business partners, Maitland Carter and Lenny Fritz, may not be the two sharpest pickle forks in the picnic basket, but they have big hearts. And they are just now coming around to the fact that maybe their hearts are caught in a bit of turmoil.

Diving headfirst into a whirlwind of animal mayhem, these two self-proclaimed pet detectives strive to earn a living, reunite a few poor lost creatures with their lonely owners, and hopefully not make complete twits of themselves in the process.

When they stumble onto a confusing crime involving venomous reptiles, which is rather unnerving since they're more accustomed to dealing with misplaced puppy dogs and puddy tats, they take the plunge into becoming real-life crime stoppers.

While they're plunging into that, they're also plunging into love. They just haven't admitted it to each other yet.

www.dreamspinnerpress.com

WORDS

JOHN INMAN

The world of writers, readers, and reviewers is a close-knit family of friends, fans, and fiction fanatics. That's the world Milo Cook and Logan Hunter reside in—thriving on the give and take of creativity, the sharing of stories and ideas, and forever glorying in their boundless love of books and the words that make them breathe.

But sometimes words can cut too deep. And when they do, there is inevitably a price to pay.

What begins for Milo and Logan as a time of new love and gentle romantic discoveries, becomes before it's over a race for their lives and for the lives of everyone they know.

Who would ever suspect that an entity as beautiful as the written word could become a catalyst for revenge? And ultimately—murder?

www.dreamspinnerpress.com

www.ingramcontent.com/pod-product-compliance
Lightning Source LLC
Chambersburg PA
CBHW070119260626
47160CB00004B/1532